MW00715516

ESCAPE TO ERIE'S END

WADE VERMEERSCH
& PAMELA MUNTEAN

Copyright © 2018 by Wader Likes Media
Authors: Wade Vermeersch & Pamela Muntean

All rights reserved. This book or any portion thereof may not be reproduced or used in any manner whatsoever without the express written permission of the publisher except for the use of brief quotations in a book review.

This is a work of fiction. Names, characters, businesses, places, events and incidents are either the products of the author's imagination or used in a fictitious manner. Any resemblance to actual persons, living or dead, or actual events is purely coincidental.

Book layout by www.ebooklaunch.com

Release year, 2018

ISBN 978-1-7751025-0-2

Wader Likes Media
24 John St. East
Blenheim, ON
N0P 1A0

www.waderlikes.com

www.facebook.com/waderlikes

To the Vern Kellys of the world. And to my Mom.

- Wade

"No love, no friendship can cross the path of our destiny without leaving some mark on it forever."

- Francois Mauriac

There are too many people I'd like to dedicate this book to - too many friendships that inspired me, too many adventures, too many late night conversations, and too many moments that will last a lifetime in my heart. This book is for those of you who have crossed my path and left a mark. xoxo

- Pam

CHAPTER 1

The windows of the pickup truck were open as it laboured down the highway. It was two in the morning, and Jess's hair was blowing as she rested her head on the pillow she had wedged between the passenger seat and window. The silence of the otherwise vacant highway was broken by Emm Gryner's "Summerlong" booming from the radio. Jess and her mom, Steph, had discovered after countless hours on the road that the only music they could agree on was courtesy of whatever indie station was in range. Jess hoped that this station would hold for a while, and feared that her mom would scan to an easy-listening station - or worse, talk-radio - if they lost it.

If they had rented a car, or taken their own, he would find them. There was no time to wait, and Jess remembered seeing the For Sale sign on the powder blue-and-white 1986 Ford F-150 when she walked past it on her way to school. He would never suspect that they'd go from a Mercedes sedan to a 1986 pickup truck. It already seemed like a lifetime had passed since that night when they banged on the door of the darkened house, until the seller of the truck appeared in his robe, not at all impressed.

When the man in the robe took one look at Steph, his demeanour changed. He could tell that they were in trouble.

"We need to buy your truck," Jess said to him. "We have four hundred dollars, and can get the rest to you in a few days. I promise we will not rip you off." The man looked uncomfortable.

Jess watched her mom remove her jewellery and her expensive watch, and without saying anything place them in the man's hands. She could tell the man saw the desperation in her mom's eyes. He grabbed the keys, and walked out to the truck with Steph and Jess, grabbing the ownership out of the glove-box.

"Who should I sign it over to?" he asked.

"We'll fill in the rest, thank you so much."

Steph waved the cab away. Jess took a deep breath; they were leaving.

When she woke up, Jess glanced at her mother now in the driver's seat and was struck by her beauty, despite what had happened, and despite the black smudges of mascara that were left from the tears she shed while Jess was sleeping. Jess studied the contours of her mother's face. She was gorgeous, but what she'd endured showed in the lines of her face - the lines that forged their way too early for someone her age. Her face was still swollen and sore, and under her makeup it was different shades of red and purple.

Jess turned her glance from her mom back to the sky. She leaned her head as far back on the pillow as she comfortably could. She could not believe how the stars looked when there was nothing else to interfere with the sight of them - they were almost magical, illuminating the night sky with their sorcery. They were nearing the end of the three-day trip from Richmond. Somehow, Jess thought the vastness of the night sky and the possibility it represented gave meaning to the unknown, to what was happening, and she felt a strange sense of security. She glanced quickly at her mom, who was still focussed on the road, and then up again - her mouth curved into a subtle smile, and she felt like they were headed in the right direction.

There was a smell of sweetness in the night air - it was the smell of spring turning to summer. But the crisp chill in the air hinted that spring hadn't entirely departed just yet. As Steph looked over at her daughter and saw her admiring the sky, gazing at the stars, she felt for the first time like it was going to be okay. Steph hadn't known in which direction to drive the old pickup truck after she and Jess managed to acquire it. At first, she just started driving. They were an hour outside of Richmond when she remembered a short pit stop she and her parents took while on a family vacation. She was just a kid, and they had only stopped for a few hours. They had a picnic on the beach and she remembered how beautiful it was, how peaceful. She and her parents always said they wanted to go back again and stay longer, but they never did. The only thing Steph knew for certain as she drove the unfamiliar pickup was that Erie's End, on the shores of Lake Erie, had to be their destination. It was a treasured memory, and it held the possibility of their best future.

She knew this little village was safe, a community where the residents would notice change: a place where neighbours were friends, and everyone not only knew each other's names, but knew each other's business too. She looked in the rear-view mirror, happy to see that she wasn't being followed, and relieved to think that maybe their old life could be left in the rear view as well. They had to start over, somewhere no one would ever suspect, especially him, and Erie's End was the place.

CHAPTER 2

Val focussed on the lighthouse at the end of the pier, because she knew if she looked into Jay's eyes, she'd lose what was left of her composure. The lighthouse was not like most - it was an uneven tower of white cinder blocks whose base formed a crooked pyramid. It looked as if the tip of the pyramid had been stretched toward the sky and instead of having a peak, reached up to form a flat-topped tower. It had a bright green door to match the enormous green light-bulb that sat unprotected on top, where most lighthouses would've had a lantern room. The word "fierce" was spray-painted carefully across it in big green block letters, and it was a mystery how the artist was able to get high enough to leave such a mark. The lighthouse was more than a beacon; it was the heart of the village. Val couldn't help but think of all of the secrets, all of the encounters, all of the life-changing moments the old lighthouse must have been witness to.

At first glance, Jay fit into the cliché of every girl's dream. He was tall and charming, and had a kind smile that conveyed his easy-going nature. He was well dressed, and his clothes hung off his shoulders in a way that emphasized his lean but solid frame. He was wholesome; Val used to tease that he was the picture of an all-American Scrabble player. She loved his gentle soul and his sincere heart. He was notorious for his love of romantic comedies and 1980s love ballads. He continuously referenced scenes from movies in conversations, and was known for being able to quote any line from any movie.

He laughed at her for being an emotional wreck; he said she always wore her heart on her sleeve. As she stood there on the pier, she hoped that the rush of emotions she was experiencing was not so obvious. The tension in the air was rigid and harsh in contrast to the soft breeze that swept between them and tousled their hair.

Jay stood defeated with his shoulders slumped. "I just don't -"

"Get it," she said. "I know, Jay. I just can't handle us right now. I've got too much going on."

Val was on the verge of tears. She looked up at Jay, staring not at him but past him, wanting to keep her distance.

"Too much going on, Val?" Jay looked at her with confusion in his eyes, and Val realized that this was all news to him. "What the hell? What do you have going on? I can help you through it...or is it something I've done?" He grabbed her hands and pleaded apologetically, "I'm sorry...please, tell me how I can fix this?"

Val gently slid her hands out of his. "Jay, it's not you. I promise. You're great." Tears were now streaming down her cheeks. "It's me." She nervously bit her lip. "I'm sorry." She turned around, and at that moment knew that she had to just will her feet to keep moving forward, one in front of the other. *Walk,* she told herself. *Just keep going, don't look back.*

Jay stood on the pier motionless, emotionless - and just watched as she briskly walked away toward the shore, half hugging herself. He could not believe what had just happened. He was waiting, wanting, hoping that she would turn around, and see him standing there and come back, and take it all back. But she just kept going - taking everything they had and making it mean less with each step she took. As she disappeared into the distance, a lump in his throat swelled and a sudden pain burned in his chest. It was over. He sat down on the concrete of the pier - and put his head in his hands.

Nobody from the outside looking in would ever have expected this. Jay did not see it coming either. He thought they were happy. They were just supposed to *be* - they were Jay and Val. They were in each other's lives since they were five. They shared toys in the sandbox, then first flirts in the schoolyard, and on his fourteenth birthday after they shared their first kiss, she officially became his girlfriend, and had been ever since.

Recently they had been discussing taking their relationship to the next level - physically. It started with casual discussion - it was like they were both thinking it, they were both curious. Jay didn't mean for the topic to be so serious. Maybe that was it, he thought. Maybe he had given Val the wrong idea, maybe she thought he was too eager to experience their first time - but it wasn't true. He'd thought about it, but he was happy just the way things were. Jay wished he could tell her that it was okay, that he would wait as long as she needed him to…that he loved making out with her. But he knew that nothing he could say would change her mind. He sat on the pier, listening to the waves, trying to take it all in.

Val's feet continued their task of carrying her forward, one foot in front of the other through the streets of Erie's End, toward her house. She hoped that she would not meet anyone along the way. She just wanted to get home and disappear within the four walls of her bedroom. She wasn't expecting to break up with Jay, and was slightly stunned by what had just happened. What surprised her even more was the fact that she didn't want to change what happened. It was over, and she didn't even know herself until the words came out of her mouth on the pier. Jay held a special place in her heart, but she couldn't be his girlfriend and deal with everything else that was going on.

She started walking up the front path towards her house. Val could already hear the arguing through the open kitchen window. *Not now,* she silently wished.

"Jesus, Janet! Get off my back!"

"What, Kent? *Where are your priorities?*"

Val quietly opened the front door, and stood in the entrance. She didn't know whether she should make herself known to her parents, or try to sneak up to her room. She just stood there without making a sound, not sure if she would be able to endure another episode of her parents' fighting. Not now. Not today. She wanted to disappear, she wanted them to disappear. She wanted to return to the time when they were all happy, and when they needed less from each other to be that way.

"Ohhh, I'm so sorry, *Janet!* That's what you want isn't it? You want an apology?" Her dad sounded ridiculous. He tended to over-accentuate and over-pronounce his words when he was arguing with her mom. Val wished he knew that it just made him sound like an idiot.

"Actually, Kent - yes, I would love for you apologize and to take some responsibility for what you're doing to us. Look at how you have been treating all of us lately - not just me, the kids too. I don't understand why you've been acting like such an incredible *asshole?*"

"Jesus, Janet - *I'm* the asshole? Well - then - I - am - sorry. I am so, so, sorry - so sorry *that I ever married you in the first place!*"

Val's silence expired with a loud, uncontrollable gasp - she felt like she had been punched in the stomach. She briefly leaned against the wall, gained her balance, and as her soft tears progressed into audible weeping she darted for the stairs. She stumbled on the first step, revealing her presence to her parents.

"Val!" her mom cried, and she picked herself up and continued to run up the stairs.

In the mirror at the top of the stairs she could see the look of disgust her mom gave her dad. She heard her mom, through gritted teeth, seethe, "Look what you have done now." Val stood there, trying to catch her breath and stop sobbing.

"Don't put this on me, Janet. I'm about up to here," he raised his hand above his head, "with this shit." She watched her dad stand up from the kitchen table, walk over to the fridge and grab a beer. He shot a look of loathing at her mom and walked out the door. She heard the abrupt crash of metal as her dad kicked the garbage bin before entering the garage.

Val quietly closed her bedroom door, not wanting to draw attention. Not wanting to create any sort of invitation for her mom to come and check on her. She lay down, holding one pillow close to her chest and sobbing into the other - sobbing so hard that she felt like she could hardly breathe. She closed her eyes, and held them shut. She imagined that she would open them again and all of this would have just been a bad dream. She would open her eyes, and this day wouldn't have happened.

CHAPTER 3

Meg sat in the dim living room, staring into space. She was amazed how the house she had grown up in her whole life could feel so different now. It used to be so vibrant and full of life - and now it was dull, and grey, and sad. She realized that her mom was the soul of the house. With her mom gone - the house seemed to have no heart. It was just walls, and a roof, and a place to stay. Meg sat there and watched as her dad struggled through the pile of bills. He would write things out, punch something into the calculator - then he'd curse, cross something out and run his hands through his hair.

He never really had to deal with bills much before this. Her mom used to take care of all of it. They got married just after high school, and Meg was born shortly after. Meg's dad used to be gone a lot. He was a fisherman - it was a job he was able to do right out of high school, and it provided a pretty solid income - but he had to give it up; he just couldn't be gone all the time after what happened. Meg's dad was a bit younger than all of her friends' parents. Everyone used to love coming over to Meg's place: her parents were the fun ones - they were always joking and teasing or dancing around and making fools of themselves. *It's amazing how things can change*, she thought.

"Now Meg, I don't want you to get too comfortable." He looked at her through his reading glasses. "I really want you back here, living with us, I really do - but you know how Grandma and Grandpa are. If they don't think we're pulling things off, they're likely to have you move back in with them come September."

Meg thought her dad looked like an overgrown teenager trying to be an adult when he wore his glasses. He was wearing sweatpants and the same Hollister t-shirt that was part of every sixteen-year-old boy's daily uniform.

"I'm gonna try, I just don't know," he said, "maybe they *can* take better care of you than I can." He crumpled up a piece of paper and threw it across the room. "I don't seem to be doing too good of a job so far," he grumbled.

Meg got the impression that her dad allowed her to come home from her grandparents' house out of obligation. She knew he must have blamed her for what happened. Why wouldn't he - she blamed herself for what happened, too.

"I know, don't worry Dad - I'll keep Grandma on alert, in case you decide you want me to go back," she replied, trying to keep the tone light. Meg was the spitting image of her mother. She overheard her grandmother say it to her grandfather one night, after which she couldn't help but wonder if that was why her dad couldn't bear to look at her.

She, like her mother, had flawless skin that looked like she had a tan year round. Her eyes were an unusual glacial blue that stood out against the tanned look of her skin. Her hair was chestnut brown with natural golden highlights that made it look like she had spent hours in the salon. She was a natural beauty. When she first started staying with her grandparents, her grandmother would plead with her to dress more like a lady. Meg tried to explain that how she dressed was just who she was and what she liked, but her grandma was relentless. "Show off that dynamite figure of yours," she would say. "You're hiding behind these baggy cargo pants and t-shirts. And your hair - oh, what I could do to your hair if you would take it out of those baseball caps."

"As for now," her dad continued, "your brothers and I are glad to have you back around."

Meg shot a soft smile in her dad's direction. "Thanks, I'm glad I'm back too." She knew her dad was trying, but couldn't help but feel that he was so distant. It was like she had lost both of her parents.

Matthew sauntered into the living room and curled up on the couch beside Meg. He started to have a coughing fit. Meg covered him up with the comforter she'd been using and put her arm around him. Even though he was nine years old, he still seemed so little to her. He had always been small for his age, but holding him against her side, she could feel that he was truly skin and bones. She had missed her brothers so much when she was gone - it was like her whole world had been ripped away from her in an instant. She worried about Matthew the most; ever since she was little she'd worried that he would just die from his illness, and then she would feel guilty for even thinking the thought.

"Do you want some chocolate milk, Matty?" she asked. Her brother nodded, and smiled - she knew it was a special treat for him. She got up, tucked the blanket around him on the couch, and went into the kitchen. It made Meg feel good to take care of her brothers - she wished her dad would see that she could.

Meg, although she loved her grandparents and appreciated their intentions, did not want to be forced to live with them. She wanted to stay with her dad and her brothers, in her home, in her room, in Erie's End - where she belonged. Being away from Erie's End made her realize how much she really loved it. She loved that it was a place seemingly stuck in the past. Living in the city caused her to realize that Erie's End had a culture that was not the norm. In Erie's End, people still stopped to chat with one another, neighbours looked out for each other; kids played outside more than they played on tablets.

They didn't even have high-speed internet in Erie's End, but no one who lived there seemed to mind. Music people listened to was not necessarily the most current. The internet they did have was too slow for Netflix, so people still rented movies. It was a place where technology had not yet infringed on the quality of people's relationships, and where those relationships were built on face-to-face conversations instead of through texts and Facebook posts. It was the place she wanted to be, and the place where she wanted to stay.

CHAPTER 4

"Got a letter from your mom today," Jay's grandma said as she passed him a bowl of homemade potato soup. It was his favourite, and although he hadn't told her about what happened with Val, she knew that he needed a bit of subtle comfort. The soup reminded him of when he was little and he used to help her in the kitchen - his job was always to add the secret ingredient, the TLC. "Every recipe needs a dash of tender loving care," she would say. Jay had been spending summers with his grandparents for his whole life. He had his own room there, and their house might as well have been an extension of the home he shared with his parents.

His parents were both teachers, and every summer they volunteered with their church and travelled to perform missionary work. This year they were in Ghana, and although Jay wasn't involved in the church like they were, he was proud of his parents for the work they were doing. He couldn't wait to hear the stories they shared through letters, and of course when they returned in person. Jay's grandma chuckled and said, "Your mom says the mosquitoes are the size of hummingbirds over there."

Jay loved spending the summers with his grandparents. They were pretty easygoing; they made sure they provided whatever he needed, but otherwise they left him to his own devices. They didn't impose any rules or curfews on him, and once his grandpa actually advised him to take advantage of his youth. There was no harm done if he wasn't going to be home for dinner - but Jay always made a point of letting them know where he'd be and when he'd be home. He respected them and appreciated the freedom they allowed him.

Jay finished his soup and put his bowl in the dishwasher. He kissed his grandma on the cheek and walked toward the screen door. Before he left he said, "See ya tonight, Gram!" She gave him a flimsy wave, while still chuckling about something she was reading in his mother's letter. The wooden screen door banged behind him, and Jay made his way down the lane.

His best friends, Vern and Dave, were already waiting for him when he arrived at their usual meeting spot at the lookout. They started walking toward the centre of town, and Jay told them about what had happened with Val.

"No. She. Didn't." Vern stated in disbelief.

"Yeah, man," Jay assured him.

"Are you telling me she actually pulled the whole, 'it's not you, it's me,' routine? You're not shitting me?"

Jay was getting slightly annoyed with Vern, as it seemed like he was finding this overly entertaining.

"No. I am not shitting you, Vern - for the last time," he replied, completely unenthusiastically.

"Classic!" Dave piped in, and Vern responded with "You're telling me, bro!"

"Wow," Jay said. "You guys are making me feel great about this, so much better, thank you!"

"Not gonna lie, man," Dave said, "I saw it coming."

"What?" he said to Dave with irritation in his voice. "Well, thanks for the heads up?" He was annoyed that they weren't taking this more seriously.

"Nah man, not like that," Dave said. "It's just that Val - Val is *really* hot, man. No offence."

Vern reached around Jay, who was standing between them, and offered Dave a high-five and a "Hey-O!" Jay wished he had just stayed home.

Vern looked at Jay and realized that his attempt to make him laugh had failed. He wasn't used to seeing him so bummed out. His clothes didn't match, which was unusual for Jay; his hair wasn't gelled, and nothing he was saying caused Jay to even crack a smile. As out of character as it was for Vern to have a sense of someone else's feelings, he recognized that his friend was not himself and might actually need a little boost.

"Don't get us wrong, J-Slice," he said. "Like, we're stoked you're single again! Think about it dude. We haven't done anything awesome together for quite some time now. Plus, your parents are in Tasmania or some shit trying to save the world, so you have free rein, man - this summer will be epic! It's gonna go down in the books, bro."

Impressed by Vern's little pep talk, Dave responded with an "Amen," and Jay cracked the first smile he had since before yesterday's breakup on the pier.

Jay had a couple of movie rentals in his backpack that he wanted to drop off at the video store in the mini mall. He loved that Erie's End was probably one of the few places left in the world that still had a movie rental store. "Hey guys," he said, "What are the plans today? I need to stop and return some movies on the way."

Vern gave Jay a little shove. "Are you carrying rom-coms in that backpack?" he asked. "Or something from the more intense drama variety - like the movies where she says, 'It's not you, it's me?'"

"Shut up Vern," Jay said - although he couldn't help but laugh.

CHAPTER 5

Meg and Val sat on the patio outside Dougie's Diner at the mini mall; they had a lot to catch up on over their Dougie Burgers and diet soda.

"I love that we both just ordered the biggest burger known to man, and then made sure we ordered *diet* soda," Meg said, and they both started laughing.

Although they spoke on the phone nearly every day when Meg was gone, it wasn't the same. There's something about a friend face-to-face that makes them more tangible.

Meg looked at Val and said, "I can't even tell you how good it is to see you. Now I understand that saying 'sight for sore eyes.' So, what's going on? I tried calling your house and your cell yesterday, but nobody answered. How's Jay?"

Val looked at Meg, unsure of how to begin. "We broke up," she said, as quickly as the words could come out, and took a sip of her drink, doing all she could not to make eye contact with Meg. She expected the next words out of Meg's mouth.

"But you two were perfect! Val, what happened?"

"I don't know. I just needed to breathe," Val said. "It's like I told him - he was great. He *is* great. It's not him. It's me."

"You didn't - *it's not you, it's me?* Tell me you didn't, Val?" Meg looked at her friend in disbelief, "You didn't?"

"Meg! I feel bad enough already! And it is the truth. It has nothing to do with him, it *is* me. Just *trust* me, okay?" Val wanted to try and explain everything, but she just couldn't, she didn't understand it herself.

16

"Consider yourself officially *trusted*, okay?" Meg joked. "But seriously, *it's not you, it's me?*"

Both friends grimaced at the realization of how trite it really was. Val was about to change the subject when out of the corner of her eye she saw the three guys walking in their direction.

"Oh shit, oh shit!"

"What? Oh shit what? I'm just teasing you, Val -"

"No, it's the guys - and he's with them." Val attempted to find another direction to look in, to pretend that she hadn't seen them.

"Don't worry, this is not going to be the most awkward first day of summer ever, *trust me.*"

Val looked at her and rolled her eyes in response to Meg's sarcasm, and for the first time, Meg realized that there really was something going on with Val - she was not acting like herself at all.

"I'm so glad you're finally back from living at your grandma's," Val said, with a look of relief on her face. "Things have been rough without you."

∞

As the three guys approached, Dave was the first to see Meg and Val sitting at the corner table on the patio at Dougie's. It was such a cool hangout spot in the summer. Each table was unique and adorned with a different promotional umbrella to provide shade. The girls looked as if they were deep in conversation. Val was leaning forward across the table, and Meg had her legs stretched out on the vacant chair beside her. "Hey, I need to go and remind Val - and oh crap…Meg's back! - I need to remind them about the party tonight."

Jay perked up, "Your parents are going ahead with it?"

Vern answered for Dave. "Come on bro; it's tradition."

"Yeah, I just wondered if they were going to have the party again this year," Jay said, "you know, with everything."

"Yeah," Dave said, "I think they considered cancelling it for a second, but thought that it would be good for everyone to try to have a good time."

"I do have a weakness for your mom's beefies," Jay smiled.

"Whoa!" Vern interjected. "That's Dave's mom; have some respect!"

Dave chuckled. "Actually, he just likes her homemade meatballs, she calls them beefies."

"Oh," Vern said, followed by a playful grin.

"You guys go tell them," Jay said to his friends, hoping they'd understand that he had no desire to face Val in that unexpected instant. "I'm going to drop these movies off."

Dave and Vern approached the girls on the patio. "Hey, ladies," Dave said as smoothly as he could. "You're both coming to the summer shindig tonight, I hope?" He winked at them and held his hands out waiting for an answer.

"It's kind of lame that we call it the summer shindig," he laughed, "but it's guaranteed to be a fun time. You gotta come, okay?"

"Or don't come - up to you, really!" Vern offered, with that playful smile still on his face.

"I don't know...-" Val started to say.

Meg lowered her feet off the chair they were resting on and turned to face the guys. "We'll be there, Dave," she said. "See you tonight."

Dave smiled; the girls had given him the answer he was hoping for.

"So Meg, can you still go toe-to-toe, beer-for-beer, shot-for-shot with the guys after spending all that time away with your grandma?" Vern asked.

"Who do you think I get it from, Vern?" She winked. "See you tonight."

Vern placed his hand on his heart, and turned to walk away with Dave.

The guys met up with Jay again in the mini mall.

"Bro." Vern stopped walking, and just stood where he was, looking happily stunned. Dave and Jay realized from a few feet ahead that he wasn't right beside them. They stood where they were, waiting for Vern to catch up - but he appeared to be lost in his own world. They looked at each other, Dave shrugged his shoulders, and they started walking back towards Vern.

"What's up?" Dave asked.

"Meg," Vern said with his eyes wide. He looked down at his chest, grinned, and then looked back at Dave.

"I know," Dave grinned, "growth spurt." The two chuckled.

Vern raised his hand, signalling Dave for a high-five. Dave pounded his hand with a closed fist. Vern looked at him quizzically.

"*Pound* five, dude," he explained.

"Epic," Vern said in awe.

The guys decided that the best use of their afternoon would be to see if Dave's parents needed any help getting ready for the shindig. They walked in the back door, which entered directly into the kitchen. Jay felt like he was walking into the Seavers' kitchen from the set of the 80s sitcom *Growing Pains* every time he went over to Dave's place.

The smell of deliciousness hit them as they surrounded the kitchen island like a pack of hungry wolves. Dave's mom, Deb, had stuff cooking on the stove, baking in the oven, and sitting out on cookie sheets to cool. The crockpot in the middle of the kitchen island, however, might as well have been a pot of gold. Deb had just taken the lid off to have a taste test when she noticed all of the boys staring at her with looks of primal hunger on their faces.

She chuckled, "Anybody want a taste?"

Vern couldn't control himself. "I want your *beefies!*"

Dave gave Vern a solid elbow in the ribs.

"What?" Vern said, with that mischievous smile of his.

"So how are you boys enjoying summer so far?" Deb asked the group.

"It's decent," Dave replied.

"It's okay," Jay said. "Better than gym with Watkins."

"Seriously, Dave's mom," Vern started, "I love the freedom, and no school, and all that - but my day today - my day was so awkward. Like, *so* awkward."

"Vern, I've known you since you were a toddler. You need to stop calling me Dave's mom. It's Deb, okay?"

"Sure, sorry Dave's mom," Vern laughed, realizing he did it again. He shrugged. "But back to my day being awkward already... you know..." He couldn't stand still - he was pacing all over the kitchen, and his words were even more chaotic than his movements. "...And her, I think I love her...but she hates me. Well, I think she does, I'm pretty sure she always used to."

Deb shot a *help-me-out-here* look at Dave.

"Apparently he has a crush on Meg, Mom, that's what he meant."

Deb nodded, "Ah, I see."

"You're telling me," said Vern, "you're telling me."

"Too bad Val broke up with me yesterday," Jay said. "We could have gone on a double."

Deb grabbed Jay's hand and gave him a look of motherly comfort, as if to say, *it'll be all right.*

Vern piped up, "Yeah! Way to screw that up, you jerk!"

Jay just shook his head, and smiled at Dave's mom to let her know that he would be okay.

Dave, feeling the need to put Vern in his place, said, "Hey Vern, you know I was thinking...maybe we could set Jay up with one of the Polanski sisters?"

"Dude," Vern said, "the guy just got dumped, what kind of monster would feed him to the piranhas after something like that?"

Dave laughed to himself.

"The Polanski sisters?" Jay asked.

"Don't ask," Vern said.

"We went over to their place during the last week of school," Dave explained.

"What?" Jay was shocked. "How did I not know about this? The two of you, hung out with the two of them?"

All three boys smiled at each other, as Deb appeared to remain oblivious to what it meant to "hang out" with the Polanski sisters.

"You guys will have to fill me in on this," Jay said.

"I never kiss and tell," Vern grinned.

Dave started to laugh, maybe a little too hard - and Jay wondered what was so funny, but figured the guys would fill him in when Dave's mom wasn't around.

CHAPTER 6

Meg leaned back in the Adirondack chair, hugged her knees and stared ahead, fixated on the dancing flames. It seemed amazing that if she really listened, she could still hear the crackle of the fire through the multiple conversations and over-accentuated laughs of neighbours and friends who'd gathered for the Listers' annual summer kick-off shindig. She felt safe and secure sitting by the fire. She could just stare at the flames and her mind would go blank - no thoughts, no worries, no guilt.

Her dad had dropped her off a few minutes earlier, but none of her friends had arrived yet. She'd really wanted him to come - and tried, without being too pushy, to convince him that he should.

"I'm really sorry, Meggy," he said, "I have to work on the truck and tonight is the only free time I'll have for the next while."

She knew the truck was about to explode or something, but she also knew that the real reason he didn't want to attend the shindig this year was because he didn't want to answer questions about how he was doing, and he didn't want to face people's phoney looks of concern, and obvious looks of pity. It hit her that last year, at this time, her mom was sitting beside her at the fire, roasting marshmallows for everyone so that they could make s'mores.

Suddenly Meg felt like the fire was the last place she wanted to be. She made her way through the huddles of familiar faces, hoping that friends her own age had now arrived. She approached the deck and heard Vern, talking with his mouth full.

"Dave's mom, Jay was right, your meatballs rule. Seriously, I love your beefies." Vern was speaking partly to Deb, partly to himself, and partly to the meatballs themselves.

Meg saw Jay sitting off to the side, away from everyone else on the deck. He was sitting on the edge of the deck's railing, with his back against the cedar shake of the house. She hadn't had a chance to speak to him since she got back to the End, and she really wanted to say hello, but wasn't sure how to approach him. She knew it would be awkward because of the breakup, but wanted to make things as easy as possible for him and Val within their close-knit group of friends. She wanted to let him know, without saying as much, that she still valued his friendship. She started walking towards him, and as he made eye contact, she gave him a wave. He smiled and motioned for her to come over.

"Meg!" He jumped down onto the deck and gave her a big Jay-style hug. "It's so good to see you, when did you get back?"

"Great to see you too," she said. "A couple of days ago. I see you still give the best hugs ever."

Just then, Val walked out the patio door onto the deck. She noticed Meg and Jay, and smiled an awkward smile in their direction. She hoped Meg would come over, knowing that she wasn't quite ready for an awkward meeting with Jay. Val knew that he'd be there tonight, and she knew that at some point they would have to speak to each other. Their friends were always mutual friends. That meant that the breakup wasn't only between them, it was tough on their friends too. She hoped that it would get more comfortable for her to be around him in these kinds of situations, though. She just felt so guilty every time she looked at him.

She was relieved when Meg started making her way over. "Will you come and sit with me in the yard?"

They managed to snag a couple of vacant lawn chairs resting on the side of the house.

"Sorry," Val said, "I just think, I think I might need a bit of time, and maybe a drink - then I can be around him."

"I get it, no worries," Meg said. "I'm here for you - whatever you need. Seriously, I wouldn't have gotten through these last six months without you - anything you need, I got it babe." Val smiled at Meg in appreciation.

"How's this for a subject changer?" Meg said. "Ever since I've been home, I feel like I'm being watched. It's creepy, I can't shake this feeling that somebody is always watching me - think it could be my mom?"

Val smiled sympathetically. "It could be, if you believe in that, but I think that it's probably been Vern." She pointed at Vern, who was leaning on his elbows at the edge of the deck, supporting his head in his hands, blatantly staring at the girls. "He's been staring over here since we sat down." When he saw them both look in his direction, he stood up straight and shot them a peace sign, seemingly oblivious to the fact that he still had sauce from the beefies all over his face.

"Has he?" Meg blushed, but hoped that Val couldn't tell.

"I don't know," Val said. "Maybe I'm just imagining things - it's so weird with Jay over there - but he seriously hasn't taken his eyes off you."

Meg laughed, and was about to continue the discussion about Vern, when Val's parents walked through the gate.

"Hey, your parents are here!" she exclaimed - but as she looked at Val's face, it became apparent that she already knew, and that she was not as excited about their arrival. The smile vanished from Val's face, and she looked over at Meg with fear and desperation in her eyes.

"This isn't good," she said and leaned forward in her chair. "Do you remember what I told you about my Dad? I don't think it's good that they're here."

Meg put her arm around Val's shoulder. "It'll be okay," she reassured her, "maybe he wants to make things better. Maybe he's trying." Val looked at Meg with a slight grin of appreciation, but Meg could tell that she wasn't buying it.

∞

Dave had been helping his mom with final touches on the food, arranging platters, and walking around serving guests, ensuring that they all had food and drinks in hand. He bumped into his mom, who was chatting to some neighbours in the yard.

"Thanks for all your help, Love - you're officially off duty." Deb squeezed his hand. "Go and enjoy yourself."

Dave made his way to the deck to catch up with Jay and Vern. As he walked past the girls in their lawn chairs, he winked at them - and it hit him that he hadn't asked Jay if it was okay to invite Val. He ran up the stairs to the deck, skipping every second step, and over to where Jay was again perched on the deck railing, staring off into space.

"Crap, Jay," Dave said. "I'm sorry man! I'm an idiot! Must be awkward, but I didn't even think to ask you if it was okay to still invite Val to the party - sorry about that!"

"It's cool man, excuse me for a second, though," Jay said. He got up, walked past the girls in their lawn chairs without a look or a word, and passed through the gate. He sat on the Listers' front steps.

Just before Dave came running up the steps, Jay had decided he needed a few minutes away from the crowd. While he was sitting there, watching the party happen around him - he realized that he was actually okay with the breakup, and somehow, that awareness made him feel even more confused.

He was flustered, but it wasn't because of Val and the breakup. It wasn't really Val that he was upset about losing; it was the idea of losing the habitual life he was accustomed to. He didn't know what he was supposed to do now, now that he was just Jay. He smiled to himself with the thought that he was kind of like Julia Roberts in *Runaway Bride* - he didn't know what kind of eggs he liked without Val.

∞

Val looked around the yard and saw the clusters of people talking and chuckling; the group by the fire had already started singing cheesy campfire tunes. Last year at the shindig, the five of them had spent the whole party together, laughing their asses off. "Great," she said to Meg, "this whole situation is going to make for a great summer." She rolled her eyes. "Should I go talk to him?"

Just then, she heard them start. Her parents were standing a few feet away, between where she and Meg were sitting and where the stairs led up to the deck. They were in the middle of everything that was happening; they might as well have been on a stage. Val wished there was a place where she could run and hide, or a rock she could crawl under, because she knew what was coming, and she couldn't believe that it was going to happen outside the walls of their home.

"So can we leave already, Janet?" Val's dad snapped. "We made our appearance, let's go."

"We just got here, Kent," her mom replied. "Give it a rest."

"Yeah, well, I've already had enough," Kent replied in his long, drawn out, over-accentuated arguing words.

Val knew that her Dad hated it when people got involved in his business. She could clearly see that the party-goers were all aware of the spectacle, as many of them stopped their conversations to gawk. She was mortified when he turned to one of the Listers' neighbours and snidely said, "Hello there, am I wearing something of yours?"

"For God's sake, Kent! Have some manners, these are our friends," Janet said desperately, "unless you've forgotten that?"

"They are your friends," he said through his teeth. "I'm outta here."

They continued to yell at each other, but Meg and Val could no longer hear what they were actually saying. All eyes seemed to be on the arguing couple, but it was now as if they didn't even realize anyone else was around. The humiliation of it wouldn't sink in until later; until someone saw Janet in the grocery store and smiled with concealed judgement, or until one of the guys at work reminded Kent of the adage, "happy wife, happy life." In that moment, however, it was as if they were alone, and unaware that everyone was witnessing the death of their once impeccable marriage.

Meg grabbed Val's hand. "Now I get it."

Val put her head on Meg's shoulder and wondered if things could get any worse. Kent stormed past the girls and slammed the gate as he left. Janet put a fake smile on her face and walked over to the deck. "What a beautiful spread you have here," she said with exaggerated oomph. "I've really been looking forward to this party."

CHAPTER 7

Jay didn't know how long he'd been sitting on the Listers' front steps, enjoying the solitude, when he saw her walking from a few lamp posts away. She had long, auburn brown hair that bounced behind her as she walked. She was wearing black Chuck Taylors, jeans and a plain white V-neck t-shirt. He could no longer hear the muffled conversations and background noise from the party - the only sound was her voice, speaking to someone on the phone.

"Yes, Mom - I have my key. You need to lock the door - and no, I won't go far."

She tucked her phone into her back pocket, and continued walking in his direction - he was fascinated by her; he knew he had to find out who she was. She walked past Dave's house, and Jay realized she wasn't stopping there for the party.

"Hey, wait up!" he called out to her.

She turned around, and smiled as Jay skipped over the curb. He suddenly felt a buzz of nervousness. *This is crazy,* he thought to himself, but she was captivating. He thought this must have been how Noah felt when he first saw Allie in *The Notebook*.

"Who, me?" she asked.

"Yes, you - hi, I'm Jay." He reached out his hand, wondering if that was weird, and wondering if it was obvious how intensely he was staring at her.

"Jess," she said, with a smile, as she looked up at him with the most inviting green eyes he'd ever seen. She shook his hand,

and giggled - indicating to Jay that he was right, the whole situation was a bit awkward.

"Pleasure to meet you, Jess. You're new here, I take it?" He was still holding onto her hand.

"Yeah," Jess said, "we moved in last night. We moved into that little cottage on the bayside, with the garden in back, and the blue shutters - the one that has the wraparound porch." Her smile revealed how much she liked her new home. "We've been setting up all day, so I decided to take a break - and walk around for a bit, you know, to kind of scope out the town."

"Well, welcome to the End!" Jay said. "But first things first - one, we're a village, not a town, and two, have you been to the beach yet?"

Jess laughed. "Okay, village police, got it - *village, not town* - and no, I haven't been to the beach."

As the breeze swept through Jess's hair, Jay was intrigued by the enchanting scent. Jess had always individualized her shampoo by mixing her mom's drugstore brand with various essential oils. This time she had used lavender. He felt his stomach flutter, and his heart was pounding so hard he wondered if she could hear it.

"Would you like me to take you? I mean, to the beach?" Jay wondered if she could tell that he was blushing under the glow of the street lamp.

"That would be nice," Jess said, sort of bashfully.

"C'mon." Jay motioned in the direction of the beach. "You're going to love it here."

Jess smiled and followed Jay - *I think I am going to love it here,* she thought to herself.

CHAPTER 8

Steph put on a pot of coffee, and started mixing eggs into the pancake batter. She wouldn't risk putting breakfast on the table these days without coffee - even though her daughter was only fifteen and it seemed like she was breaking the laws of motherhood by allowing it. She forced herself to open the kitchen window to let some fresh air in, even though the little voice in her head was saying no. She was struggling to accept that she was safe.

You came here for freedom, she thought to herself. "Open the damn window, would ya?" she said out loud with a self-scorning chuckle. Steph had become so accustomed to walking on eggshells and living in fear it was as if there was no other way.

It took everything in her to allow Jess to leave the house, alone - their first day in Erie's End. She was terrified of what might happen, who might see her, if they had been followed - all the possibilities of what could happen while she walked through the village had raced through her mind. She paced the whole time Jess was gone, she could barely wait ten minutes before calling to speak to her on her cell phone, and she nearly broke down in tears when Jess returned safe and sound two hours after she left. That's when she decided to call the counsellor from Richmond, the one who encouraged her to leave in the first place. The one she met in the hospital that night.

Steph did not want her daughter to live in fear, and she knew that in order for that to be possible, she would have to encourage Jess to live outside her own insecurities. She looked at the blue wooden door, and realized that it might be difficult to encourage self-assurance and freedom with deadbolts on the door of a cottage. It seemed that everyone else in Erie's End left their doors unlocked, even when they went out. Steph wondered if she'd ever manage to get to that point. For now, opening the kitchen window was a start. The counsellor from Richmond gave Steph the name of a therapist in the city, one she said would help her to adjust to her new life and to feel safe. She looked at the name on the calendar and traced it with her finger: *Dr. Lindsay Taylor.*

∞

Jess loved waking up to the smell of her mom making breakfast. It was the bacon that got her every time. She rolled over in her white cloud of a bed and stretched her arms above her head. She loved this cottage. Her bedding was like heaven - white cotton sheets and a white down duvet that literally made her feel like she was in the middle of a cloud. She knew she was supposed to be cautious and nervously on the lookout, but she wasn't. She felt good here. She felt safe and like this place was too good, so good that someone as evil as him wouldn't even know it existed. She had decided from the passenger seat of the old F-150 that she was going to make the best of this new opportunity. He already ruined their old life; she wasn't going to give him the power to ruin their new one.

She recognized that her mom would have freaked if she knew, but Jess had been sleeping with her window open since they moved into the cottage. She loved the smell of the fresh air and the grass, and even hearing the sound of the birds chirping at the crack of dawn. She could smell the coffee brewing, which was the persuasion she needed to throw the covers off and jump out of bed. She closed her bedroom window, and closed the curtains so that her mom would be none the wiser.

She stood back and admired how her painted curtains had turned out. She picked out white canvas curtains when she went shopping with her mom, and then took acrylic paints and created an abstract that instead of hanging on the wall, hung from her windows. Her new room was coming together; her plan for the day was to string mini Christmas lights strategically throughout.

Jess grabbed the jeans that were hanging off her vanity chair, and sand poured out of the rolled-up cuffs onto her floor.

"Mom, do we have a vacuum yet?" she asked as she walked into the kitchen. "I got sand all over my floor."

Steph poured her daughter a coffee. "Where the heck did the sand come from?"

Jess grabbed her coffee off the counter. She took a sip, smiled at her mom and started telling her the details of her walk and the first friend she met in Erie's End, and the beach - and more importantly, she said, "Mom, I think we're really going to like it here."

CHAPTER 9

Val waited for Meg on her front porch while she helped her dad with Matthew's treatment. She was wearing a blue sundress over her bathing suit. She'd packed a bag for the beach, and her mom had packed a cooler with enough food for her and Meg for the day. Janet was going to the city for the next couple of days to visit her sister. She said that she needed a shopping weekend and a bit of girl time, but Val knew she just really wanted to get away from her dad for a little while. She dropped Val off at Meg's on her way out of town.

Through the open screen door, Val could hear Meg's dad pounding on Matthew's back to loosen up the mucus from his lungs. He had to have it done a couple of times a day. Val thought it must be so uncomfortable for Matthew. She heard him start to cough, and then she heard Meg say, "That's it buddy, great job!"

Meg's other brother Mark stepped outside the door and sat down beside Val. Mark was eleven. He offered Val one of the two chocolate chip cookies he had in his hand.

"No thanks Mark, I'm good…how's your summer going?" she asked.

"It's okay," Mark said, "but I wish my brother's cystic fibrosis didn't take up so much time. We never have time to do stuff."

She put her arm around him. "We all wish that he didn't have CF too, Mark." She tried to comprehend how difficult the past six months must have been on him. "I heard you've been a great help for your dad," she said.

He gave her a little smile, she gave him a little squeeze, and she was convinced that she'd at least made him feel better in that moment. "Dad's taking us fishing when they're done with Matt," he told Val, "I hope."

"Awesome," she said. "Guys' day out!"

Mark nodded, trying to conceal his excitement.

Meg walked out the door with a towel draped over her arm. She was dressed in her cargo shorts, flip-flops and one of her many baseball caps, with a tank top covering her swimsuit. "Dad," she called, "I have my cell, call me if you need anything - we'll just be at the beach."

"We'll be fine," he hollered, "have fun!"

The girls had been looking forward to this day at the beach. "I can't believe it's been a week since the Listers' party already," Val said as they starting walking.

"Speak of the devil," Meg replied as she saw Dave and Vern in the distance - on their way to the beach as well.

"Wait up!" Val called, and they stopped dead in their tracks. While they were waiting for the girls to catch up to them, Dave and Vern started whipping their beach towels at each other and laughing.

"This bonfire's going to be the highlight of our summer," Val said to Meg, "I'm so excited for tonight."

"Do we know anyone who can play guitar?" Meg asked. "We need campfire tunes."

"I don't think so," Val said. "Wait - Vern might, I don't know why, but I think he might."

"Okay, otherwise, we're set," Meg said as she half skipped, half walked down the centre of the street. "Did your brother get us beer?"

"Yeah," said Val, "I have to go back to the house for it later, though. He said his train from the city gets in around dinner time...don't worry though, he's got it covered."

Ever since Val's brother went away to college, it seemed to Val like he was more willing to do decent-older-brother stuff for her - like get her alcohol for parties. She figured it was because he felt guilty for leaving her alone to deal with their parents' issues.

"Uncle! Uncle!" Vern yelled and laughed at the same time. "When you say uncle it means stop, you jackass."

Dave reined in his towel when the girls were a couple of feet away. "Are you ladies heading to the beach?" he asked.

"Sure are!" Val smiled. She was happy today; she hadn't felt this good in a long time and was enjoying every minute of it.

"You would waste all of your time at the beach," Vern teased, fully aware that time spent at the beach could never be considered time wasted.

"Whatever, Vern," Meg said. "Oh hey, do you have a guitar?"

"Maybe I do, and maybe I do," he said in his *I'm-oh-so-clever* voice.

"Why are you always so difficult?" Meg asked him with a sense of exasperation.

"You're attracted to me right now, aren't you Meg?" he replied as he broadened his shoulders and his smile. It was more of a statement than an actual question.

∞

Jay had been spending a lot of his time with Jess since the night of Dave's party. He showed her around Erie's End, and was someone other than her mom to hang out with. They had gotten into a routine of meeting up and finding new places in Erie's End for Jess to be introduced to. Today they were going to sit at the end of an old wooden dock that belonged to a retired fisherman, Mr. Johnson. He had reluctantly left the End to live with his daughter and her family in the city. He wasn't able to take care of his home on his own anymore, but he refused to sell it.

Jay stopped along the way, as they walked through the village and along the beach, to pick up as many skipping stones as he could find. Jess was curious about what he was doing with so many rocks. As they crossed the lane toward Mr. Johnson's the thought occurred to her that maybe he had some kind of collection and she found it endearing.

The dock was starting to warp and some boards were rotting or missing, or awkwardly sticking out, making the walk to the end of the dock a bit hazardous. Jay warned Jess to be careful as they made their way to the edge - he grabbed her hand at one point to help guide her so she wouldn't step through one of the rotten boards. He felt a flutter when her hand was in his - but brushed it aside.

He had heard his mom tell one of her girlfriends once that "sometimes people come into our lives just when we need them." He couldn't help but think that was the case with Jess. She managed to come into his life just when he needed a friend who knew nothing of his history with Val, and who he could be himself with. He could have an independent identity with her: he wasn't Jay of "Jay and Val."

As they sat at the edge of the dock, Jay pulled all of the stones he'd collected out of his pockets and placed them in a big pile between them. "I'm kind of an expert at skipping stones," he proclaimed with a laugh. "How about you?" he asked. "Do you partake in this generally underrated sport?"

Jess laughed. "I'm afraid not," she said. "I've actually never skipped a stone in my life."

"Okay," he said, "I'm going to give you all of my secrets, but you have to promise to never tell anyone else."

"Promise," Jess said, "cross my heart," and she drew a cross over her heart with her finger.

"First" - Jay picked up one of the stones - "you have to make sure that you choose stones that are pretty flat. Most people think round stones are best - but I'm telling you if you can find triangular ones, you're golden. You hold the stone with your thumb and your middle finger" - he picked up another stone and showed Jess how to place her fingers - "then you hook your pointer finger on the edge like this." Jess paid close attention and nodded to show Jay that she was following. "When you throw the stone," he said, "and this is key - throw out and down, and throw it fast." Jay threw the stone he was holding and it skipped across the surface of the lake.

"That's amazing!" Jess said. "Can I try?"

"Absolutely," Jay said, "don't feel bad if you don't get it the first few times - it takes some getting used to."

Jess carefully picked what she thought was the best stone. She placed her fingers the way Jay had shown her, and she threw it out and down as fast as she could. The stone skipped over the surface of the lake like a grasshopper sweeping over grass in a field. Every single stone that Jess threw was a skipper. Jay was in awe. "Must be beginner's luck," Jess said with a grin.

Jay laughed and said, "I've been practicing my whole life, and look at you...you're here for a week and you're already out-skipping me."

Jess smiled. "I'm all out of stones." Jay handed her the rest of the ones he had been holding.

"I was wondering," Jess raised her eyebrow in a sideways glance at Jay.

"Yes?" He smiled and raised his eyebrow in response.

"Well," she said, "I was wondering if you're going to introduce me to your friends? It'd be nice to know a few more people. I mean, don't get me wrong -"

"Awesome!" Jay interrupted. "They'll love you. We're actually planning a bonfire at the beach tonight - want to come?"

"I would *love* that!" Jess could not contain her excitement. She had fallen in love with the beach that first night when Jay brought her there. "Do you think your friends will care that I'm younger than all of you?" she asked, with her excitement fading a little as the possibility entered her mind. Through the discussions they'd had, she'd deducted that Jay's friends were all sixteen like him.

"Seriously," he said, "they will love you."

She smiled and said, "I better get home and let my mom know my plans - she can be kind of protective. She'll probably want to meet you before we go if I'm going to be out late - would that be okay? Could you pick me up tonight?"

"I can do that," Jay smiled. "Be at your place at seven, okay?"

Jess grinned; she couldn't wait. She skipped her last stone, and stood up.

∞

"No, Vern," Meg said, "I really don't think you should order a Borat Mankini!"

"C'mon," he said, "if anyone could pull it off, I could." Meg shook her head and laughed - she wouldn't put it past him.

"Oh, I bet that's my brother!" Val said as her phone chirped. She picked it up, and read the text from her brother out-loud to Meg.

"*Hey Val, sorry - but I'm not coming home this weekend after all. Mom told me she wasn't going to be home, and none of the guys are there this weekend either. I know I said I'd get you beer for the fire - sorry! Listen though, I have a full bottle of tequila in my room - it's yours. It's in the shoebox that my Jordans came in - back of my closet. Just be careful with it dude.*"

"Meg! Did you hear any of that?" Val asked, a bit irritated that Meg had spent most of the afternoon in relentless banter with Vern. She thought it was bizarre how much Meg and Vern seemed to be enjoying each other's company. She gave Dave a quizzical look; Dave nodded with the same puzzled look on his face, indicating to Val that he thought this new connection in their circle of friends was surprising too.

"Okay, let's go," Val said. "I want to get everything ready and leave the house before my dad gets home from work."

The four friends started collecting the stuff they'd accumulated throughout the afternoon at the beach. They picked up their empty soda bottles and packed up the magazines they'd brought. Val stuffed her sunscreen back into her bag and asked if anyone wanted the leftover sandwiches from the cooler. "Come to Papa," Vern said as he reached for them. Dave picked up the small pieces of driftwood he'd collected - he got into the habit of collecting it for his mom whenever he could; she used it for crafts.

"See you guys tonight," Meg said as she started walking away from the group.

"Ooh - I hate to see you go, but I love to watch you leave," Vern said under his breath as he watched Meg walking away. As he stared, Meg turned her head back over her shoulder and shot a sweet smile in Vern's direction. "How cute are you today?" he said, this time loudly enough for her to hear.

"That's a nice," Meg said in her best Borat impression. She winked and turned away again, hoping that Val would catch up soon. Dave rolled his eyes towards Val, who returned the gesture and ran after Meg.

Dave grabbed Vern's shoulder, and started walking him in the opposite direction of the girls. "See you ladies tonight," he said over his shoulder. "You're all starting to sound like Jay with the movie references."

"Yeah, see ya tonight," said Val. "And Vern - don't forget the guitar."

"Yeah - bring the guitar," Meg added.

"Your wish is my command," Vern said, as he continued to stare at Meg - and the tank top she'd put on over her wet swimsuit.

Val and Meg walked down the street towards Meg's house in silence. It seemed to Val like Meg was in a blissful daze. As much as Val was irritated by it at the beach, the more she thought about it, the more she thought it was good for Meg to feel like someone wanted her around.

"What's with you and Vern?" she teased and gave Meg a little hip bump as they walked down the street. Meg shrugged her shoulders as if to imply that she didn't know what Val was talking about.

As they approached Meg's house, they saw Matt and Mark sitting on the front steps, Mark was hunched over with his chin resting on his hands. The truck was sitting in the driveway with its hood open and pieces of its engine scattered around it.

"We didn't go fishing," Mark said in a matter-of-fact way to nobody in particular as the girls approached.

"Where's Dad?" Meg asked. Matt pointed, and the girls started walking towards the open garage.

Meg put her hand out to suggest that Val stop - she saw her dad sitting on a milk crate in the garage. His face and hands were blackened with dirt from working on the truck; when he looked up at Meg, it appeared that the only part of his face that wasn't covered in dirt was where tears had rolled down his cheeks. She realized that he had just spent hours working on the truck, trying to get it to go, so that he could take the boys fishing.

"I just don't know what I'm going to do," he said, and another tear made its way down his cheek.

Meg waved at Val, and called out to her from the garage. "I'll see you at the fire tonight!"

Val understood that this family just needed to be with each other right now. She waved back at Meg and blew her a kiss as she made her way down the driveway. It had been a great day in the sun, but it had tired her out and she hoped she'd have time for a quick nap when she got home.

Meg pulled up another milk crate and sat beside her dad. She put her arm around him. He put his head on her shoulder and began to sob. She held him as tears streamed down her face, too. He didn't even cry like that when her mom died. She didn't know what else to do but just sit and let him cry, and she cried with him - and in some strange way it felt good.

∞

Val walked the rest of the way to her house thinking about Meg and her dad. It was hard to see them like that, but she knew they both needed it. She hoped that Meg would still be coming tonight, and that they could talk about what happened over roasted marshmallows and tequila.

As she walked in the front door, she could hear loud music coming from Kevin's room. He had a really great stereo - every once in a while when just the two of them were home, they would blast music through the entire house and dance around - and the thought of it made her miss her brother. She realized that since his music was on, he must have come! *Maybe he was just messing with me to surprise me,* she thought. Val dropped her beach stuff in the front entrance and ran up to his room. She swung the door open - but discovered that he wasn't in his room. She figured she'd wait and grabbed the shoebox from the back of his closet. She took the forty-ouncer. "Thank. You. Kevin," she whispered.

She closed his door behind her and continued down the hall towards her own room. She noticed that the door to her parents' room at the end of the hall was open a crack. She thought that maybe in the chaos of rushing out of the house that morning her mom forgot to close it all the way. She always kept it closed so that the cat, Lucy, wouldn't nestle up and leave tufts of white fuzz on her pillow.

She passed her own bedroom and continued towards her parents' room, thinking she'd inevitably find Lucy on the bed, and planned to bring her into her room and close her parents' door. As she got closer, she could hear that someone was in the room - but wasn't able to discern who it was because Kevin's music was so loud.

"Kev," she yelled as she pushed her parents' bedroom door open, "is that you?" She stood in the doorway, unable to move or speak. She felt sick to her stomach, as she stared - unable to remove her gaze from the sight of her dad on top of another woman. They were both completely naked.

The woman saw Val, and gasped. "Kent," she said, "you told me nobody was here!"

He turned his head and saw Val standing in the doorway. "Get outta here, Val," he said, as if he was asking her to pass the peas.

"Asshole," was her response - but she wasn't sure if the word actually came out of her mouth. She pivoted around. She was in shock, but willed herself to walk down the hall with the bottle of tequila still in hand, and out the front door.

CHAPTER 10

"Vern!" Dave's mom yelled into the living room.

"S'up, Dave's Mom?" he answered, and Deb appeared in the doorway between the kitchen and living room, smiling and shaking her head. "It's Deb," she said. "Are you joining us for dinner tonight?" she asked.

"Oh, thank you!" he said, momentarily taking his gaze away from the video game he was playing. "You know I'd love to, but I have to go home and shower and change before the fire tonight."

"Okay," she said, "if you change your mind, you're more than welcome - dinner's in an hour," and she went back into the kitchen.

"Dude!" Dave groaned. "What the hell?"

"You should know by now to never mess with the Vernmeister, bro." Vern was revelling in the fact that he just beat Dave in another level of 007. "It's so wicked that your uncle gave you his old Nintendo 64, dude - but I told you it's impossible to beat me."

Dave rolled his eyes as Vern danced around the living room with the controller in his hand. "I think Meg really has a thing for you," Dave said, knowing that it would stop his gloating.

"You think?" Vern stopped in his tracks and threw the controller on the couch.

"Oddly enough," Dave said, "yes - I do."

"It's so weird," said Vern in an unusually serious tone, "in the most awesome way imaginable."

He was interrupted by a knock at the door, followed by Deb's voice greeting Jay and advising him that they were in the living room.

"Thanks, Dave's mom!" Jay said.

"Not you too, Jay - it's Deb, for God's sake."

Jay walked into the living room with a bounce in his step and a smile from ear to ear. He saw Dave sprawled out on the blue-and-green plaid couch as Vern did his victory dance in front of the fireplace whose mantel was adorned with photos and handmade crafts. "Guys, Jess is coming to the fire tonight," he announced.

"No way," said Dave. "You mean we actually get to meet this mystery girl you've been hanging out with?"

"I bet she doesn't even exist," Vern interjected, "not like my girl." He smiled to himself, and then shared a big grin with the guys.

"Your girl?" asked Jay.

Dave answered for Vern. "It seems as though Meg likes Vern, and well - we all know how Vern feels."

"That's awesome, man!" Jay said.

With the utmost look of concern on his face, Vern then asked, "Dude, you bringing this girl...is it going to be cool with Val?" He clumsily leaned back on the mantel and caused a couple of the picture frames to fall over. He started standing them back up without watching what he was doing, but looking intently at Jay. "Because if Val's upset, then Meg's going to want to comfort her, and if Meg's comforting Val, then she's not going to be comforting me - if you catch my drift?"

"Vern, seriously," Jay replied. "First of all, Val broke up with me, and secondly, it's not even like that with Jess. We're friends, and she needs to meet more people - I think she'll get along great with Meg and Val. Anyway" - Jay put his hands in his pockets and shrugged his shoulders - "I just wanted to let you guys know that she's coming. I better go home. I still have to get ready, and let my grandparents know what's going on tonight. I'll see you later."

"Yo, this stud muffin better get ready too," Vern said, with each of his thumbs pointing back towards his shoulders.

Jay and Dave both laughed, as they had never seen Vern so eager to impress. Typically, he was absurdly self-assured and confident. The way he dressed, and the clothes he wore often demonstrated how audacious he really was. Sometimes they were too big, sometimes they were from a different decade, sometimes the colour choices were questionable - but Vern always seemed to wear those clothes with purpose, and people got the impression that whatever he was wearing, it was intentional.

His entire walk home, Vern could not contain his excitement for the bonfire. He actually jumped and clicked his heels together when he passed through the weeping willows at the entrance to the path. The path started at the end of Dave's street and wound through to the centre of Erie's End, where he lived.

Vern lived in Golden Acres, the trailer park in the centre of the village, tucked discreetly behind a few storefronts and the local watering hole. It wasn't the trailer park that campers and tourists went to for summer retreats with their RVs and family photo ops. Golden Acres was a beautiful name for a not-so-beautiful place. A place that Vern felt he had no connection to whatsoever, and a place that he worked very hard to ensure did not define him.

Vern approached the front steps of the double-wide he lived in with his mom. He only spent as much time there as he had to. His mom didn't notice if he was there or not, so when he slept out at Dave's or Jay's, or on the beach in his tent, it made no difference to her. She was sitting on the floral wooden-framed couch when Vern walked in. She took a long drag of her cigarette, and as she exhaled her coarse voice asked, "Where the hell ya been?"

Surprised by her asking, Vern stepped back and looked into the living room, about to answer, when he saw that she was on the phone. As Vern closed the door to his room, he smiled at the thought that Meg really had been flirting with him that afternoon.

∞

As he approached the cottage, Jay could see why Jess loved it. It was directly on the bay, and the only thing holding the waves back from crashing onto their lawn was the steel break wall. It was just what Jay would have imagined for her. It was small, but it stood out on the lane more than any of the other houses. Facing the lane was a garden of mostly wild tulips and marigolds. There were sculptures made from driftwood placed throughout the garden. One looked like a dog, but had a scary-looking face painted on it, that would likely scare small children walking by. There was one that looked like a stick figure, wearing actual sunglasses and a goofy smile made from an old bicycle chain. There were wind chimes made of old cutlery and glass beads hanging from the tree that was in the centre of the garden.

Jay didn't remember seeing these things at the cottage before Jess moved in, and he'd learned enough about her over the past week to realize that she had to be the one who created them. The orange, red and yellow flowers stood in contrast to the blue wooden door and shutters, which in their own right stood out against the white stucco of the cottage. The wraparound porch was sweet and romantic, and when Jay saw the swing at the far end of it, he pictured himself sitting there with Jess and experienced one of the flutters he'd been feeling at the thought of her. He realized that even though it wasn't the right timing, and even though they were just friends, he felt more - and he wasn't sure what to do with those feelings, except to just ignore them.

He knocked on the blue door, which was quickly opened by Steph. She was watching as Jay walked up, but hoped that it wasn't obvious. "You must be Jay," she said with a welcoming smile.

"That's me," Jay smiled back. "It's a pleasure to meet you, Ms. Carmichael."

Jess rushed into the room, and as discreetly as possible, slid on her socks in order to be at her mother's side before their conversation could go any further.

"Well, aren't you just a charmer?" Steph said to Jay. "Jess tells me you're taking her to a bonfire at the beach tonight?"

"Yes, our first one of the season," he replied. "We'll be at the beach closest to the lighthouse. I'm excited to introduce Jess to my friends."

He smiled at Jess, who appeared to be just as excited about the bonfire as she was earlier that day when they discussed it on the dock. He had noticed her slide in on her socks, and gave her a wink.

She lifted her foot up behind her and ripped off one sock, then did the same to the other. She tucked them into a ball and tossed them down the hallway. "Flip-flops," she said to her mom, with a smile.

"Alright, you two have a nice time," Steph said, "and Jay, bring her back by twelve, or there will be consequences."

"Mom!" Jess objected, as her cheeks flushed.

"No problem, we can do that." Jay smiled at both Jess and her mom.

Jess said goodbye and gave her mom a hug. "I have my cell phone," she whispered, "don't worry, okay?" Steph hugged her a bit tighter at that point.

"Thank you," Jess whispered, knowing that this was difficult for her mom. She turned towards Jay, and Steph said, "Have fun!" and waved them out the door.

∞

Dave, Vern and Meg were the first ones to make it to the beach for the fire. Dave and Vern walked around collecting driftwood and logs to sit on, while Meg lit kindling and started building a fire in the pit that had been left by a previous group.

"That's so hot," Vern said to Meg.

She smiled at him, but didn't respond. She was a little preoccupied with Val: she hadn't been able to reach her before she left, and found it odd that she just didn't come by so they could walk to the fire together.

As the three friends sat on logs and watched the fire, Jay and Jess appeared.

"Oh man! Jay's imaginary girl really exists," Vern chuckled.

"Not only does she exist," Dave said, "she's cute!"

"Who is she?" Meg asked, and it became apparent to both Vern and Dave that neither Meg nor Val knew a thing about how Jay had been hanging out with Jess since the breakup.

"She just moved here," Vern explained, "and Jay's been keeping her a secret all week."

"Interesting," Meg said, in a curious but not necessarily impressed tone.

"We figured it was just him making up some story to help him get over Val," said Dave. "But maybe he really has gotten over her."

As Jay and Jess approached the fire, Jess started to feel pangs of nervousness as she realized that all eyes were on her. She knew this was part of being the new kid, but she couldn't help but notice how uncomfortable it felt. She smiled at everyone.

"Hey guys," Jay said, "Dave - Meg - Vern - this is Jess. Jess, this is Dave, Meg and Vern."

"Why am I always last?" Vern asked with an insulted look on his face.

"Nice to meet you," Jess said to the group.

"You too," Dave smiled, and reached up his hand for Jess to shake.

"Yeah," said Meg. "Welcome to Erie's End." She smiled and moved over a bit, making a spot for Jess to sit on her log.

"This is just a great start to the summer," Dave said, "bonfires and a bunch of beauties."

"I hear ya," said Meg. "It's so good to be back in the End."

"Yeah, this fire does rule!" Vern added, a bit out of sorts. He was a little annoyed that Jess was invited to sit beside Meg and he wasn't.

The group shared funny stories with Jess about some of the adventures they had growing up together in Erie's End. It seemed like their main priority was to try and embarrass Jay, but every story they told, made him seem just a little bit more endearing to Jess.

"You gonna play anything on that guitar, Vern?" Meg asked. "Or just look at it?"

Vern was holding his spruce top acoustic guitar. Its back and sides were a darker mahogany, and what made Vern love it when he saw it at the pawn shop was the one-of-a-kind pick guard that appeared to be hand-carved with images that might be found in a tattoo shop.

"I can't play guitar, as if," Vern chuckled. "I just bought one for the chicks!"

Meg and Dave looked at one another and shook their heads in amusement.

"Would it be okay if I tried?" Jess asked Vern. The combination of the stories, and the laughs and the wine cooler that Vern had given her caused her inhibitions to fade away.

"Sure!" he said as he passed the guitar over to Jess. "Jay, you didn't tell us your new friend was a musician."

Jay smiled at her and said, "I didn't know either - what are you going to play for us?"

Jess smiled, and started to put the guitar strap over her shoulder.

"I'll be right back," Meg said. She had just seen Val in the distance and got up to go and meet her. She noticed that she was still wearing what she had on at the beach earlier that day. She was staggering as she walked, and she was slurring gibberish to nobody in particular. It was pretty clear that she was drunk, and as Meg got closer to Val, her suspicions were confirmed by the half-empty bottle of tequila in her hand.

"Oh Val," she said. "What's going on? Are you already drunk?"

"No!" yelled Val. "I mean yes," and she started laughing. Meg guided her to a log and helped her sit down by the fire.

"Don't let Drunkie McGee over there stop you," Vern said to Jess. "What were you going to play for us?"

Jess suddenly regretted offering to play guitar, but started strumming "Breakfast at Tiffany's" by Deep Blue Something and then quietly started to sing, *You'll say, we've got nothing in common - no common ground to start from ... And we're falling apart...You'll say the world has come between us..."*

"Who is that?" Val demanded. "And what is she doing at *our* bonfire?" She had noticed the way Jay was looking at Jess in awe as she was singing.

"She just moved here," Meg told her. "She's Jay's new friend."

"Ugh," Val grunted, and rolled her eyes. She took another huge swig out of the tequila bottle. She got up and started staggering towards Jess - who saw her approaching and stopped playing the guitar. "I do not know who you think you are," she slurred, "but these are *my* friends and you can leave."

Jess felt her eyes swell up with tears, but she did not shed one. She felt the lump in her throat which made it difficult for any words to come out, but she simply looked up at Val and said, "No."

"Well at least stay away from my boyfriend then!"

Jess looked at Jay, with hurt in her eyes.

"We are not together," Jay said. "She broke up with me." He then looked at Val with desperation and said, "Val - you're being a jerk! You should go."

"That's exactly why I broke up with you, Jay!" Val cried. "You're completely insensitive."

Meg got up and stood behind Val. "Sorry guys, it really was nice to meet you, Jess." She put her hand on Val's shoulder. "Let's go, Val."

"No!" Val screamed. She bent down until she was face-to-face with Jess, "She needs to know that she can't just come to the End like she belongs here - this is supposed to be *our* fire - and you," she paused, "can back the fuck off." She slapped Jess across the face.

The sting of it caused the tears that were captive in Jess's eyes to be released, and she couldn't control the urge to cry anymore.

"Chick fight!" Vern yelled, trying to use humour to break the tension.

"Do you think this is funny?" Val yelled at Vern, and she shoved Jess, who fell backwards off the log.

"Val, don't," Dave shouted as he stood up, not sure what to do. "Just go home."

"Chick fight!" Vern continued to shout.

"Stop it, Vern!" Meg demanded.

"Chick fight, chick fight," he continued. He wasn't trying to be an asshole. He just wanted to get Val's attention away from Jess so that she'd stop.

"Vern!" Meg yelled.

"Chick -"

Meg pushed Vern. "Seriously, shut up!" she insisted. She realized that nothing she could say would make him stop. She had been away for too long, and was worried to see Val so messed up. She had to do something. Vern's teasing would only aggravate things, and Meg could only think of one way to shut him up. She stepped forward and kissed him right on the lips - ensuring that not a single word would escape them.

Vern felt everything in his body tingle as she kissed him. He couldn't believe this was happening, and he realized that it was most likely only to stop him, but he thought to himself, *I don't care, I'll take it.*

"I can't go home!" Val screamed, and she collapsed in the sand and began to sob.

Meg ran over to her and put her arm around her. "What's going on?" she asked. "Val, what is this? C'mon, you can sleep at my place tonight," she said.

"No!" Val cried. "Do you think I want your dad and brothers to see me like this?"

Jay bent down to help Jess up, reaching out his hand to her. "I'm so sorry, are you okay?"

Dave got down beside Val and Meg and put his hand on Val's back. "You can come to my place," he told her, and put his hand under her arm to help her up.

"Dave, what do you have in mind?...what naughty things are you going to do to me at your house?" she said half laughing and still crying. She was clearly drunk, and not making much sense.

"I'm taking you to my couch," he said, "where you are going to sleep." As she got up, Dave put her arm around the back of his neck, and started walking her away from the bonfire.

Once Dave and Val were out of earshot, Meg stood up to face Vern, her hands on her hips. "I can't *believe* you would yell 'Chick Fight' when that was happening". Vern looked up at

Meg apologetically, "I was just trying to help," he shrugged his shoulders.

"I'm so sorry," Jay said again to Jess. "That's not her. She's better than that."

"It's fine, Jay," Jess said. "You couldn't have predicted it." She wiped a tear away with her sleeve.

They both sat back down on a log and watched intently as the flames of the fire danced against the dark backdrop of the night sky. As Jay put his arm around her, Jess put her head on his shoulder. He knew in that moment that his feelings for her were too strong to keep ignoring.

They sat like that, in silence, for a few minutes, before Jay noticed what was happening and started laughing silently.

"What's so funny?" Jess whispered as she looked up at him.

Jay pointed discreetly across to where Meg was now sitting with Vern. She had her head on Vern's shoulder, and he was awkwardly trying to comfort her. "I'm just so worried about her," Meg said, "that was not my Val in any way, shape or form."

Vern rubbed Meg's back and said, "It's okay," as he leaned in towards Meg's face for an attempt at another kiss. Meg planted her palm on his face and pushed him away.

"Vern," she said, "give it up - I just wanted to shut you up."

"Chick Fight?" Vern repeated, hopeful that she would want to shut him again.

Meg was truly worried about Val — she was the one in their group who always had it together, and something was terribly wrong. Meg appreciated Vern's efforts to try and make her feel better. In between his attempts to kiss her, he really was trying to make her feel better. He was the last person she'd ever have thought to turn to for solace. Although she would never admit it, she was a little bit enticed by Vern's attempts to kiss her again. It was when he took her hand, and said, "Seriously

Meg, Val will be okay - she will be because she has a friend like you," that Meg finally surrendered and leaned in to kiss Vern.

Meg heard Jay apologizing to Jess for what happened and suddenly pushed Vern away. "Oh my God!" she cried, "I'm late for curfew!" She grabbed her bag off the log, and started running. "I gotta go," she called and waved, and was gone before Vern could get any words out.

Vern sat there on the log, smiling, with his head whirling. Finally, in his Vern way, he said, "Nice" - maybe to Jay and Jess, but mostly to himself.

∞

When it was getting close to midnight, Jess and Jay were the only ones left. "I guess we should head out too," she said. They stood up and wiped the sand off their bums. Jay grabbed the bucket of water they had prepared earlier and dumped it on the embers that were still glowing in the fire pit.

As they approached Jess's front door, Jay wanted to tell her again how sorry he was for what happened, and he wanted to tell her about all the feelings that had been rushing through him - how he did feel like maybe there was potential for them to be more than just friends. "Well, here we are," he said.

"Here we are," Jess replied with a shrug.

Just then the blue wooden door opened, and there stood Steph with a smile on her face. "I think I like this boy, Jess," she said, "he brought you home on time and everything!"

"Hi, Ms. Carmichael," Jay said.

Jess smiled at him with an apologetic look. "Night, Jay," she said as she stepped inside.

"Night," Jay replied as he put his hands in his pockets.

The door closed behind Jess and her mom, and Jay turned around and started walking home. *What a night.* His thoughts were not consumed by the "chick fight," but by what might be next for him and Jess, if anything. Or was the snuggle they'd shared by the fire just a response to her being upset by what had happened? He knew that only time would tell.

∞

It was dark in the house as Dave guided Val into the living room. He was going to set her up on the couch, but as they approached they noticed that Dave's mom had fallen asleep there while reading her book.

"Dad must have decided to just let her sleep," Dave whispered. "Just come up to my room, you can have the bed, I'll sleep on the floor."

As they started walking towards the stairs, Val bumped into one of the end tables beside the couch, and let out a giggle. Deb did not stir, and the two headed upstairs.

Dave pulled down the covers and tucked Val into his bed. He was feeling buzzed, and she was more drunk than she had ever been.

She felt so much affection for Dave in that moment. He seemed to be the one who knew best how to listen to her, to hear what she was saying without trying to offer her solutions. She just needed to talk.

"He is such a dick," Val said as Dave handed her a glass of water.

"I don't think they're more than just friends, Val," Dave replied. "He just brought her to the fire because he thought you'd all get along, and she's new and needs to meet people."

"No," said Val, beginning to crumble beneath the weight of everything she'd just witnessed. "I'm not talking about Jay. I don't care about Jay and whoever she is - I'm talking about my dad."

"Oh," said Dave, feeling a bit like an idiot. "Why, what happened?"

"I walked in on him today." Val started to get choked up. "I walked in on him today," she started again, "and he was in my parents' bed with another woman, and he just looked at me when he knew I was there. He just looked at me as if he wanted to know what the hell *I* was doing there."

"Oh, whoa, Val," Dave said in sincere shock, "I'm so sorry."

"It really sucks," she said, "and how am I going to tell my mom?"

"Val, I'm no expert but - I'm here if you need to talk, anytime, okay?"

"You're too good, Dave," Val said, and moved over to make room for Dave to lie beside her. She was crying, and Dave was facing her, wiping her tears.

"That's all," she said. "I'm just confused."

"It's going to be okay," Dave said. "You'll figure out what you have to do. I'm here and you know all of us are here for you."

"Thanks for listening," she whispered.

"Of course," Dave said. "Get some sleep though. Good-night, Val."

He got out of bed and put a pillow and his sleeping bag on the floor beside the bed. He walked over to the lamp on his desk which had been providing a dim light for their conversation. He turned it off, and then heard Val say, "Dave..."

She had gotten out of bed and was standing beside him. As he turned, she grabbed his hands and wrapped them around her waist. She put her arms around his neck and pulled his face to hers.

CHAPTER 11

This is a record of guilt. The diary of a coward. I have not said a word of what happened to a soul - but this secret, keeping it inside is killing me. It feels like a living thing that could eat me from the inside out. I don't know what else to do, but to write it here. When I die, they will find it, and they'll know. They'll understand that what happened to her, happened because of a coward. It should have been me, not her - and when I die - and someone finds this - they will agree that mine has been a wasted life, a life that the universe should never have allowed. They'll curse me, and hate me, and their pain and anger will be rekindled.

This is the diary of a coward. The diary of a monster. The diary of a man who continues to cause pain. I watch them now, and I see their pain. I see how their lives have fallen apart. How they have fallen apart, and how they're trying so hard to live. What have I done?

Something I can never make right; something that has changed the course of so many lives. Something too awful to be acknowledged out loud, so will remain here only - on these pages.

-A.D.

CHAPTER 12

The pounding was almost unbearable; she couldn't tell if it was coming from her head or her heart. She was having a difficult time deciphering the events of last night, the events that led her to this moment, naked, in the bed of her ex-boyfriend's best friend. As Val squirmed beneath the blue cotton sheet, her foot grazed his. That's when flashes of last night came flooding back and she started spinning.

She didn't know if the spinning was from the after-effects of the tequila or if it was caused by the reality of last night sinking in; she decided that it was most definitely a bit of both. It all rushed through her mind - the rude remarks, the girl she shoved, her breakup with Jay, her parents' humiliating, public, hurtful war on each other. *God,* she thought, *don't they know innocent civilians get hurt in war too?* Her mind was racing, her stomach was churning, and as the sheet brushed against her naked body, the room seemed to be revolving around her. She felt so lost and vulnerable, and hungover. The worst night of her life was also the night she lost her virginity.

Most would consider it a drunken mistake, but it was more than that. Dave was secretly in love with Val. He had been since before she and Jay were ever together. It was Dave, not Jay, who came up with the sweet text messages and flirtatious emails that would help Jay win Val's affection. It was Dave who suggested flowers and a romantic walk on the beach to Jay as a way to celebrate their first anniversary. It was Dave that Jay depended on anytime he needed advice on how to impress Val.

It was Dave who sat on the sidelines in envy as his best friend dated the only girl who'd ever caused him to feel this way.

As Dave lay there next to Val, his eyes remained closed and he pretended to sleep, afraid of what might happen if they were to wake up and face the truth about last night. Was it a mistake? Was it love? Did Val feel the same way he did? Would she think he took advantage of her? Worse, did he take advantage of her? Did he become a complication instead of a friend? Had he messed up his chances with her, the only girl in Erie's End his heart had ever wanted? For now, he would remain still, pretending to sleep, allowing more time to pass, breathing her in - and hoping with all of his heart that when Val awoke she wouldn't regret it.

Dave's hopes were interrupted by a sudden loud and intrusive *knock, knock, knock* on the door.

"Have any laundry on that floor of yours?" Dave's mom called through the door.

Dave shot out from beneath the sheet, and out of the bed, inadvertently forcing Val off the other side of the mattress in his ungraceful jolt. He heard the loud thud as she hit the floor, and hoped that she hadn't hurt herself on the way down. He quickly spotted his boxers, and attempted to get into them - although it seemed more like he was hopping into a tangled mess. *This is so not sexy.* Things could not get any worse.

"Everything okay in there?" his mom asked.

"Uhhh, yeah!" Dave said as he finally had both feet on the floor and felt slightly more dignified in his underwear. "Just startled me, Mom!"

Val jumped up with the sheet barely covering her, looking at Dave as if to say *what the hell?* Dave looked at her and silently mouthed his apologies.

"Well, does the startled one have any laundry or no?" his mom chuckled.

"No, Mom, floor looks clean - I'm good!" he replied, hoping she would run downstairs to start the laundry and leave them alone.

"Okay, either way you need to get up - Vern's already called twice; who knows when he'll be at our door."

Dave listened as the sound of his mom whistling "You Are My Sunshine" became more and more distant.

It was in that moment that Dave knew everything was ruined. This wasn't the way it was supposed to happen. Val looked at him from across the bed, as if this was the last place on earth she wanted to be.

"Phew, that was close," Dave said to Val, with an air of hope in his voice.

She had turned her back to him, and with her voice shaking she replied, "I gotta go."

∞

Jay and Vern walked down the bayside path. The weeping willows that surrounded them always emitted a fresh scent in the morning that made it seem like it had just rained, even when that wasn't the case. Jay and Vern often had one-of-a-kind conversations on their way to Dave's house, mostly because Vern tended to do most of the talking.

"Do you think she's like, in love with me?" Vern asked with both confidence and inquisition.

"Probably..." Jay replied, knowing the answer Vern wanted to hear. Over the course of their friendship Jay had learned that it was crucial to go along with what Vern was saying, and to show an appreciation for his wild ideas. Otherwise, a form of verbal diarrhea would ensue that was unique to Vern, the likes of which no one should ever have to tolerate.

"I can't have Meg messing up my game, it's summer - should I hire a bodyguard?"

Jay wasn't sure if Vern was joking, if the question was rhetorical, or if he was really asking - so he replied anyway. "Wasn't that your first legitimate kiss, man?"

Vern put his head to his chest and mumbled something to himself, before saying, "Describe legitimate?" Vern looked at Jay with a goofy smile, and all they both laughed.

As they continued their walk, Vern decided to turn the attention to Jay. "Is Jess okay after last night? Val definitely crossed the line."

Jay was quiet for a moment. He knew the way Val treated Jess had hurt her. "I hope so," he said. "I know Val wasn't in a good place, but Jess shouldn't have been her punching bag because of it."

The boys neared the end of the path, and in the distance they could see the hazy blur of someone walking in their direction. Vern's vision came into focus first, and he looked to Jay and said, "Well, look who it is." It was none other than Val herself, walking towards them.

Val knew that the boys had no idea yet about what happened between her and Dave. Still, she couldn't help but feel so exposed. She wondered if people would just be able to tell. She was also still embarrassed about how she had reacted to Jay's new friend, and wasn't sure how the guys felt or if they'd even want to speak to her. As she neared them, she gave them a dejected look, one that Jay recognized as Val feeling ashamed. As she passed them she said, "I've got to get home, but I'm so sorry…"

Jay suddenly felt a rush of compassion come over him and felt sorry for his ex-girlfriend. He could tell she was frazzled and heartbroken. "It's cool, Val," he said, hoping that she'd know he was sincere. "We'll see you later."

As the boys neared the *Welcome to Erie's End* sign, Vern yelled "Chick fight!" as only Vern could do, and Jay elbowed him - knowing that Val was probably not ready to laugh about what had happened just yet.

He chuckled and said, "I could try and get you to shut up the way Meg did - you'd like that, wouldn't ya?"

"You know it buddy!" Vern said, laughing. "Pucker up." And he pursed his lips and leaned his head toward Jay, who started running - not knowing how far Vern would actually go.

∞

Meg stepped out onto her small front porch. She sat on the concrete steps, holding her tea and taking everything in. Her eyes followed the seagulls flying above and the beauty of the clouds as they shape-shifted across the morning's blue sky. After returning to Erie's End, Meg promised herself that she would begin living in the moment and taking pleasure in life itself. She knew that at any point she could be sent away again. Her instincts told her that she was living in Erie's End on borrowed time.

She worried about her dad, how he'd manage it all. Taking care of the boys, and the expenses that went with Matt, and the mortgage and not being able to work like before, and not knowing if he'd ever laugh again. When Meg began thinking that way, it caused her to ache with how much she missed her mom. She felt a deep sense of guilt and responsibility for her mom's death; in her mind her mom died because of her - it was all her fault. She would close her eyes and see the crushed Impala, its jet black body, crumpled against the white snow. She sometimes had nightmares in which she could hear her mom crying in pain, calling her name.

At the school Meg had attended while living with her grandparents, one of the school clubs was selling cookies one day to raise money and create awareness to stop drinking and driving. She walked by the table in the hallway, and when she found out why they were selling cookies, she started yelling, "Do you think *cookies* are going to stop drunken bastards from driving? You stupid assholes. What are cookies going to do?"

She swiped the cookies off the table and collapsed on the floor in tears. "Cookies," she wept, "fucking cookies."

Her grandfather had come to the school to pick her up from the guidance office less than half an hour later. He quietly left a generous donation for the bake sale.

The months since the accident had been difficult, to say the least, but being back in Erie's End made Meg realize that her mom would have wanted them all to continue living lives that were not dull, and grey, and sad. She would have wanted them to live every moment to its fullest. Meg had a million reasons to hide from the world, but the realization about what her mom would have wanted inspired her to face things head-on. Meg was mature beyond her years. She was cool in a way that prevented anyone from knowing how much she was suffering inside.

Placing her empty mug on the table inside the door, she yelled, "I'm heading to the beach, see you tonight." As she bounced down the stairs, Meg took a step towards what she hoped would become a glorious day under the sun.

∞

Dave was dressed and sitting in the sunroom at the front of the house. He knew that his mom was right and that if Vern had already called twice it was only a matter of time until he showed up. He was worried about how things had left off with Val, and he sat there and felt rushes of mixed-up emotions go through him. He didn't know what was next with Val, but he hoped so much that there would be more. Dave's wandering thoughts were interrupted by Vern's boisterous voice. He could see, as he looked up with his shoulders still hunched, that Jay was with Vern too. Dave was nervous - he felt like he wasn't the same person after last night, but he knew that the guys had no idea about what happened. He made his way out the front door as his friends got closer.

"Boys!" Dave said with fake confidence as he stepped out of the house.

Without hesitation or consideration, Vern chuckled before saying, "David Emmanuel Lister..." knowing that Dave hated any mention of his full given name.

Dave usually laughed at Vern's jokes and teasing nature - but this time he gave his friend a shove and told him to shut up. Vern laughed, and Dave realized that today, Vern's antics were the least of his worries.

He wondered what Jay might say, or how he would feel when he found out about Val. Thankfully, at that moment, everything appeared to be okay, as the first words out of Jay's mouth were, "Got the Holey Board, dude?"

Dave realized that he just needed to be with his friends right now, and not worry about the details. He hoped that everything between him and Jay would be copacetic, but for now he replied by saying, "You know it!" He smiled awkwardly while he stood with his hands in his pockets, staring off into space.

"Well, are you going to grab that shit or what?" Vern said, talking about the Holey Board.

"Yeah, yeah, one sec," Dave said, realizing that his thoughts had wandered off again, to the whirlwind that was last night.

"Well, hurry up, Big Poppa's gotta impress some bitties at the beach!"

It was impossible for Dave and Jay to determine how Vern had gained his obnoxious confidence. He came from the worst family situation in all of Erie's End, and to Vern's dismay and despite all his efforts, everyone seemed to know it. He'd grown up hearing whispers, but never really became accustomed to them. People would say things like, *There's that kid, that's Drunk Doris' son, keep an eye on your wallet - he's from*

Golden Acres, you know; just a matter of time before he ends up in Juvie."

He'd never known his father, and whenever he asked his mom about it, she'd look at him with disgust, swallow down whatever she'd been drinking at the moment, and walk away. Eventually, Vern learned not to ask. He assumed that she never answered because she probably didn't know. From early on it was as if Vern was raising himself.

From the time they met as small children, Dave and Jay recognized that Vern's life was different from their own and they grew up looking out for him. They made a conscious effort to include him in anything and everything they did. They invited him to family functions as if he was their brother. To Vern, the unspoken truth about Dave and Jay was that they were not just his best friends. He knew that they were his opportunity to break away from an otherwise doomed identity and destiny. They were his brothers, his liberators and his most cherished family. It also didn't hurt that they laughed at his jokes.

∞

Everyone in Erie's End had a Holey Board that had been passed down for generations. As the washers clanked against the board, and Vern's laughter filled the air, a sunbather nearby packed up her things and decided to move to a more peaceful spot on the beach. The intensity of their game however, made the boys oblivious to the fact that anyone else was around. "You couldn't hit water if you fell out of a boat," Vern bellowed.

On this particular day, Dave just couldn't seem to hit a shot. Luckily, this wasn't the NBA Finals, and his misses merely came as a talking point for his friends.

There was no breeze on the beach, the kind that's needed on a hot summer's day to make the heat tolerable. The boys loved the heat for at least one reason, which was obvious after their game ended, and their eyes instinctually scanned the beach. The hotter it was, the more women there were in scanty swimsuits. Vern's eyes kept returning to one beach babe in particular. *I need to investigate that,* he thought to himself. "Take five," Vern said, "I'm going to do some P.I. work."

Vern made his way over to the beautiful girl catching some rays on her towel. As he neared, he realized it wasn't just any beautiful girl, it was Meg.

"Hey, Lips," he chortled. "How's it going?"

"You're delusional, Vern," Meg said nonchalantly, without moving or looking up from her towel. "I just wanted to shut you up. You talk too much."

"I don't think that's how your lips feel," Vern said with self-assurance.

Deep down, Meg had enjoyed kissing Vern. She struggled with the fact that she enjoyed last night; she'd known him forever and although she always considered him a fun part of their group, she had never ever had stronger-than-friendship feelings for him, until now. She'd been thinking about it since she got to the beach. She'd get flutters in her stomach and feel excited, and smile, and then she'd think...*but he's Vern!*

∞

Val scurried up the hill towards the beach with her towel spilling out of her beach bag, and her flip-flops in her hand. She was late meeting Meg. It seemed that she was late for everything lately. She had always been known for having everything together - good grades, great fashion, and a cool, collected composure. It seemed that lately, though, she was falling apart, and she wondered if it was evident to the outside world too. On this particular day, it didn't help that she was also hungover.

As she reached the peak of the small hill at the edge of the beach, she scanned, looking to see where Meg had set up.

She spotted her, and realized that she and Vern were deep in conversation. Her heart sank a bit, as she was really looking forward to just having a bit of alone time with her best friend today.

She looked towards where the boys were playing Holey Board, and saw Dave and Jay standing there, talking to each other, likely waiting for Vern. *Oh God,* she thought at the sight of seeing them both together. Dave saw her and started waving for her to come towards them. She looked back at Meg and Vern, who were still in a conversation that made them seem like they were their own separate entity on the beach, unaware that anything or anyone else was around them.

Val took a deep breath. *This is going to have to happen sooner or later* she thought, as she started walking towards the guys. She said hello to Jay first, and then grabbed Dave's arm and whispered, "Can I talk to you for a sec?"

Dave looked over at Jay and asked, "Hey man, time out?"

Jay thought it was weird that Val wanted to talk to Dave, but figured after everything that happened last night at the fire, she needed someone to talk to.

"Yeah, you know what, dude?" he replied. "It's too frigging hot out here today - think I'm going to head home for a bit." He walked over to Dave and Val, and wrapped his arms around both of them. "But first a big sweaty group hug," he laughed. He knew that Val was not herself, and he knew that he couldn't be pissed at her for what happened - something was up with her, and although he couldn't be the one to help her, he wanted Val to know that things were cool.

Dave and Val both laughed as they pushed him away, Val with her nose turned up.

"What? Do I smell that bad?" Jay asked. The look on Val's face suggested that he did, so he smiled, saluted his friends and started running towards the lake for a dip before heading home.

Dave and Val walked through the hot sand towards the treed area at the edge of the beach. They were both feeling uncomfortable and awkward, and neither was really sure how to be around the other in that moment. Dave kept walking closer to Val, and she seemed to want to keep her distance. His heart was pounding, her stomach was uneasy.

Val sat on top of the picnic table under the tree, and patted the table beside her, suggesting that Dave sit too. He sat beside her, with disappointment already showing on his face and a sinking feeling in his heart. He suspected that this wasn't going to be a good conversation.

"Dave," said Val, "I haven't been able to stop thinking about you and about last night. I'm not sure what any of it means. We've been friends for so long," she said as she looked at him with a gentle, introspective smile, "and I love you."

Dave smiled back at her. "But..." he said.

"But friends like us are not supposed to cross that line. I have so much going on in my life that my feelings don't make sense to me - not just my feelings about you - but my feelings about anything. I don't want to take you on this roller coaster with me. I'm not me right now. I am falling apart - and more than anything, I just need my friends right now. Friends with no expectations or uncertainty, or confusing emotions - and friends without amazing sex while their parents are sleeping on the couch."

She smiled at him, hoping he would at least appreciate that last night was a big deal, but that she didn't want to make a big deal out of it. She hoped he knew that she didn't want him to feel bad about what happened. She hoped he understood that it was big and complex and she was so afraid that it would change things, and that their friendship would pay the price.

Dave put his arm around Val, and pulled her closer to him. She rested her head on his shoulder.

"Val," he said, "sometimes, that's exactly what friends like us are supposed to do - but only when it's what both friends want. Whatever happens, you know I'll always love you. I'll always respect you. I'll always want what is best for you - I will always want your happiness." He was being sincere, and he hoped that he'd be able to find the words to tell her where he stood. "The worst thing that could ever happen would be that we regretted loving each other too much. Our friendship will always come first; whatever else happened or happens is gravy. We decide if and how this affects our friendship. You'll always have a place in my heart Val," he said, "and I'll respect however you decide you'd like to take up residence there," he winked at her. "Whatever you need - I'm here, okay?" They looked at each other and smiled with a mutual understanding and the sense of a strong connection they shared, a connection they hadn't consciously identified in each other before. "Especially if what you need is more amazing sex," he teased - and Val shoved him so hard that he fell off the picnic table.

They were both laughing when Meg and Vern approached. "There you are!" Meg called over. "I thought maybe you stood me up."

"I didn't want to interrupt you two love birds," Val called out. Vern smiled with pride; Meg rolled her eyes.

"I'm sleeping at your place tonight, okay?" Meg said to Val. "You know, for old time's sake."

"Yes, oh my gosh, yes," Val said, "that would be so fun!"

Dave was still sitting on the ground beside the picnic table. Val reached out to help him up.

"Can we keep all of this between us for now, please?" she quietly asked in Dave's ear as he got to his feet.

"Whatever you need," Dave said with a wink.

∞

It was the hottest day Erie's End had seen in a long time. Jay turned onto the path that acted as the entrance and exit to the beach, where the pavement met the sand. His wet swim trunks dripped onto the pavement, causing little waves of steam to rise from the blacktop with each step. He walked with his head down, wanting to get into the shade of the willows - he loved summer, but today was too hot. He heard a girl's voice call out, "Looking pretty hot over there!"

He lifted his head, and much to his pleasant surprise saw Jess. *She's incredible,* he thought, as she started walking towards him. "Hey now, we've only just met," Jay said with a flirtatious smile.

Jess raised her eyebrow in her own uniquely sweet way. "I was talking about the pavement," she giggled, "but hey, you're not so bad, either."

"Umm...want to come over and watch a movie tonight?" she asked nervously. "My mom's going into the city this afternoon, and I don't really feel like being alone."

Jay immediately felt his heartbeat quicken and flutters of excitement in his stomach. He hoped that he still seemed unruffled on the outside.

"That sounds perfect," he said. "I'll be over after supper?"

Jess smiled and nodded. "See you then," she said. As she began walking away, she looked back quickly. "I'm glad you're coming, Jay."

Her words made his stomach flutter.

As Jay hurried down the path, his mind raced through his selection of favourite movies. The guys constantly teased him about his love of rom-coms, but he really loved all movies. What the guys didn't realize was that girls love romantic comedies, and they love watching them with guys. He argued with himself over what movies to bring to Jess's place. Pretty Woman, he thought, *no - can't bring a movie about a prostitute;* Some Kind of Wonderful - *no...don't want her to feel like Watts.* Breakfast at Tiffany's - *it was the song she played at the fire -ohhhh...definitely no.* Princess Bride. *Yes.* Princess Bride.

Jay continued to analyze movies the entire way home, not yet feeling confident about any of the titles his mind was producing.

As Jess walked home, she was thinking deeper thoughts. She really liked Jay, but she had hoped she'd be able to ignore her feelings. She was beginning to realize that might not be possible, and it worried her. She wondered what would happen if *he* found them. She worried that if she let Jay in, Jay could get caught up in a complicated mess that he didn't deserve - and she wondered if there would be an expiration date on this wonderful place for her and her mom. She didn't want it to hurt more than it had to, and she feared that letting Jay in would make things so much more difficult. But the feelings she had, the butterflies she felt, they'd been there since the first day Jay approached her from Dave's front yard. *I have to try,* she thought, *that's why we're here.*

CHAPTER 13

The girls rounded the corner of Val's street; it was dusk and they had just picked up stuff from Meg's for the sleepover. Val's house was a yellow Cape Cod with white shutters and a perfectly manicured yard. It looked picture perfect, from the outside. As they got closer, Val realized that her mom had returned from her trip to the city. She felt a rush of heat that seemed to travel from her toes and settle in her cheeks. Her hearing became muffled and her vision became blurry, but their yelling became louder and clearer.

"Just go, you liar! Just leave!" Janet screamed. Val could see, even from a distance that tears were streaming down her mom's face. Her dad walked briskly out of the house with his duffle bag, and past her mom without a second glance, as she stood cross-armed on the front stoop.

Val froze at the corner of their property, unable to take another step.

When Meg was away, Val had called her one night. She broke down crying and had told her that it seemed like everything had changed. She explained how her dad had been acting like an asshole. "He's a perfect stranger," she said. "Tonight he came home and just lost his shit on all of us. The thing is, none of us have done anything differently than usual. He started yelling at my mom and told her she looked like shit. When Kevin tried to defend her, he called him out - like basically invited him outside for a fight. I couldn't believe it. I started crying, because I couldn't help myself. When he saw that I was upset, he told me that I was a spoiled brat and that I needed to learn how to deal with life. I just don't get it. He's not the same person; he's not my dad. I miss the dad I had who would come home and try to make us laugh; he would ask about our day, and tell us the funny things that happened in his." Val sobbed that night on the phone and she told Meg how her dad's behaviour had left her mom an emotional wreck, and how she herself just didn't know how to deal with any of it.

"There's nothing to talk about - you delusional bitch!" Kent roared as he walked to his mosquito-covered '98 Cherokee. He stopped before getting in, and turned his hateful gaze toward Val. He shook his head and got into his jeep. The door slammed shut, the engine bellowed abruptly, and as the tires squealed the SUV gunned out of the driveway, leaving rubber marks that tarnished the perfect picture of the West residence.

Val looked on, tears forming in the corners of her eyes. Her mom had gone back into the house. She sat down on the curb.

Meg wrapped her arm around Val's shoulder and whispered, "It's going to be okay."

It brought Val a sense of comfort knowing there were people with a shoulder she could put her head on. She didn't want to talk about it. She didn't need someone to understand. She just needed to rest her head.

∞

Jay laughed when he arrived and Jess told him that *Dirty Dancing* was playing on cable. He had painstakingly selected three movies to bring with him. He loved how easy Jess seemed to make everything. He didn't mention that he had movies in his backpack; he simply said, "I love that movie," with a smile.

Jess made popcorn, and the two of them started watching the movie. They were sitting on opposite ends of the couch, neither quite sure what to do, but both fully aware that this was the first time since the beginning of their friendship when things felt so awkward. Jay wondered if he should move closer.

His palms began to sweat, and he hated that he wasn't quite sure of the rules. With Val, he never had to make the first move: most of their relationship had been initiated by her, or he'd been nudged by tips from Dave. This was new territory. It was terrifying, exhilarating, invigorating and everything in between. Though Jess was only a sofa cushion away, he couldn't help but want to be right next to her. *I want to hold her hand,* he thought, but his nerves wouldn't allow him to reach for it.

"What?" Jess asked. "Are you thirsty? Oh my gosh, I'm a terrible host, I'm so sorry." *Why am I messing this up?* she thought to herself.

Jay hadn't realized until then, but he'd stopped watching the movie and had been inadvertently gawking at Jess instead. "No, no, I'm fine," he insisted.

"Are you sure?"

"Yeah, I just zoned out, I'm fine."

"Okay," Jess replied.

She turned her gaze back to Baby and Johnny Castle practicing the cha-cha. Johnny was trying to put his hands all over Baby. "Hey spaghetti arms," Baby teased, "would you give me some tension please? You're invading my dance space…" *Wait, was he staring at me?* She'd caught him. Jess smiled, trying not to let on that she knew.

Jay had been looking at her, studying her flawless skin and her beautiful smile, and getting lost in her gorgeous green eyes. He could not look away; he was fascinated by her - and by how oblivious she was to her own beauty. He was fascinated by the fact that every time he saw her, she had some sort of personalized addition to her clothing or jewellery - something added that always just made her seem a little bit more unique.

Tonight it was a bracelet she made by wrapping copper wire around a skipping stone, and then around her wrist.

Jay didn't want the awkward air between the two of them to last any longer. "You know what, we should get a drink," he said.

Jess paused the movie on the DVR remote, hopped off the couch and said, "Come with me," while motioning him toward the kitchen. She opened the fridge. "We have diet soda, orange juice, milk...there's this wine that was in the fridge when we moved in..." She turned around, holding the neck of the bottle, and realized that Jay was right behind her.

She closed the fridge and started laughing. "Do you think my mom would notice?" she asked.

Jay grabbed the bottle out of Jess's hand, and while he reached over her to put it on the counter, the weight of his body gently compelled her to move backwards until she was leaning against the counter. They could feel the warmth of each other's breath. Jess looked up from the floor and her eyes met Jay's; he leaned down and his lips pressed against hers. The intensity of it made everything else in the universe seem non-existent.

He lifted her up onto the counter. She sat there with one hand holding his, and the other on his shoulder. She was now leaning down to him, kissing him, as he stood in front of her - and she thought it was the best feeling she'd ever felt or would ever feel again.

"Wait," she whispered and pulled away with her hand still in Jay's, not wanting to ruin the moment, but not wanting to continue without letting Jay know what he was getting into. "I have to tell you something."

"Are you okay?" he asked, sincerely concerned that she didn't want this, that maybe he'd moved too fast.

"With you," she replied, "how could I not be? But, Jay, you need to know why my mom and I moved here to Erie's End. I need to tell you before we can let this, let us, get any further."

Jay looked up at Jess, into her green eyes, and thought that nothing she could tell him would ever change the way he felt about her.

"It's my dad..." she started.

CHAPTER 14

S teph was beginning to question her decision to go to the counsellor in the city. She kept wondering if Jess was safe and couldn't wait to get to her room so she could call. She worried that this would be the most opportune time for him to take Jess. She had booked a hotel room for the night, knowing that after a session that would require her to relive some of what had happened, she would not be able to drive. She didn't want Jess to come, to have to see her like that again. They had come so far, and ultimately - her goal was to create a life in which Jess could feel normal, and confident and safe.

She slid the key card into the door and the light flashed from red to green; the unmistakeable and peculiar aroma that seemed to belong to every hotel greeted her as she stepped inside. It was combination of bleach and dust, and other people. She left her shoes on and carefully checked the bed before sitting down. She propped herself up with pillows and dialled the number for the cottage on her cell phone. Her heart pounded with each ring. Finally on the fourth, she heard Jess say, "Hello?"

"Hi Sweetie," she said. "How are things going?"

Jess told her that Jay was still there and they were just watching movies, and that he was going to spend the night, but not to worry - he was sleeping on the couch.

Steph smiled and told Jess that she'd see her first thing in the morning. Under normal circumstances, there was no way that she would allow her fifteen-year-old daughter to have a boy spend the night. But now, she felt safer knowing that Jess wasn't alone and Jay was there. For some reason, she trusted him. "He can take my bed," said Steph. "There are clean sheets in the closet."

"Goodnight Mom, I love you," Jess said.

"You too, 'night."

Steph heard the dial tone - and that's when she felt it. The darkness, the fear, the vulnerability - and she started to cry. She curled herself up into a ball, and she went over all of the things she'd told the counsellor again in her head, and she cried, and cried.

∞

The clock ticking on the wall above the receptionist's window was the only sound that Steph could hear as she sat in the waiting room earlier that day. She had concentrated on straightening her back and keeping her feet together. She held a handkerchief that she twisted over and over in her hands, until she looked down and realized that her knuckles had actually turned white. She relaxed her grip, took a deep breath, and reminded herself that she was here because she was not going to let what had happened impede the quality of her future, and more importantly, the quality of her daughter's life.

Her racing thoughts brought her back to a conversation she had with her college roommate years before. Her roommate sat on the edge of her bed in their dorm room while Steph was getting ready for a night out. With admiration her roommate told her that she wished she could be as certain about herself as Steph was. She told her that she wished she had the guts to take life by the horns, like Steph did. *That's why I'm here,* Steph thought as she looked up at the irritating clock. I need my self-assurance back, and to feel like taking life by the horns is actually an option, and to show Jess that there is no other option.

"Ms. Carmichael." The receptionist was standing at the door adjacent to her window; her purse hung over her forearm and she had rested her sunglasses on top of her head. "Dr. Taylor will see you now."

It was clear to Steph that she was the last appointment of the day, and the receptionist was eager to go home. She was guided into the therapist's office, and invited to sit in an oversized leather chair. Steph's nerves were causing her to feel shaky as she sat and was consumed by the chair. She assured herself that this would help, and that she had to do it in order to move forward, and she took a deep breath.

Dr. Taylor walked in after a few minutes and introduced herself. She sat in the chair across from Steph and told her that the counsellor from Richmond had been in touch and explained the basics, that she was fleeing from a dangerous situation, and that she wanted to be able to live a life without constantly being afraid. Dr. Taylor seemed kind, and warm and trustworthy. But no words would come. Steph sat and studied the doctor. She was young, too young, maybe, to be qualified for this? Beautiful. She had long, straight, jet black hair that shimmered even in the dimly lit office. Kind. Something about her made Steph know that she was safe - that this was right.

"Why don't we start at the beginning?" asked Dr. Taylor. Steph was aware that this tactic of asking vague, open-ended questions was one that counsellors used often as a starting point, as a way to establish a baseline or get some sense of direction as to where their patient needed to go.

"The beginning," said Steph softly, with trepidation, "well, I met Greg in college." After that first sentence, Steph found it much easier for the words to come. Her heart rate slowed, and she continued.

"Greg was also completing a double major in Business Administration and Accounting, but he was a year ahead of me. When we met, he was a few months away from graduation. We started dating, and everything was truly wonderful. He was charming and funny, and good-looking. He had many friends and seemed to know everyone. We made a good pair - because at that time, I was also very involved in a lot of different clubs, and causes, and if there was a group for it, I had probably signed up for it. I knew a lot of people then, too, and had a great social life.

"At that time in my life, I felt like I could do or be anything. I felt good about who I was and who I could become. At the time, meeting Greg just seemed like it was adding to my life's potential for possibility. What's that saying? It's like 'the world was our oyster.'" Steph smiled as she reminisced.

"At first we were just having fun - but after he graduated, our relationship got more serious. I would spend the night off campus at his apartment often - I knew he was the one and that I was in love. He would always talk about his dreams of opening his own asset management and investment accounting firm, that it would be run by the two of us, we'd be partners - and for a student in her last year, that seemed like a dream.

"It was just after second semester started. I was a few months away from graduation and I realized that something wasn't right - I felt terrible, I was exhausted, I had lost my energy and zest for life. I was barely making it through classes. I was dishevelled and felt like I was falling apart. I figured it was just from being in my last year, and the demands of trying to complete my degree with honours. However, after eight tests came back positive - it all made sense - I was pregnant. I was so nervous to tell Greg. I knew that a baby was not in line with his goals of starting his own firm, and he was miserable at the firm he was at. He talked about quitting every time anything about work came up.

"I was shocked by his reaction when I did tell him. He was thrilled. He picked me up and spun me around, and as he put me down on the ground again, he got down on one knee and asked me to marry him. I couldn't believe it. I was so happy - everything in life seemed right. I would still be able to graduate before the baby came, and Greg promised that everything would be all right until I was ready to go to work. It only took us a few weeks to decide that a city hall wedding would be best, and within a month we were married. I moved into his apartment. Things were great - for a while.

"The first time my false sense of reality and security was shaken was the day that Greg came home after finally being fired from the firm he hated being at. He was so angry. I'd been sleeping when he stormed in - I had just finished a midterm, and was exhausted - intensive studying when you're pregnant takes a lot out of you. He pulled the quilt off me and started yelling that the place was a mess. I'd never seen him in that state before. I was confused, and his behaviour was scaring me. I started to cry, and locked myself in the bathroom. Eventually he stopped yelling and I could no longer hear him throwing and slamming things.

"I stayed in the bathroom, sitting with my back against the door. I heard him slide down the door on the other side. 'Stephie,' he said, 'I'm so sorry. I don't know what got into me.' He started to cry - and then my heart melted for him. I thought of what he must be going through, knowing there was a baby coming - a wife without a job, and rent to pay. I opened the bathroom door, and we sat there and held each other, both of us crying silently.

"The next day, I was nervous as I stepped over the threshold of the apartment after returning from class. I wasn't sure what I was coming home to. It was jaw-dropping. Greg was dressed in a full suit and tie. He was sitting at the desk on the phone. 'Yes, sir - of course it's a priority. I'll be in touch,' he said as he hung up the phone. He was literally jumping up and down. He started taking my coat off for me. 'Stephie - I did it,' he said, 'I'm doing it. I've called some of my old clients, and they're going to follow me - I'm starting our firm. Now. Today.'

"I had so many concerns and objections and fears about the whole thing, but I kept them to myself. I knew that it wasn't the time to question Greg. He explained his plan to me - that if things got really busy, I would help him - but otherwise he could wait for me to become partner until the baby was old enough to be left with a nanny. My heart sank - it wasn't the life I had planned on. I wanted to be a partner in a firm - and I wanted my husband and I to start our own firm - but I hadn't even graduated yet, and I wasn't sure if either of us had the experience to pull it off. I smiled at Greg, though - at his enthusiasm - and I told him I was proud of him. He kissed my forehead, and I apologized, telling him that I was exhausted and had to lie down. He covered me up with the quilt - and as he shut the door, I couldn't control my tears. I think that was the day I lost my faith in possibility.

"It was a struggle, but somehow we were managing. Between dirty diapers and two a.m. feedings, we were managing the growing number of client portfolios that were coming in. It was time to move into an actual office space and out of our apartment. It wasn't fair to our daughter, Jessica - and we thought it would be best for our family to have separation between work and play. I had an inheritance from my grandfather in trust that I had never mentioned to Greg - the time never seemed right - but I was willing to use it to fund the transition of our firm from our apartment to an actual office.

"Before I mentioned it to Greg, I called my parents - and told them what I wanted to use it for. They refused to release it to me. They were still upset with me for marrying Greg the way I did. After I announced our marriage to them, my mother tearfully told me that she'd never liked or trusted him. I was hurt. Looking back, I can see that she had an intuition and I understand how much it must have hurt them."

Steph got choked up at the mention of her parents. She dabbed her eyes with a tissue, but looked back at Dr. Taylor's concerned, kind face, and continued -

"The most joyous part of my life for the next few years was being Jessica's mom. She was such a good kid, and she made me laugh. When she would smile or wrap her little arms around me and say she loved me - nothing else mattered. Greg continued to preside over our little firm. We had managed to open a storefront, which attracted more business - we were growing and becoming more financially secure. We were able to leave the apartment and buy a nice three-bedroom house in a subdivision with a yard for Jessica.

"Greg was proud of our firm. He managed the books, he managed the clients and their investments and he managed the PR. He really did it all - I just worked on a few simple client portfolios. When Jess started school I got more involved in the firm. I took on my own clients and was able to grow the business a little more.

"As time went on, Greg became more and more distant. All he seemed to care about was the firm, and his clients. It was next to impossible to ask him to make time for Jess and me. At first, I chalked it up to his drive to succeed - thought maybe his goal of growing the firm and bringing on more partners was what was keeping him so involved with work.

"That was until the day I decided to look through the books - the real books. It wasn't his drive, or his ambition that was keeping him at work all hours of the day. It was his greed. I felt weak in the knees and sick to my stomach when I realized what was happening. Greg had been embezzling from a number of our higher-profile clients. I also realized when I started looking through the *real* books, that there were clients I didn't know about. Clients whose businesses were shady, and whose books had to actually be off the books.

"I called him on it - I asked him about what I had seen. That's when things started to get bad for me. That's when Greg no longer tried to keep up the appearance of being a decent husband. It started with really demeaning remarks. He would tell me I was useless, and that I was lucky he was carrying me - that I was a shitty accountant. He would say I was a bad mother, and that I was repulsive. He would say that I belonged in a barn - that I couldn't keep a clean house if I tried. The more things he would say, the smaller and more defeated I would feel. I knew what was happening. I'm a smart woman. But somehow - he managed to whittle away at my self-confidence and my pride, and my spirit.

"Time went on - and things got worse. The demeaning remarks became a part of my daily life with Greg, and often every interaction with him. It got to the point where I didn't even notice it was happening anymore - and I don't even know if he realized what he was saying anymore either. His disrespect soon became more threatening. He would speak to me with his fists clenched. He would yell and threaten to throw me out on the street. I continued to look through his books, and continued to see that he was cheating our clients - skimming off the top. The list of shady clients was growing. The more money he embezzled, and the deeper involved he got with disreputable clients, the more concerned I became about our future, and our firm - and ultimately our daughter. I again asked him to stop - and to run this business we had legitimately and with dignity.

"He got so angry. He told me that I was no longer to have any involvement in the firm - and that I had to keep my mouth shut. He told me that I should thank him for the privilege of staying home with our daughter. He said that as long as I kept my mouth shut about what I had discovered, I could stay and he wouldn't take Jessica away. I was devastated. I felt so trapped - but I didn't want to tear our family apart. Saying it now, it seems so stupid. But at the time - even considering everything - I still had hope. In my lack of clarity - I thought that even though I wasn't happy, he was still a good father to Jessica. She was such a happy kid - I didn't want to take her away from her happy life. Again - I was so stupid.

"I begrudgingly became a stay-at-home mom. Not because I didn't want to spend every moment with Jess, but I really valued contributing to society in a professional way too. I worked hard for my credentials, and was devastated when I was told I couldn't use them. When I started staying at home, things got worse yet again. I no longer had to be seen by clients, or by the public much, for that matter. That's when I started getting bruises. He would grab my arm too tight and leave his handprint. I had a lot of tender spots that never really seemed to stop throbbing. Greg would remind me often that I had used the kind of Pine-Sol that smelled too strong, or I didn't make the proper lunch, or anything he could think of as an excuse - it was how he felt justified to take his stress out on me.

"He became increasingly suspicious of me over the next couple of years. I think he realized that all I ever really daydreamed about was leaving. He was smart, though: he took away any means I had of doing that. He controlled all of the finances. All I had was the inheritance from my grandfather that was still in trust. My parents told me that they would transfer it into Jessica's name for a college fund. I never did tell Greg about it - and I'm glad - because when I left, I was only able to escape to Erie's End after I called my parents, and explained why I needed that trust and what I was going to do with it. I couldn't tell them where I was going to take Jess - but they understood. They had seen it for so much longer than I did.

"The worst night of my life is why I'm here now. Why I can't keep a window open, or a door unlocked. It's why I feel sick and dizzy and like the walls are closing in whenever my daughter leaves the house." Steph put her head in her hands and started sobbing. "I'm sorry," she whispered as she looked up at Dr. Taylor and tried to wipe away the tears, which just wouldn't stop.

"You're doing great, Stephanie," Dr. Taylor said. "Take your time, take a breath - this is a safe place. Tell me what happened that night."

CHAPTER 15

Vern inhaled the morning summer air as the old rust-ridden door of the trailer slammed behind him. *Today is going to be boring,* he thought - and he took a hard sip of the day-old Slurpee he'd left on the picnic table. He spat it out immediately, making a mental note not to do that in the future. He sat at the old wooden picnic table, with the sun shining, and the birds chirping - and listened to the neighbours yelling at each other.

"I have to get out of here," he said out loud, to no one, but with purpose. His heart jumped at the thought of the canoe he found the night of the bonfire. It was a tad ragged and old, but it had been put out in front of a Slickers' cottage as if it were trash. It wasn't trash, at least not to Vern.

The Slickers would come and take over the waterfront of Erie's End for eight weeks every summer, with their plaid shorts and polo shirts, and their snobby friends and snobby families. They were from the city, mostly, and they were the epitome of the kind of condescending, arrogant assholes who snickered at anyone from Golden Acres. Jay had come up with the name "Slickers" for them because of a movie he made them all watch with Billy Crystal in it. They were nowhere near as impressive as Billy, who Vern loved, but it didn't matter because the name worked. They needed to be called something. Vern had wanted to call them the Invaders - but the guys pointed out that it made them seem like they were from outer space.

"They might as well be," Vern had said, but Slickers worked for him too, so he conceded.

The Slickers' cottages were in the opposite direction of where Vern lived. He had stopped to laugh at himself, when he realized he was staggering home the wrong way from the bonfire. He was distracted by thoughts of Meg, and realized he'd had far too much to drink. He had stopped to orient himself when he noticed the canoe. Vern walked up to it, and as he slid his hand over its tattered, abused surface, he stumbled and fell to the ground beside it. He got into the canoe, and sat there - and he didn't know if it was the beer or fate, but somehow he felt as if he was connected to that old canoe.

As Vern sat there in the darkness in front of the Slicker's cottage, he had the sensation that the boat was actually bobbing in the water. The distant sound of waves crashing against the shore certainly didn't help. *Only one cure for this,* he thought, and he swung his backpack around, unzipped it, and took out the last beer. He leaned back, and as he sipped his beer, he reflected on his life.

"Canoe," he chortled, "we have so much in common."

The canoe had been left to the road, with no one to care for it - and in a way, that was how Vern felt about his own life. He thought about how nobody cared. His mom definitely didn't. He didn't know his dad, and he didn't even know if his dad knew he existed. And sure, he did have good friends, but was that because of their pity?

As he sat there in the old trashed canoe and got even more trashed himself, Vern forged a bond with the wooden boat. As he stared at all the dings and damaged spots, all the rough edges and rotten wood, it occurred to him that he was meant to find it. He threw his empty bottle on the Slicker's lawn and rolled out of the canoe. He knew that he was in no shape to make it back to Golden Acres. He put his backpack on, and hoisted the canoe above his head. It took him a few tries before he could actually stand and walk with the canoe. Old Man Johnson's place was just down the road - and he decided that he and his new canoe would spend the night there.

"Fucking brilliant," he slurred as he staggered, covered by the canoe and dragging the tip of its other end on the ground behind him.

He arrived at the old man's empty estate - and decided that it would be less like trespassing if he slept in the boathouse instead of the house itself. The lock on the door was easy to pick. Vern marvelled briefly at the fact that the boathouse alone was double the size of the trailer he shared with his mom. It was as if the building was on stilts above the water, and he knew that if you looked out the east window in the daylight, the rickety old dock could be seen stretching out into the bay, attached to the break wall as if it were holding on for dear life.

In one corner of the boathouse was a sitting area with two couches covered in white sheets which were now blackened from the layers of dust. In the centre of the floor was a hole, opening right up to the bay, where Old Man Johnson used to store his boat. Across from that, a large garage door opened up onto the lawn; it mirrored the one on the opposite end that opened to the bay for the boat. The back of the boathouse was the workshop.

Perfect, Vern thought, and he hoisted the canoe, one end at a time, onto the two vacant workhorse trestles that seemed to be there just waiting for it to arrive.

Sitting in the dark, listening to the gentle waves beneath, Vern had vowed to fix up the old canoe. He would keep it in Old Man Johnson's boathouse, and work on it over the summer. Mr. Johnson was never around to check on things. He'd found a project - he'd found a purpose for his summer. First, whatever it was that was happening with Meg; and now, a canoe in need of rescue. Somewhere in his heart Vern began to think, maybe hope floats. "That one was for you, Jay," he had chuckled out load, thinking that Jay would appreciate the movie reference.

The cloud of a boring day quickly dissipated when Vern decided that this was the day he was going to start working on the canoe. He took another sip of the day-old Slurpee, and then groaned with disgust - remembering his mental note to never do that again. He tossed it, and ran inside to grab his stuff. With his backpack emptied, he headed towards town to get supplies. He realized he'd need some paint thinner to clean up the remnants of the old paint. He wanted to see what he could accomplish with some hard work and determination. He wanted to reinvent that canoe. In typical Vern fashion, he began whistling the tune to "Hi-ho, hi-ho, it's off to work we go" as he set off in the direction of Erie Mart.

Erie Mart was a small general store that had been a staple of life in Erie's End for as far back as the town had a history. It was in all the old black-and-white photos of Erie's End that the record-keepers had; all the photos that hung on the walls in the town hall, the diner and the high school library. It had evolved over the years, but it was the closest thing to a grocery store, or a department store that the little peninsula had. The city had big chain grocery stores, but that was an hour drive that most Enders rarely wanted to make. Of course there were planned trips to the city to do what locals called "a big run," in which they'd get enough supplies to last long enough that they could avoid the city again for a while.

As he walked in the door he could feel the clerk's eyes following him. Vern knew the only way to shed the perceptions and misconceptions others had of him was to be a good person - and to be so good that it would be impossible for anyone to think badly of him. He wasn't his mother. He looked over to the clerk with a smile and went about his shopping. He found the TSP, rubber gloves, and some heavy-duty cloths to wipe down the boat. He paid cash for his order and thanked the clerk with a big grin.

"I'll be back throughout the summer for more supplies," he said as he headed for the door.

"Come back anytime," the clerk said.

She wants me, Vern thought with satisfaction as he pushed the door open.

∞

The truck breaking down couldn't have come at a worse time. Mr. Cole was at his wits' end. He had no money left, and none coming in. He had a kid with special needs. *In fact,* he thought, *all of my kids have special needs - they just lost their mother, for Christ's sake.* Fathers were supposed to provide for their kids, and the thought of it gave reason for that burning lump in his throat to stay stuck there. If only his wife were still here.

"Dad, are you okay?" Meg asked as she walked into the office.

"Nothing Meggy, everything is okay," he assured her as he shook his head back into the moment, not really sure of what she had just asked. "Are you going to hang out with your friends today?" he asked. "I sure do like those kids. Hot days like these make the best memories," he smiled.

Meg could tell he was somewhere else. "Dad, I want to help you," she said. "I'm not a little girl anymore. I can get a job. I'm sure I could work at the diner, or at the Erie Mart. I could apply to be a lifeguard - there are a lot of tourists this year - I'm sure they could use a little extra help at the yacht club. I want to be here for you and the boys. I can help with Matt. I'm only two years younger than Mom was when I was born, Dad," she said.

The mention of it made them both freeze in mid-conversation. They continued to look at each other, but neither was sure what to say next. Mr. Cole felt the lump in his throat.

"Meggy, like I said, go and see your friends, we'll be okay," he replied. "These years of your life are the fastest, and the ones you'll miss the most."

"Fine," she grumbled, wishing he would consider what she was saying even just a little bit.

Meg's brothers were in the living room playing video games. Matt had just finished a pretty violent coughing fit. Meg had helped pound his chest and back earlier to loosen the mucus, and it seemed like he was still coughing some of it up.

"Do you think we can go fishing today?" Mark asked.

"That's a great idea!" Meg replied, and Mark grinned.

She ran up the stairs, and before entering the room, started, "The boys want to go fishing, Dad." As she stepped into the room, she again saw him just staring into space, and it occurred to her that maybe he wasn't okay. Maybe he needed help. Maybe his numbness had finally left, and he didn't know how to manage the cataclysm of what he was feeling.

"Dad," she said softly, "the boys would really like to go fishing."

He smiled at her, nodded, and said, "Great idea, Sweetheart - I'll take them out in a bit."

Meg wasn't convinced by her dad's smile, but told the boys that he was going to take them fishing in a little while. They were both excited, and started doing happy dances on the couch.

"Be good for him, okay?" she asked. "I'll see you guys later. Group Hug!" she yelled, and held both boys as they continued to jump around.

She stepped outside. If nothing else, a walk would be a good way for her to clear her mind.

Meg was walking along the bayside boardwalk when she spotted the ridiculous throwback outfit. At first she laughed to herself, and then realized it was in fact none other than the one and only, Vern Kelly. He was wearing his favourite worn-out jeans - they had holes in both knees - a white T-shirt, and a tweed vest that belonged to a three-piece suit in 1974. To top it all off he was rocking a pair of Westbrook shades with the lenses flipped up. As he walked down the road with his Erie Mart bag in hand, Meg giggled because she couldn't help but think he would fit in with Dwayne Wayne from *A Different World*. She smiled as she remembered snuggling up with her mom to watch it as a kid.

"Vern!" she shouted, startling him out of the plans he was making for the canoe while he whistled *hi-ho, hi-ho*.

"Oh, hey," Vern replied, and that was all he said. Meg wondered what was going on; the fact that he didn't suggest she wanted him, or ask her to make out, was very strange. He was usually excited to see her, and she hoped something wasn't wrong.

"Where are you off to?" she asked, now walking alongside him.

"Nowhere special," Vern said nonchalantly.

She pointed to the Erie Mart bag. "What do you have there?"

Vern didn't want to give anything away; he wasn't planning on telling anyone about the canoe until it was all said and done. *But it's Meg, for frig's sake,* he thought to himself.

He stopped walking, and Meg followed his cue and stopped as well. "Can you keep a secret?" he asked, looking her directly in the eyes.

Meg had never seen Vern so serious before. It was the first time she could recall in the history of knowing him that he was looking at her with such a weighty stare. He looked contemplative and was not quick to offer a wisecrack. "Of course," she said. "Is everything okay, Vern?"

"Yes. Follow me."

"Where are we going?" Meg asked, confused and amused.

Vern stopped in his tracks, and with a playful smile, said, "Do you want to come or not?"

Meg grinned and held her hands out as if to say, "After you."

∞

"This is so neat!"

"I found it the other night after the bonfire. Someone had just thrown it out." Vern grinned at Meg. "Like, I just think it has so much...what's the word...?"

"Potential?" Meg replied, causing Vern to over-enunciate the word, *"Yesssss!"* - which he followed with what Meg deemed to be an idiotic but cute laugh.

"So," Vern asked, "are you going to help me give this beauty a makeover?"

∞

As Vern sanded the worn wood, he looked across the canoe with admiration, subtly (he hoped) gazing at Meg as she worked hard at her end. She was so cool - and she wanted to do this with him. She had been tasked with TSPing the wood that Vern had sanded. It was important to remove any dust, and she was so *damn* beautiful and Vern knew it. He wanted to stand on a stage and yell it out to everyone. She made him feel like a rockstar, and he loved it.

As Vern and Meg worked away on the canoe, a comfortable silence fell over them. Meg began assessing the situation and considering the answers.

"Wait, does Mr. Johnson know you're using his boathouse?"

Vern looked up from his sanding with a sly smile. "In a word, no."

"Oh, Vern, what if he comes home and catches you?"

"Meg, I honestly don't care... I just want to work on this boat and spend time with you."

Meg smiled softly. "I think that's the sweetest thing I've ever heard, Vern."

"Nice," said Vern in his customary obnoxious fashion. On any other day it would have been enough to ruin a moment, but this was different. Meg was beginning to find Vern's quirks endearing. It showed in her inability to control her smile, and the way she uncharacteristically tucked her hair behind her ear. She laughed at all of his jokes, and she didn't want this day to end - until she looked at her phone.

"Oh god, Vern," she said, realizing she'd missed dinner. "I'm late, I've gotta go." She walked over to Vern and kissed him on the cheek. "Thanks for today," she said before heading for the door.

"Thanks Meg," Vern replied as she made her way out the boathouse door. Meg was gone and the sun was sinking into the horizon. He stood and stared across the canoe to where Meg had been working, and it was there in the quiet orange glow, that he thought to himself, *holy crap, I'm in love.*

∞

Meg was worried as she walked up to the house. She didn't want to give her dad any reason to send her back to her grandma's, and missing dinner was not a good start. When she got there it was obvious that he'd been crying. She was confused, however, because it seemed that this time they were happy tears.

"What's going on?" she asked.

"I took the boys to the mechanic's to pay for all the work," he said, "but when we got there the bill was already paid for."

"What?" Meg said in disbelief. "That's amazing...but who?"

"I was going to ask you if you had any idea, or if you've told anyone about our financial troubles," he laughed, and shrugged. "Whoever it was even ensured there was a credit for the next time the truck acts up," he said. "Meg, are you sure you don't know who might have done this?"

"No clue," she said, puzzled and relieved at the same time.

"The mechanic wouldn't say who paid for the work - he said that whoever it was only left a vague note." Meg's dad shrugged and put his arm around her. "At this point," he said, "I really hate to feel like a charity case, but I don't know what we would have done."

CHAPTER 16

The little café was bustling. As Janet sat and drank her coffee, she admired how the ceiling had been painted black and somehow gave the industrial lighting a sense of class. The walls were the original aged brick. Val introduced her to this place during one of their mother-daughter days out, and she'd loved The Loft Café ever since. It was an escape for Janet, a place she always felt comfortable and at ease.

It had the appeal of a big-city loft, with exposed heating and venting pipes and bare electrical. Janet loved the place's character, especially in the winter when the one-of-a-kind fireplace was crackling. She'd told Val, that first day they were at the café, that she wanted the fireplace to be transplanted into their living room. She loved the sharp matte black of the slate hearth and the oversized, aged beam that had been fashioned into a mantel. In the summer the fireplace contained several different-sized candles that contributed to the café's heart-warming ambience without the intense heat of a burning fire.

"Today is a hot one," Deb said as she approached the table where Janet was enjoying her coffee.

"A bit like hell," Janet replied sarcastically with a smile. A local musician was playing bluesy music in the corner of the café, and the old friends started catching up on each other's lives.

Deb listened intently as Janet discussed how she found out about her husband's affair. She still didn't know who the mistress was. Kent had come clean about what happened after Val walked in on them, thinking she would have told.

"He broke my heart," she said to Deb, "but the worst part was hearing Val describe what it was like for her to walk in on them." She hung her head, and knew that Deb heard the crack in her voice as her words trailed off.

Deb was empathetic; she had been friends with Janet for a long time and thought of her as one of the sweetest people around. She told her that she did not deserve this pain. "I'm here whenever you need to talk about it," she said softly, "okay?"

"I'm heartbroken, but I'll be okay. It's Val. I can tell she's hurting, she's not herself, and I don't know how to help her," Janet said while taking a deep breath to help fend off the tears.

Janet appreciated Deb's concern, but didn't want to talk about all the shit that was happening anymore - she was tired of feeling like she was on the brink of tears. "I love how they support local artists in here," she said to change the subject. "I haven't been able to stop looking at that painting" - she pointed across the café to the brick wall where a number of local artists had paintings on display. "The one of the woman's silhouette," she said, "it's amazing how a few brush strokes can make you feel so lonely."

Deb smiled as she noticed the painting. "You know, Janet," she said, "I didn't even notice the art in here. I was so concerned about you, I just wanted to make sure you were okay after what happened with your asshole husband." Deb blushed; she rarely swore, but when she did, it was most definitely called for. They both laughed. "Oh, enough about that," Janet said, "let's change the subject. How's Dave?"

"Dave?" Deb repeated. "Oh, he's doing pretty well," she said, and put her hand on Janet's, "although I went to see if he had any dirty laundry the other morning and he was really weird." Deb cleared her throat before whispering, "I think he may have been masturbating," which caused both women to laugh awkwardly, and the coffee that Janet had been sipping went up her nose.

"Oh god, Deb," Janet said, trying to sympathize with how it might feel to have a teenage son. "Does he have a crush on someone?"

"I really hope so," Deb said. "He's never had a girlfriend, he's always just palling around with Jay and Vern."

The friends spent the afternoon catching up, listening to the live music and admiring the art. Janet was grateful for her friend, and for the distraction. "Thanks for listening, Deb," she said as she got up from her seat. "You always have known how to make me laugh, even if it is at Dave's expense."

"Anytime," Deb said and laughed. "Although next time we should include some daiquiris and a nice bayside view - how's my place?"

"That sounds perfect." Janet smiled at the thought.

As Deb pushed through the door, she spotted Kent getting out of his vehicle with who she assumed was the other woman. Without allowing Janet to see, she guided her out the door in the opposite direction, saving her from the pain the sight of it would have caused.

∞

Dave was playing Nintendo 64. He was determined to improve his skills in the James Bond 007 game, because he could not tolerate losing to Vern one more time. He could not understand how Vern could just come in, with no practice or strategy or second thoughts, and kick his ass every time. Dave was beyond bored, and he really wanted to hang out with someone. His options were limited, as he knew Jay was going to the city zoo with Jess and her mom, and he didn't think he could handle Vern today, especially if hanging out came with another N64 loss.

He put the controller down and turned on some summer league basketball. He loved watching the recently drafted rookies showcase their skills before the true season started in October. It was something he looked forward to every summer. He got a thrill out of watching the teams run up and down the court, firing outlet passes for open looks, the definition of run and gun. There was a beauty to the simplistic dysfunction that was summer league basketball. The lack of defence allowed for several dunks a game, and with each one Dave would usually jump out of his seat with a boisterous cheer. He loved basketball, playing it and watching it. But he was so distracted that even watching hoops seemed to have lost its appeal.

This shit isn't cutting it, he thought. Val would just not escape his mind. She said her life was too complicated for a relationship, but he didn't buy it. Dave didn't mind being in the friend zone; he just wanted to be around her. And he wanted to tell her that he had feelings for her - that he always had. He grabbed the remote and shut the TV off. He was suddenly walloped with the courage he needed - he decided that he would go to Val's and invite her for a picnic.

It was a scorching hot day, but he had the perfect spot in mind: the big oak tree at the edge of the bay. It was like the hidden gem of Erie's End - maybe the most beautiful spot in the area, and no one was ever there. It was in a grass-filled clearing tucked back off the usual path, and you'd have to know it was there to get to it. There was an old cast-iron park bench that had layers of paint chipping off, revealing that it had been there for probably a hundred years itself. It was right on the bay, but not touristy enough for the Slickers to pay any attention to it. It was the perfect spot for relaxation and reflection - *or for hooking up,* Dave thought. He hoped she would want to go.

Dave worked up the nerve to knock on Val's front door. He had to wait a second, as a group of young kids rode by on their BMX bikes. After they were way down the road, he took a deep breath and knocked.

Val was brushing her hair, furiously trying to detangle the crazy mess that had taken hold of her head. In that moment, she felt so much frustration and she couldn't decipher if she was madder at her hair, at her dad for being a jackass, or at herself for losing control of her life. She was a mess, and even something as simple as a bad hair day was liable to set her off. Either way, the damn knots weren't coming loose. *Fuck all of this,* she thought as she let out an exasperated sigh.

Her mom wasn't home, and she wasn't expecting company. As she opened the door, Dave couldn't help but stare.

"Oh my God," she said, "I didn't realize you were coming over. Did I forget plans?" When he didn't answer, she said "Dave?" in a *Hello, are you there?* kind of tone. She suddenly realized she wasn't wearing a bra under her white t-shirt and went flush with embarrassment.

All Dave could do was smile and try to conceal the fact that blood had started flowing south. *Not now, not now, be cool.* "I just came by because I thought we could hang out, well, maybe, if you're into it." He then looked down and made a point of showing her he'd packed a picnic lunch.

"I would love that," Val said with appreciation. "Give me ten minutes to get dressed?" and they both blushed.

Dave sat on Val's front porch, glad that he decided to come over and relieved that she said yes. Val returned wearing a purple sundress and had managed to wrangle her hair into a bun on top of her head.

As they walked down the street, Val realized that nothing could ever happen between her and Dave that would make them uncomfortable with each other. He was one of her oldest and truest friends. She was glad to have someone like him in her life who she could trust with her thoughts, and her fears, with herself. She looked over at him and smiled, as they passed a neighbour who was power-washing the mayflies off his garage door.

"Where are we having this picnic?"

"I thought we could relax at the old oak tree?"

"That's perfect." Val's eyes softened, and her mouth perked into a smile.

Dave placed the blanket over the grass near the tree trunk, taking full advantage of the shade. Dave and Val both lay down clumsily on the blanket - trying not to brush against one another, yet each secretly hoping they would. As they looked out over the bay, they began exchanging impressions of what the clouds above resembled.

"That one looks like a T-rex trying to eat a donut," Val chuckled.

"Oh yeah! I see it," Dave said, although he had no idea where Val was looking, and could not see anything that looked like a dinosaur eating a donut.

"That one looks like boobs," Dave said as he pointed towards the sky.

"Dave! I thought you were the mature one of the guys!" Val said, sounding offended - although she wasn't.

"You didn't know that I'm the awesome, yet incredibly modest one? Jay's mature - he's seriously such an old soul, you know that...and Vern, well, Vern - what can I say?" Dave laughed.

"You are awesome," said Val, "but that cloud does not look like boobs." She was trying extremely hard to contain her laughter. "I'd say you've never seen boobs, except..." She blushed as the words escaped before she could stop them.

Dave popped onto his side to look at Val and began to chuckle. "I don't remember seeing any boobs. Can we try that again?" He looked deep into her blue eyes, wondering how any of this could possibly be wrong.

Val was surprised by how much she was enjoying this day - she loved the way Dave looked at her. He made her feel special. Lying on the blanket next to him, looking up at one of the most beautiful skies she'd ever seen; she found comfort. She wasn't stuck in her head, consumed by all that was wrong in her life. She wanted to savour the peaceful ease of every moment under the tree. She listened to the squawks of seagulls in the distance, and the quiet splashing as waves rolled up and crashed against the break wall. She breathed in the fresh air and wished they could stop time and stay there forever.

Before long, Dave poked Val and joked, "Admit it: boobs, really nice boobs."

"You're such a perv!" Val chuckled. "Seriously!"

As the two laughed, their bodies inched closer, and their hands connected and then intertwined. Dave could feel his uneasiness creeping in, but his desire gave him the nerve to sweep Val's hair out of her face and behind her ear. *Now or never.* "You are so…perfect, Val."

"Dave…" Val looked at him, not sure how to react.

Dave leaned in to kiss her. The second their lips touched, the nervous awkwardness they both had been feeling faded away. At first each soft brush of their lips sent chills through Dave's spine. As their kisses got steamier, his hands seemed to move on their own, feeling her body and pulling her closer. As sure as time passed, it also stood still.

When they finally stopped kissing, Dave looked down at Val, who was still in his embrace and looking up into his eyes. He didn't know what the expression on her face was. He hoped content. They continued to look at each other for a long time, partly because they were lost in the moment, and partly because neither of them knew what to say or do next.

"Val, that PB&J was incredible." He looked in her eyes with a tease of a smile.

"You made it," she said with a cute wink. "Clearly you are a whiz in the kitchen." They didn't have to talk about their make-out session; words would have only diminished it.

As the breeze from the bay picked up, Val rolled up the blanket and Dave grabbed the basket filled with the remaining food. They had just spent a dream of a day together. A lazy day, a special day, the kind that comes completely unexpected. It was like going to a baseball game with no expectations and being rewarded with a grand slam - a day that leaves a mark on your memory. As they walked away from the oak tree, Dave grabbed Val's hand. He didn't have to think about it anymore.

"Great day," he said. Val squeezed his hand and nodded. Nothing else was said, nothing else had to be.

∞

Jay walked up the path to the cottage, and as he saw Steph standing by the pickup to welcome him, he felt such sorrow for her. She was such a nice lady, and he couldn't imagine someone hurting her. He was shocked, the other night, when Jess told him about how she found her mother the night they left.

While she was in the city Steph had seen a billboard promoting the zoo, and she thought the three of them could go on the weekend. Steph passed Jay and Jess each a travel mug with fresh coffee as they piled into the pickup. She realized that the early morning start would be harsh for any teenager on summer holidays.

Jess grabbed her purse and pulled out a mixed tape she made for the trip. She loved that the old pickup had a cassette player. She conscientiously chose each song, carefully considering the lyrics. She wanted to ensure that her song choices provided a fun, light-hearted soundtrack for their drive to the city. When they arrived in the zoo's parking lot, all three were singing "Sweet Home Alabama," at the top of their lungs.

Jess could not stop smiling and laughing. The zoo was turning out to be more fun than she could have hoped. She loved looking over at her mom and seeing the quiet look of satisfaction on her face. She could tell that Steph's contentment was a result of the genuine good time that all three of them were having. Jess also recognized how uplifting it felt to be doing a normal thing that normal people do on normal summer days. The sight of the penguins, and the lion cubs, and the giraffes reminded Jess of how enchanted the world could be.

Jay stood beside the monkeys and pulled on his ears and puffed out his cheeks. Jess started laughing, and Steph couldn't contain herself and also spit out her laughter at the sight. It was amazing how such a good-looking kid could actually also look so much like a monkey.

∞

As they drove back to the End, Jess fell asleep on Jay's shoulder and when Steph looked at the two of them, she felt a strong sense of hope come over her. This sense of normalcy felt new, and blissful. Jay noticed her gaze, and gave her a soft, kind smile.

As Steph put the pickup into park in the driveway, Jess slowly snapped out of her sleepy state and lifted her head off Jay's shoulder. She looked over at her mom with an apologetic look, and Steph looked back with an approving nod, as if to say, "It's all good." They all hopped out of the truck - each with the intention of making it to the washroom first after the bumpy ride.

Jay made it to the cottage first, and after Steph unlocked the many deadbolts to let them in, pushed his way through. Jess and Steph looked at each other with disbelief. "Just joking," he called out. "Ladies first."

The two laughed and made their way inside. "You can go first, Mom." Still a bit drowsy, Jess rested her head on Jay's chest, for a snuggle as much as for a place to lean.

"Next," Steph said as she walked into the kitchen. Jess tiredly pulled away from Jay's embrace, and dragged her feet towards the washroom.

Just as Steph had begun putting away the extra snacks she'd brought for the trip, the phone on the wall rang once, then twice.

"Jay, would you mind picking up the phone?" she asked.

On the third ring he picked it up. "Hello, Carmichael residence."

There was nothing but silence on the other end. "Hello?" Jay continued. "Hello, anyone there?"

Steph looked up from her task of organizing things in the pantry. The puzzled look on Jay's face made her realize this wasn't a normal phone call. She hurried over and grabbed the phone from Jay's hand.

"Hello," she demanded. "Hello, who is this?"

Immediately, she started to shake. Jay had never seen someone tremble so visibly in his life. Steph gasped and her hand covered her mouth; tears started streaming from her eyes. She dropped her hand with the phone still in it to her waist, and Jay came and took it from her as she crumpled to the floor.

He put his ear to the receiver, and all he could hear was someone whistling a happy tune. He hung up and sat down beside her.

"He found us," she barely whispered.

Just then, and none the wiser, Jess opened the door to the bathroom. "Oh my God! What happened?" she cried as she ran over and dropped to the ground, embracing her mother.

CHAPTER 17

Steph, wrapped in an afghan on the porch swing with her knees to her chest, quietly stared at the police car sitting in the lane. The last thing she wanted was to draw this kind of attention from the neighbours. She felt far away from reality. She could see Jess speaking to the police officer, and Jay standing behind her, protective but so unaware of what he was getting himself into.

What happened had Jay stupefied, and it hit him that Jess and her mom were in actual, real danger.

"Explain to me again what the voice on the other end said," Officer Parker directed.

"It was just whistling," Jay interjected, feeling the need to take control of answering questions; Steph and Jess both needed someone to lean on after what happened. The officer looked confused, almost questioning why whistling would be a problem - but without saying as much.

"The Devil Is in the Details," Steph said in a monotone from the swing, without taking her eyes off the police car. "He was whistling 'The Devil Is in the Details' by the Chemical Brothers." She turned her head and looked at the officer, suppressing her belief that there was nothing he could do to protect them.

"Do you know who the caller was?" the officer asked Jess and Jay.

Jess looked over at her mom. The officer walked over and sat beside her on the swing.

"Ma'am, it's very important that if you feel that someone is putting you in danger, and you know who that person is, that you let us know. It's the only way we'll be able to protect you."

Steph turned her head and looked at the officer; she couldn't hold back her tears. Jess walked over and stood behind her with her hand on her shoulder.

Steph put her hand on top of Jess's. "It's my husband, her father," she said. "I never thought he'd find us here." She looked up at Jess. "I'm so sorry, Sweetie," she said.

Jess gave her mom a hug. "It's going to be okay mom, I swear, everything is going to be okay." She walked over to Jay and leaned into him.

Steph gave the officer a brief, and incomplete synopsis of the circumstances that led up to her flight from Richmond, and how she decided on Erie's End, convinced that he would never find her.

"Can you give me a description of your husband, so we can take every precaution?"

"Yes, actually, come inside," Steph said as she got out of the swing and onto her feet. "I can show you a photo from his website."

Jess looked up at Jay who was still holding her. "Thanks," she said. He smiled. "I'm sorry you're involved in all of this," she said.

"I'm not sorry," he replied and tightened his embrace. "I just wish you didn't have to go through this at all."

∞

Jay had a handful of rocks, and he whipped them one at a time as he walked along the tracks. The train tracks that ran just outside of Erie's End were a part of the landscape to the locals. Once in a while, Jay would remember that they were a manmade addition, and that their wooden beams and steel rails were not as native to the area as the corn fields that ran along one side of them, and the thick forest that bordered the other. The tracks seemed like they belonged there as a natural partition. The sun was rising in the distance, and it seemed like the perfect backdrop for Jay to suddenly realize how real and how fucked up things were for Jess and her mom. He could not believe how helpless he felt about the whole thing. He let out a yell of frustration and threw the rest of the rocks in his hand as hard as he could. As gravity returned them to the ground they clanked and pinged loudly against the tracks.

All Jay could think about was what Jess had told him the other night when they were watching movies. How could something so horrible have happened to someone so amazing? After Jess explained that they had run from her dad, and were kind of in hiding, it made more sense why sometimes Ms. Carmichael seemed so nervous and on edge. And after last night, it made perfect sense.

He thought about what Jess had said - that her dad beat her mom up so badly that she was bleeding and bruised; that she had to drive her mom to the hospital that night, because she couldn't drive herself.

She told him about how her mom wouldn't let her come into the exam room, and all she wanted to do was know if she was okay. She couldn't understand why her mom refused to speak to the police, or to tell them that her dad was the one who hurt her. They were at the hospital for hours that night. Jess told her mom that she never wanted to see him again, and her mom asked her if she was willing to leave everything, in that moment - to not return to the house, to not speak to any of her friends or tell them where she'd gone - to just leave. Jess had said that she would of course go - she was so afraid for her mom, and so ashamed of her dad, that of course she would leave. Jay approached the abandoned junction house that was the halfway point to home - he didn't want to go home. He didn't want to explain to his grandparents what was happening.

He didn't want life to be more complicated. He didn't want to leave Jess and her mom for even a second. He didn't want what was happening to them to be happening, and he wished he knew what to do to stop it.

He wanted the world to be the place it was yesterday. Where shit like this happened only in the movies. Somehow, he thought now, it was disgusting that people watched this happen in movies and found it entertaining. He ran up the stairs of the junction house and sat on its rusty metal platform - watching the sunrise. He didn't fully understand what he was feeling. He felt like he'd been punched in the gut. Though he was a bystander, he felt like he'd been given some kind of dark insight, an unwanted introduction to world's injustice. Jay leaned his head back and closed his eyes. He burned with anger, and fear, and love - real love - and he dozed off as the warmth of the rising sun remained the only thing in the world that was unchanged.

"Hello up there! Hey, what is this? Did you find a new summer home?"

Jay opened his eyes and heard Vern's cackles, and saw him and Dave approaching. He looked at his watch. It was after eleven in the morning; he couldn't believe he'd slept for so long. He jumped and made it down to the tracks just as his friends reached the junction.

"S'up?" he asked them - feeling a bit out of sorts, and not quite awake. Vern gave him an unwelcomed noogie - and Jay pushed him away and told him to fuck off.

"Whoa dude," Dave interjected. "He's just being Vern, give him a break, man. Why did you wake up in such a pissy mood? And what's with sleeping on the junction house? Trouble in paradise?"

Dave's reaction caused Jay to realize that he wasn't being himself, and that maybe he shouldn't be taking it out on his friends. The two people in the world he trusted the most. "Sorry, guys," he said, "it's just…"

"What's up, man?" Vern asked, recognizing that something was really wrong.

Jay stopped walking and told his friends about some of what was happening to Jess and her mom.

"No way!" Vern said after Jay had finished. "Finally, something interesting in Erie's End! Nice!"

"Just don't talk," Jay said to Vern.

"You love it when I talk," Vern joked, and Dave this time interjected on Jay's behalf.

"Shut. Up. Vern. This is serious." Dave put his hand on his friend's shoulder as they walked. "Things are going to work out, buddy," he said. Vern nodded in agreement and acted as serious as he could.

"Let's just talk about something different," Jay suggested. "What ever happened with you guys and the twins that day?"

Jay was remembering their brief conversation before the Listers' summer bash, before Jess came to the End, before the summer. It seemed so long ago and far away now.

"It went like this…" Dave grinned a wide, mocking grin.

"Let's not talk about it," Vern mumbled, looking down at his feet as he walked.

Dave dismissed Vern's concerns with a wave of his hand. "It went like this," Dave started, as he began to tell the story of the day he and Vern spent with the Polanski sisters.

"Vern and I had English with Riley and Julie - and it was the second-last day before summer break. They met up with us at our lockers before class started, and suggested that instead of going to class to watch the 1968 version of *Romeo and Juliet*, that we go back to their place and make our own version. Of course, Vern and I were stoked. You've seen the twins, how could we have said no?

"We got to their place - and they led us down to the basement. Of course, it was just the four of us, and Vern and I just kept smiling at each other with the anticipation of what was coming. Julie - who Vern decided we should call Jules - took off the cardigan she'd been wearing at school and just had a tight tank top on - and oh, man I could not keep my eyes off her. She asked if we wanted to play a game, and I was like yeah, uh huh, and nodding my head." Dave laughed, realizing how dazed he must have looked.

"Anyway," he continued, "she grabbed an empty bottle from behind the bar and brought it back to where we were sitting. And then, apparently Vern decided that, I guess since they're twins" - he shrugged his shoulders in Vern's direction - "that Riley should be called Riles, because as Julie was coming back, Vern was sitting with his arm around her, telling 'Riles' that she was so hot." Dave started chuckling again.

"Shut it - Dave," Vern said under his breath, with an unusually serious tone.

"Not a chance, man," Dave continued. "Jules said, 'It's time for a little Seven Minutes in Heaven, boys.' You should have seen Vern, man." Dave nudged Vern's shoulder - letting him know that he wouldn't spare him the embarrassment. "I thought he was going to jump out of his seat and maul one of the twins right there. 'Riles' spun the bottle first - it pointed at Vern. He looked over at me and nodded with the hugest smile you've ever seen, and that look like 'I got this,' then Riley grabbed his hand, led him over to the closet and shut the door.

"I was just sitting there, not quite sure what to say to Julie. I was kind of drumming on my leg, I looked at the closet, and I looked back at Jules - and smiled, and looked away, I was such a dork - I even asked her how she thought she did in English. Then she started inching toward me on the couch. She had her head tilted to the side, and I could tell she was coming in for the move…and then…" Dave started laughing to himself, to the point where he couldn't continue the story.

"Come on, man," Jay said. "What happened?"

Dave pulled himself together, putting his hand over his mouth as if to stop the laughter from escaping. "Well, then we got interrupted by Vern stumbling out of the closet - yelling at Riley. 'That did NOT happen in Romeo and Juliet - you sicko….'"

Dave let out some of the laughter that was building up. "He grabbed my hand and pulled me off the couch, and he said, 'We have to get out of here, man - these girls will eat us alive.' And he pulled me by the arm until we were outside the twins' house, and I had no idea what had just happened."

"Vern," Jay said, "I don't even know what to think."

Jay and Dave started laughing. Vern started to say something, but Dave interrupted. "The best part of the whole story," he managed to say through his laughter, "is that now, whenever we see the twins, they go 'Oh, Romeo' to Vern."

Dave and Jay started belly laughing, and Vern stood there with an unamused look on his face.

"Are you losers done?" he asked. "I hope neither of you ever find yourself in a closet with one of those lunatics."

Dave and Jay laughed harder - and Jay said, "Sorry man, but I needed that."

Vern pushed Jay into Dave. "Alright, alright," he said, "but we won't be talking about that again, okay?"

"You got it, Romeo," Dave said - at which point he and Jay were doubled over laughing.

Vern smiled, realizing that the whole situation was pretty funny - and if it had happened to someone else, he'd be the first one to razz them about it. His thoughts wandered to Meg, and he kicked the dirt and rocks in front of him, waiting for his friends to snap out of their fit of hysteria.

∞

Meg was sitting on the pier, looking out on the water and the boats sprawled across the lake. She loved the smell of the fresh air, and the fact that there always seemed to be a breeze if you sat on the far side of the lighthouse. She remembered being afraid as a kid, because no matter what the weather, the pier was always wet from the waves crashing on the concrete. Her dad had taught her to stay away from the very edges because they got slimy and slippery from the algae. As time went on and she got older, however, the pier had become one of her favourite thinking spots. She found herself there a lot since she returned to Erie's End.

She had so much on her mind. It was more than just the grief she was feeling for her mom. She was concerned about her dad, and the boys. Matthew seemed to be sicker than ever, and his treatments were helping less and less. She was worried that if anything happened to him, it would kill her dad. She wished he would talk to her more about what he was going through. He seemed like a blank man - like he was living on autopilot. His body was working. He could pour the cereal from the box to the bowl. And he could give Matthew his treatments - but Meg would have to hold Matthew after, and rub his back, and tell him he did a great job and that everything would be okay.

She was worried about poor Mark, who just wanted to spend time with someone. Matthew got attention because of his CF, but poor Mark was lost without their mom and was trying to find his footing, and to figure out how to be an eleven-year-old in the circumstances that life gave him. He wasn't old enough to handle it like an adult, but he was too old to be treated like a kid. She just wanted to hold him and hug him - and tell him it was okay if he wanted to cry. She realized that he kept asking to go fishing not because he loved fishing so much, but as his way of trying to get their dad to do something he loved, and to live a bit of a normal, eleven-year-old boy's life.

Meg felt incredibly confused. In the midst of all of the difficult feelings she was trying to understand and manage, she was also experiencing happiness. The time that she was spending with Vern caused her to feel excitement, and gave her something to look forward to for the first time since her mom died. She felt guilty for experiencing happiness. She sat on the dock, and looked out at the bay - and she wondered how long she should wait before it would be okay to admit that something made her happy. She picked up her phone and called Vern.

"Let's work on the canoe?" she asked when he picked up.

"Awesome," Vern said on the other end. "I'll see you at the boathouse in twenty minutes."

∞

Vern was glad to be leaving Dave and Jay at the tracks. He told them he was going to spend the afternoon with Meg.

"Awww," they both replied, and Dave joked, "Just stay away from any closets."

Vern had started walking away but turned around to give Dave the finger before he hurried to Mr. Johnson's place.

When he got there Meg was sitting outside the door of the boathouse waiting for him. She smiled at him as he approached, and he marvelled at the fact that he could somehow feel her smile on the inside. He picked the lock and held the door as Meg stepped in.

"I love what you've done with the place," Meg said. Vern had taken the sheets off the corner couches and turned the corner into a bit of a living area.

"Make yourself comfortable," Vern smiled. "I'm just going to get everything ready."

As Meg waited for Vern to get all set up, she decided that one day she would love to live in a place like this. "Let's live here forever," she said to Vern, who was ready to get started.

"That would be the cat's meow," Vern said, and Meg laughed. Vern was the only sixteen-year-old who could say "the cat's meow" and sound cool.

Meg stood at one end of the canoe, and Vern stood at the other. They both applied TSP to clean up the remnants of the old paint, mold, and mildew that the years of Slicker mistreatment had left on the canoe. The two were comfortable in each other's company.

"Do you want to play a game?" Vern asked.

"What kind of game?"

"The one, two, three game," he replied. "We ask each other questions, then answer on three."

Meg nodded and smiled. She was curious where this game would lead.

"Favourite colour?" Vern asked. "One. Two. Three."

"Blue," they both replied at the same time and smiled at each other.

"Favourite movie?" Meg asked. "One. Two. Three."

"*Top Gun!*" they both shouted at the same time.

"You like *Top Gun?*" Vern asked, and Meg simply smiled in response.

"Okay, favourite singer?" Vern asked. "One. Two. Three."

"Michael Hutchence," they both said at the same time.

Meg gave Vern a quizzical look. "This is so crazy," she said. "Not many people our age even know who he is."

"Nah, not really," Vern said. "I just read your Facebook interests."

Meg gave Vern a sweet look. "I thought something was up!" she said. "But *Top Gun*, that wasn't on there - so that's kind of neat." She smiled at Vern and he gave her a wink.

"Okay, let's do it for real," Vern said. "Favourite Person: One. Two. Three."

"You!" Vern shouted, but he realized that he was the only one who'd said anything. He looked across the canoe, and saw that Meg's tears were hanging on to the corners of her eyes. Her face was white, and she had dropped her red rag onto the floor.

"My mom," she said softly as a tear managed to escape.

"I'm so sorry," Vern said, and he took a step in Meg's direction.

"It's okay," she cried. She put her hand out, as if to tell Vern not to come any closer. He leaned on the canoe. Meg sat on the floor.

"She was my favourite person," Meg whispered. "Oh my God - I miss her so much - and it's all my fault that she's gone."

"Meg," Vern said. "It is not your fault that your mom was killed by a drunk driver."

"It is my fault, Vern!" Meg yelled. "It is my fault. The only reason that she went to the city that day was to pick up my Christmas present. It was a book that she used to read me when I was little. She ordered me the special edition. She always did special things like that. She always made things special. She drove to the fucking city to pick up a book - because she wanted me to know how much she loved me. Why couldn't she have had it shipped? They found it in the car on the scene. It was the only fucking thing left intact."

Meg was bawling now. "On the inside cover she wrote, *I love you through and through, Meggie - Yesterday, Today, and Tomorrow too - Love Mom*, and it was a lie - it was a lie. Because there wasn't a tomorrow - and my dad is going to end up in the psych ward and Matthew is going to die because we can't take care of him like she did, and Mark just doesn't know what to do with himself, and I don't know how to make it better, and I don't know how to make this life work without her. And you - how dare you make me feel happy? I don't deserve to feel happy. When I'm with you, I feel happy, like I did before it happened. I feel like life is okay, and I'm not supposed to feel like life is okay after what happened - after what happened because of me." Meg sobbed into her sleeve.

At that moment, Vern's feelings for Meg overwhelmed him. He put the can of TSP on top of the canoe and tossed the rag, wiping his hands on his jeans as he started walking over to her. She watched him, unsure of what he was doing; she could feel her heart racing and her cheeks burning from the tears. He picked her up off the floor and carried her over to the couches in the corner of the boathouse.

"Nobody should ever have to feel loss the way you have," he said to her as he stroked her cheek.

The fact that he was reacting so tenderly caused Meg to feel the most vulnerable she had since her mom died. Her now silent tears spilled, and she sank into Vern's embrace. He held her and kissed the top of her head, hurting for her - wanting to take away her pain. He held her and she cried - and for the first time since her mom died, she felt like she could give in to the anguish - but that the world would not swallow her up because of it. She rested her head on Vern's chest, and when her tears stopped, she closed her eyes - just for a moment - and fell asleep.

Vern stayed as still as he could while Meg slept. He didn't want to move and wake her up and loved holding her in his arms. When she started to stir, he swiped the hair out of her eyes, "did you have a good sleep?" he asked.

"Oh," Meg mumbled, "I'm sorry - how long was I out for?" and she sat up.

Vern started rubbing and shaking his arm, "about an hour and a half," he said, "I'm pretty sure I lost feeling in my arm after twenty minutes," he laughed and so did Meg.

The radio on the end table beside them was playing flash-back songs all day. As the next song started, Meg jolted her head in Vern's direction, and as she looked at him they both called out, "Top Gun!" at the same time and started laughing. "Thanks," she said, "I needed this."

"And this is a gem from 1986," the Radio DJ said. *"Take My Breath Away by Berlin."*

Vern smiled, his mischievous smile, and said, "You know...this is the song they play in the movie when they -"

Meg leaned over and started kissing him. The two sank further down into the couch. Vern tried, numerous times, unsuccessfully, to undo Meg's bra while they kissed. Sensing his frustration, she lifted her shirt over her head, tossed it to the side, and undid the clasps herself. She smiled at him and he pulled her closer.

They were both startled by the loud bang of the boathouse door. "What in God's name is going on in here?" a raspy old crusty voice yelled. It was Mr. Johnson.

Vern's head was the first to pop up from the couch.

"My shirt," Meg whispered, "my shirt, I need my shirt."

Vern was in shock, and grabbed Meg's shirt but didn't pass it over right away. He sat, jaw-dropped, staring at the old man from behind the couch. Meg grabbed her shirt from him.

"Go home," he whispered to her without taking his gaze off Mr. Johnson. "I'll call you later."

She ran past Mr. Johnson, holding her shirt over herself, without making eye contact.

Mr. Johnson waited for Meg to leave before he started. "What the hell were you doing to that little girl in my goddamned boathouse?" he roared. "And aside from that, what in the hell are you doing in my goddamned boathouse?"

Mr. Johnson looked around. He saw the canoe. He saw the stash of supplies, and he saw that Vern had turned the corner with the couches into his own little pad. "Get your shit together, kid, and meet me on the front porch of the house in ten minutes. I'm going to call the police. Jesus Christ." And with that, shaking his head, Mr. Johnson pushed the door of the boathouse open with his cane and slowly started back toward his house.

Vern got all of his supplies packed. He covered the couches with their white sheets and cleaned up whatever indication there was that anyone had ever set foot inside the boathouse. The only thing he left behind was the canoe on the trestles. He started walking towards the old man's house, rehearsing in his head what he would say - how he would beg for him to allow him to come back for the canoe, and most of all, how he would convince him not to call the police. He had worked so hard to separate himself from the Golden Acres image he was born into. People called him a juvenile delinquent as it was, because of where he was from and who his mom was - the last thing he needed was actual charges, a record, or a ride in the back of a police car. He noticed the old '86 Wagoneer parked in the laneway. *How did we not hear it pull up?* he thought.

∞

It was dark, and Jay had been walking Erie's End for hours. That was what he did when he had to clear his head. He had made his way to the pier, and he was doing the other thing that Jay always did, picking up stones as he went and whipping them at whatever was nearby. He sat under the lighthouse and watched the water as the light from above hit it in rhythm. He looked out into the darkness, concentrating on the green bursts of light.

How could this be happening? This kind of stuff didn't happen in real life. Why couldn't the police just arrest the asshole? Or why couldn't they just get a restraining order? In that moment Jay decided that he was not going to just let Jess leave the End. If he found them here, he would find them anywhere. He started walking with determination down the pier, and when he reached the beach, Jay started running toward Jess and Steph's cottage. He had to tell them that they could not leave. He would do anything to make them stay.

As he reached the end of their street he saw the cruiser still parked in front of the cottage. Jess and Steph were sitting on the front porch, covered in the same afghan that Steph had been wrapped in the night before when the officer came for questioning.

"I've decided something," Steph was telling Jess. "I've been working with that counsellor in the city; she's been meeting me here. After last night I talked to her on the phone, and she helped me realize that running from this is not the answer." She squeezed Jess tight.

"I love you, Mom," Jess said and looked up at her, knowing that this must have been a difficult decision for her to make and that she probably made it for Jess's sake.

Jay was running down the street when the two noticed he was coming. He ran up the steps to the porch, short of breath. "I cannot let you two leave. Stay here and let me help you. I can help. This community can help. Please don't go." He was trying to be strong, but his voice cracked while he was making his plea.

Jess and Steph each pulled one of his hands, and he fell in between the two of them on the swing. Jess pulled him close. "We're not going anywhere."

He looked up at her, and she nodded; then he looked over at Steph, and she nodded too. He hugged Jess and he hugged Steph, and he swallowed the lump in his throat. He felt the greatest sense of relief he'd ever experienced in his life.

"Let's go in and celebrate," Steph said. "I think there's an old bottle of wine in the fridge."

Jess and Jay looked at each other and laughed. Jess leaned into Jay, and he put his arm around her and they followed Steph into the cottage.

As they entered, the cruiser drove away - it was shift change, and the other would arrive momentarily. Steph poured three small glasses of wine. She couldn't believe how much she was starting to feel like her old, pre-Greg self. *Bring it on,* she thought to herself. She was beginning to believe that she could protect herself and her daughter and she would do whatever it took to try.

"Cheers," she said. "Here's to forever in the End."

The three clanked glasses and each took a sip of the oxidized wine left by the previous residents, which should probably have been poured down the sink months ago.

As they laughed about their failed attempt at a celebratory drink and the fact that the world's strictest mom poured them one, the doorbell rang. "It's probably the officer for the next shift coming to introduce himself," Steph said. "Jay, would you mind grabbing that? I think I'll pour these drinks down the drain."

Jay opened the door and looked around - there was nobody there. There was no cruiser across the street, and he suddenly had a chilling feeling come over him. Jay looked down at the welcome mat and saw a nicely wrapped gift sitting there. He picked it up and read the typed tag: *To: Stephanie.*

He walked into the kitchen and Jess could tell right away by the look on his face that something was wrong.

"What is it?" she asked.

"I think we should wait for the officer," Jay said, holding the box behind his back.

"Why?" Steph asked, panicked. "Jay, tell me what you're holding - what was at the door?" she demanded as she walked towards him.

"There was nobody there, but this gift was left on the doorstep. It's for you - I think it's kind of weird."

He handed the box to Steph, who didn't know what to expect and hoped that it was innocent; that maybe a friendly neighbour just left a welcome gift and didn't want to bother them. She tried not to think the worst. She untied the ribbon and lifted the lid. She pulled out a neck tie - and read the message written on the bottom of the box: *Don't say a word,* it said in Greg's handwriting.

Steph dropped the tie on the floor and whimpered in defeat. "Lock the door," she instructed. "Close the windows." She was frozen. She couldn't get any more words out. She didn't want Jess to see her like this, but she couldn't move. She couldn't speak. She slid down the cabinets and sat on the kitchen floor. She couldn't breathe.

Jess and Jay looked at each other. They didn't know what to think, and they didn't know what to do.

CHAPTER 18

The first two days after it happened, Steph wouldn't leave the house at all. Jess called Dr. Taylor, not wanting to lose the progress her mom had made. Dr. Taylor came to the cottage and worked with Steph on some of the Cognitive Behavioural Therapy that had helped her take steps forward before the gift at the doorstep happened.

"I really think you need to talk about what happened with Jess," Dr. Taylor urged. "Steph, tell her the truth. She's a strong young woman, and she will be able to cope with it. I can help with that."

"There is no way I will ever tell Jess what really happened that night!" Steph protested. "It will be a secret I take with me to the grave. I am willing to talk to the police about the gift at my doorstep, but not about that night - never. They don't need to know that the tie in that box was the same one he used to gag me."

"You're doing well with most of your goals, Steph," Dr. Taylor said, "with being able to approach life with confidence, for the most part, but I want you to know that a lot of your remaining anxiety and the PTSD symptoms you're experiencing are a result of your avoidance of what actually happened." She looked across the table at the troubled look on Steph's face and could tell that this session had been difficult for her. "My hope for you, Steph, is that at some point, you will be able to discuss what happened to you with other people in your life who you trust. At this point, if you can't do that, then I strongly recommend that you do at least tell the police what really happened, all of the details, and press charges."

"No," Steph said bluntly. "And I know you have an obligation to break confidentiality if you believe someone is in danger. But I am telling you that if the police find out about that night, Jess and I will be in more danger than we are now."

Dr. Taylor agreed that for the time being, she would respect Steph's wishes. As she got up from the table, she told Steph to call her if she needed anything. She reminded her of why she moved to Erie's End. She reminded her of the goals she'd set for herself; and she reminded her what a truly strong person she was. Steph watched from the kitchen window as Dr. Taylor drove down the lane, and when she was out of sight, she began to cry.

∞

It was still grey in the house from the morning dusk as Val came around the corner and saw her mom hunched over the kitchen table with her hands in her hair. It looked as if she needed to hold her own head up to keep it from hitting the table. It was clear that she had been crying. She was just holding her head over the papers - the separation agreement.

Her mom looked up and saw Val watching her. "Well, it's done," she said.

Val shrugged her shoulders and opened the fridge, pretending to look for something to eat. Suddenly she wasn't so hungry.

"Listen, Val," Janet said, "I'm so sorry that you've had to go through all of this."

"Not your fault, Mom," she said, "not your fault that Dad's a dick."

"I know you're struggling. I'm worried about you, Val."

"What do you want me to say, Mom? I'm sorry that I walked in on Dad fucking that bitch in your bed, and that he told you before I could. I'm sorry that the person who I got half of my DNA from is such a loser? I'm sorry that your whole entire life was built on expectations that were unrealistic because it turns out that the person you were supposed to grow old with is a waste of breath? How could he do this?"

Val started to sob, and Janet got up and wrapped her arms around her daughter.

"Listen to me, Val," she said. "What happened with your dad hurt me - I know you know that, and there is no future for our marriage. But I really hope that you will find it within yourself somewhere, somehow, to forgive him. He wasn't always a - what did you call him? - a dick - he wasn't always a dick."

Val smiled through her tears. She had never heard her mom call anyone that before.

"The reason this is so difficult is because I love your dad, and he loves us. I think he's ashamed of how this happened, and so ashamed that you witnessed it. He loves you, Val, and admit it - before this, before he and I started fighting so much - you and your dad were close, right? Daddy's Vallerina?"

Val nodded, and the pain in her chest seemed to have a direct connection to her lower lip, which was quivering as she cried. Her brother used to tease her for being an ugly crier, and she knew that at this moment she must have been hideous. "How could he do this, Mom?" she sobbed.

Janet held Val's hands in hers and did her best to hold back her own tears. "I cannot speak for your father, Val - and I hope that one day the two of you can have this conversation. I don't know," she said. "I don't know what got us here. We had been having trouble for years, really, but our relationship hit its worst after Meg's mom died last year." Janet took a deep breath. She and Kent and the Coles had agreed that they wouldn't tell the kids. "The two of them dated, when we were kids. They were pretty serious.

"Dad was in college and Meg's mom was still in high school, so her parents made her break up with your dad - they said he was too old for her. After that is when she started dating Meg's dad. Anyway, I think that when she died last year, it really hit your dad hard. The connection didn't really occur to me until recently. In fact it was the night of the Listers' party - he had that big blow-up. When I thought about it after, I realized that he couldn't bear the fact that she wasn't there - and that everyone was laughing and having fun anyway. He loved her."

"This is why small towns suck," Val mumbled, "and it's no excuse, Mom. She was your friend too. Just because she died - doesn't mean anything, it doesn't give him the right or the excuse to have done that. And how can he have loved her and married you? And it is so gross that Dad was in love with my best friend's mom. And how can you say you still love him after all of this?"

"Val, it's okay that your dad still loved Meg's mom - she was his first love. Sometimes those feelings never leave you. Sometimes you see that person twenty years later in the grocery store and your heart still skips a beat, and you feel weak and gushy just like it was the first time you saw them. It doesn't mean that your dad loved me any less because he still loved her. I don't begrudge him that. Listen, I know about you breaking up with Jay. I didn't know how to bring it up to you, and I'm sure you have your reasons, and I respect that. But you two were together for a long time. If something happened to him tomorrow, how would you feel? Would it affect you?"

"Of course it would Mom, of course - what the hell kind of question is that? And it's not like Jay and I were together twenty years ago. I still cry because of how much I love him, and how what I did hurt him. But I knew it just wasn't right - him and I were just not all we were chalked up to be."

Val still had tears running down her cheeks. "Dad wasn't having sex with Meg's mom. If he loved her, and he loved you - and he wasn't having sex with either of you - it makes no sense. It's not like if something happened to Jay, and I couldn't deal with my life anymore, it's not like the first thing I would do is just have sex with someone..."

Val's voice trailed off and she felt frozen as the thought of Dave suddenly started to suffocate her. She put her head into her mom's shoulder and started crying even harder. "Oh my God, Mom," she said. "I don't know what to do - I don't know what I've done. Everything is messed up. Everything."

Janet held her daughter and swayed side-to-side like she used to do when Val was little. The tears she'd been holding back in her attempt to show strength now warmed her cheeks. More than anything else, the worst thing about this whole ordeal was seeing how much pain it caused Val. "It's going to be okay, sweetie," she whispered. "I promise; things get better from here."

Val gently pulled away from her mom's embrace. She wiped her eyes and took a deep breath. "Mom," she said, feeling weak in the knees from her nerves, "I think I need help." Her tears started pouring again. "I am so sad," she cried. "Ever since Meg's mom, I haven't been able to go a day without wondering if I'll ever been happy again. And with everything else that's going on - I feel like I'm losing myself, and I just want it to be okay again."

"Oh Val," Janet said and put her arm around her shoulder, "I know things have not been easy. I want it to be okay again too. I think you should talk to Dr. Greene."

Val nodded silently. Dr. Greene had been their family doctor since she was born, and she was nervous to talk to him, but she knew that her mom was right. She felt like the weight had been lifted off her shoulders. It was out. Not having to hide it anymore or pretend she was okay somehow made it easier to breathe.

Val finished getting dressed. For the first time in a long time, she actually put effort into it. She used to love fashion so much. She wore one of her favourites - a dark blue dress with a ruffled trim that rested just above her knees. The tiny white polka dots were only noticeable from close up. She put an oversized brown leather belt around her waist and slid on the matching soft Italian leather sandals that her aunt bought her while on vacation in Europe last year. She sat at her vanity and brushed her hair. It felt like she was just going through the motions, but it was a start, she thought. She put on some eyeliner, then mascara and some lip gloss. She sat, and looked at herself in the mirror. She wasn't sure of what she was feeling.

Her mom opened the door. She sat on the end of Val's bed. "You look beautiful, Sweetheart," she said. Val turned around and smiled softly. "So, I've made an appointment with Dr. Greene for tomorrow, okay?" she asked.

Val nodded. "Thanks for understanding."

Janet gave an assuring look and said, "We'll get through this together. Listen, I have to go and meet the new people in town today - it's my turn for the Welcome Wagon. I'd really like you to come with me. It's a mother and daughter - I think the girl is close to your age, her name is Jessica."

"Oh God," Val said. "Mom, I know Jessica. I kind of beat her up that day - after I found Dad. She's Jay's new girlfriend, I think." She looked at her mom with a desperate look, hoping she would say Val didn't have to come.

"Val - you didn't! Well, in that case - you're definitely coming. I think you might owe her an apology."

Val rolled her eyes but knew her mom was right. She grabbed her purse off the back of her door as the two walked out into the hallway.

∞

Vern lay awake in his bed, thankful that he was in his bed and not in juvie. Mr. Johnson had turned out to be all right, for a crusty old guy. When Vern made his way up to the porch that day, after being caught in the boathouse, the old man was sitting on the steps, waiting for him as promised.

"So kid," he said, "what's the story? Put your shit down, I poured you a glass of iced tea. Start explaining." He pointed with his cane to show Vern where to drop his stuff.

Vern wasn't sure what to think or how to start. He threw his backpack down on the ground and offered his hand to Mr. Johnson. "Hello, sir, my name is Vern Kelly."

"I know who you are, kid," he said waving away the offer of a handshake, "and I know where you're from. Your mother is a drunk."

For some reason it didn't bother Vern that Mr. Johnson so bluntly pointed out the obvious. He didn't understand why it was so easy for him to do so, but he poured his heart out to the crusty old man. He told him about finding the canoe, and about the fact that where he was from and who his mother was had nothing to do with who he wanted to be. He told Mr. Johnson about Meg - how at first he just thought she was so hot, but he'd actually started having feelings for her and hadn't really ever experienced that before. He drank his iced tea, and for the first time in his life - had a serious discussion with an adult. It was the first time in his life that an adult actually listened to what Vern was saying.

When he was done telling Mr. Johnson about himself - about how his mom, when he was a little kid, was able to sober up just enough to pass visits from Children's Services so that she could continue to collect her child tax credits, and about Meg and the guys and everything that he felt defined him - Mr. Johnson grunted.

"Okay kid," he said, "this is what's going to happen. You can use my boathouse to finish your goddamned boat, but nothing in this life is free. First of all, stop picking my lock - you're going to destroy the damned thing. I'll give you a key. I'll be here every Saturday to check up on the place. I want grass cut, I want anything that's broken fixed, and I want to see that if you're going to pursue that little girl - that you do it the right way. Show her some goddamned respect... and allow her the chance to have some for herself too. Ask her on a date, for Christ's sake. Do what you have to do -but do it right. Now get the hell out of here before I change my mind."

That was last week, and Vern lay awake at dawn anxious to see what this Saturday would hold. It would be the first time Mr. Johnson had come back since their talk. Vern worked relentlessly all week, but he did hardly anything on the canoe. He cut the grass - all the grass - the whole property's worth of grass, which had grown so long that he had to first use a manual push mower to make sure that he wouldn't blow the engine or break the blades on the regular lawnmower. He cut the grass to perfection; he used a Weedwhacker to trim all along the pathways and along the driveway; and he trimmed the hedges. He sanded and re-stained the fence. He weeded the garden. He started replacing the boards in the dock. He raked the sand on the beach. He cleaned the boathouse from top to bottom; he cleaned the outsides of the windows on the house. He did everything he could think to do. He just hoped it was enough to ensure that the old man would not change his mind.

Vern was waiting on the porch when Mr. Johnson pulled up in his Wagoneer. Vern loved that vehicle. He could picture himself driving one, and thought about how good he would look in it. He had bought a bottle of iced tea on his way over, and had two plastic cups waiting for when Mr. Johnson arrived. He ran down to the Wagoneer and reached out his hand, the gesture suggesting that he was there to help Mr. Johnson out of the truck.

"Aw, hell, kid," he said, "I'm old, I'm not a goddamned invalid." He grumbled something about his children as he continued to struggle while getting out of the vehicle. He eventually slammed the door shut, and said, "Okay, I'm dying to see what you did around here - the grass looks good."

Vern showed him around the property. Mr. Johnson, to Vern's surprise, did not complain about anything.

He put his hand on Vern's shoulder. "You did a good job, kid. I'll order some lumber from the hardware store so you can finish that dock this week."

The two walked up the path to the house. Vern could tell that the tour of the property had taken its toll on Mr. Johnson, but he dared not say anything. "I got us some iced tea on my way over," Vern offered, pointing at the bottle and cups he'd left on the porch.

"Well, it'll be warm by now, for Christ's sake," Mr. Johnson said. "Go on in the house and get some ice." Mr. Johnson sat in a lawn chair that Vern found while cleaning up the yard and set up on the porch.

As Vern walked through the front door of the house, he felt like he was walking into Mr. Johnson's own memory. There were portraits of him with his wife, and pictures of his kids and grandkids. There was a lot of wood - on the walls and the trim and the floor and the furniture - and a lot of books. There was nautical stuff, but Vern didn't really know what it was - he saw something that looked kind of like a compass, but thought it was weird that it was just hanging on the wall.

"I'm likely to die of old age out here if you keep taking your sweet-ass time, kid," Mr. Johnson hollered. "Move along, would ya? There's nothing to see, or steal in there."

Vern came back with a cup full of ice and handed it to Mr. Johnson. "I thought about what you said, about Meg - and respecting her, and doing it right," he said. "She was really embarrassed about what happened. I apologized to her, and I asked her if she wanted to go on a real date sometime. She actually said yes. She laughed a little at first; I don't think she knew I was serious. I'm going to take her to the movies at some point, but first I offered to make her dinner, but I didn't want to invite her to *Chez-Double-Wide* with Drunk Doris as the host." Mr. Johnson actually laughed - but quickly collected himself and reverted to his grumpy face. "I'm going to make dinner for her and her dad and brothers - the whole family - at their house. I'm going to do it tomorrow."

"That's real nice, kid," Mr. Johnson said, and he took a sip of his iced tea. The two of them sat in silence, and Mr. Johnson looked out over his freshly groomed property. Vern couldn't tell if the look on the old man's face was pride or nostalgia, or maybe gas. They just sat there in silence, until Mr. Johnson said, "What the hell are you still doing here, kid? Go find those friends of yours you've been telling me about. They're probably wondering what the hell happened to you. I can't get any time alone, for crying out loud. Go on, I'll see you next week."

∞

"The tie was processed with the other evidence you gave us, the box too," Officer Parker told Steph. "There are no conclusive findings to suggest that this was your husband. The police in Richmond questioned him there - and it seems that he hasn't left that area at all, ma'am. He claims to have no idea where you are. Apparently, he's been at work every day since you left."

"He's lying," she said calmly. "I know his handwriting; the tie is something significant that only he knows about. It had to be him."

There had been no activity and no threats since that night. Steph had increased her visits with Dr. Taylor, who was now coming to the cottage on a daily basis.

"Anyway, Ms. Carmichael," said Officer Parker, "I think it's safe to say that you don't have to worry. We haven't found anything to suggest that you're in real danger. I will keep my cruiser right out in front of your house as often as I can, though - if that would make you feel better?"

"I would really appreciate that," she replied - knowing full well that somehow, Greg had found them. She wasn't going to let her fear take over, though. In one of her sessions she realized that he'd already done the worst he could do to her, and that there was no way she would let him get close to Jess.

Officer Parker had just finished wishing Steph a good day, and was standing at the open door, about to head back to his cruiser, when he exclaimed, "Oh, look who it is! It must be your day for Welcome Wagon. My sister's on the committee - and look, she brought my niece, Val."

Officer Parker called to them from the door and invited them in; it was almost as if he lived there and they were his guests.

That wouldn't be so bad, Steph thought to herself. She blushed at the thought, and thanked God that people couldn't really read minds. She walked to the door and welcomed the Welcome Wagon.

∞

Vern met up with the guys on the tracks.

"Dude," Dave said as he saw Vern approaching, "where you been? We heard you got arrested!"

Vern held out his arms as if to say, *Who, me?* "No, man," he said. "You know how it is, things to do - people to see. It's not easy being Vern Kelly." They all laughed.

"So we heard that you moved into Old Man Johnson's place?" Jay asked.

"Nah," Vern said, "just using it to keep some stuff. I thought for sure he was gone for good - to the city - didn't think it would be an issue at all. Well, last weekend he caught me and Meg hanging out there - it wasn't pretty." Vern didn't want to go into all of the details with the guys. This was *his* - and he didn't know why, but he just wanted to keep it to himself.

"I thought for sure he was going to call the police, but he just basically read me the riot act and said he'd be checking up." Vern wanted to change the subject. "So what do you think about me asking Meg out, like on a more serious level?"

"I'd say it's about time," Jay said.

"You two hang out all the time anyway," Dave added.

"But what are all the other ladies going to do with themselves? Vern Kelly, off the market - it could cause mass chaos," he boasted. "Oh. Crap." He stopped in his tracks. "So, I told her I was going to make her and her family dinner tomorrow night."

"You didn't," Jay said, shocked. "Vern - you can't even make a box of macaroni and cheese. You can't make a pizza pocket in the microwave. You had to throw out your toaster because of your attempt to make pop tarts. How are you going to pull this off?" Jay asked - concerned, and also slightly amused.

Vern looked at Dave in desperation. Dave laughed. "I'll ask her - hang on," he said, knowing exactly what Vern was thinking. He called his mom on his cell phone.

"Yeah," Dave laughed, "I guess he offered without thinking about what a terrible cook he is. Thanks, Mom. Vern owes you one." He hung up. "You're covered this time, dude." Vern breathed a sigh of relief.

"So, are we going to catch anything today, boys?" Jay asked. Dave had all the fishing poles over his shoulder as they continued to walk down the tracks.

"I always catch something; it's you two amateurs that need to pick it up," Vern declared with confidence.

"A boot doesn't count!" Dave said.

"Definitely not," Jay agreed, laughing.

"A boot doesn't count?" Vern asked. "Yes it does! That's one more boot than you two!"

They all laughed, and Vern and Dave high-fived. "Nice," Vern said in his drawn-out Vern way.

∞

Val and her mom were sitting on the porch swing, and Jess sat on one of the wicker chairs that faced them. She felt entirely awkward and unsure of how to be hospitable to Jay's ex-girlfriend, who had told her straight up that she did not like her, and that she was not welcome. She had laughed to herself when she realized that Val was the *Welcome* Wagon.

"Nice sandals," she said and smiled at Val sincerely.

Val smiled back with a "thanks," and everyone sat looking at each other with fake smiles on their faces. The awkward tension was finally broken when Steph came out the screen door and announced, "Caesars for everyone!"

Janet looked at Val, and then at Steph. "The girls' are virgin Caesars, right?"

"Oh yes," Steph said, "not quite ready for that yet," and she smiled at the girls.

Jess blushed and was a bit embarrassed. Val looked at her mom with desperation, and Janet put her hand on her knee and handed her the virgin Caesar.

Janet took a sip of her Caesar, and asked Steph her secret - it was the best she'd ever had. She was concerned about her discussion with Val that morning. She sat on the swing with her fake smile and wondered how their lives had come to this point. Everything used to be picture perfect. "So, what brings you to the End?" she asked Steph.

"Well, it's a long story," Steph said, "but to make it short, Jess's father and I separated - and we needed a fresh start."

She looked at Jess, who gave her a look of encouragement. Jess knew it was difficult for her mom to speak casually about what brought them here.

"Mom told me that she came here one summer with her parents when she was a kid," Jess said.

"My parents sure knew how to make lasting memories," Steph said as she felt a pang of guilt and realized how much she missed her parents. She had held strong to her commitment not to contact anyone once she arrived in Erie's End. She knew that Jess hadn't contacted anyone either. She felt lucky that Jess was such a good kid, and didn't contact any of her old friends - although most kids her age may have tried if put in the same situation.

"Why don't you go show Val your room?" Steph suggested to Jess.

Jess felt a little bit uncomfortable but smiled at Val and got up from her wicker chair. *They say you're never supposed to invite vampires in*, she thought to herself. She held the door open and Val stepped inside the cottage.

"It's so cute in here," Val said. Jess thanked her and walked her to her room at the end of the hall.

Jess pressed play on the old tape player she had, which made her feel nostalgic for a time before her own. It contained one of the mix tapes she made, thinking she'd like a whole collection for the cassette player in the truck. "Breakfast at Tiffany's" just happened to start playing mid-song, and Jess turned it off right away.

"Sorry," she said, "I'm pretty sure you don't like that song." It was an attempt at a joke.

Val was frozen where she stood, looking around the room. She noticed what Jess had done to her curtains, the mini-lights - the perfect room. What struck her most was that this room told so much about who Jess was, and it occurred to Val that Jess was so much the right person for Jay. From the old tape player for nostalgia's sake, to the movie posters - *Dirty Dancing, Princess Bride, Sleepless in Seattle, When Harry Met Sally,* even *Star Wars* - to the antique suitcases and postcards, and vinyl records made into bowls and picture frames.

Val sat down on Jess's fluffy white bed, and swallowing her tears, said, "I'm so sorry, Jess, I'm so sorry about the fire."

"It's okay, Val," Jess said. "Jay told me that you have lots going on right now."

It pained Val to know that Jay had talked to Jess about her, but she figured that he really had no other option after how she acted. "That's true," she said. "I don't even know if I'm coming or going or if I *want* to come or go, or if I want to live or die." Val hugged one of the pillows on Jess's bed and pulled her knees to her chest.

"I'm a pretty good listener," Jess offered - and she meant it. She was starting to see clearly that Val was not a horrible life-sucking bitch of a vampire like she had originally, mistakenly thought. She was just someone who, like Jess, was going through immeasurable shit.

"Well," Val started, "last year our friend Meg's mom died. That's kind of when things started to get difficult. We tried to keep going like things were still the same, but Meg had to move away - she's my best friend, and it was right around that time that my mom and dad started fighting all the time, and my brother was away at university - and so much of what I knew was shaken to the ground. I used to want to be around people all the time, and slowly found myself wanting to be alone more and more. My mom and dad's fights got worse and I felt like the safest place I knew, home, was also about to crumble.

I broke up with Jay because I just couldn't bear for him to be the company to my misery. The night of the fire was the day that I walked in on my dad with another woman in my parents' bed. This morning my mom signed divorce papers and I told her that I'm having a really hard time coping with everything."

Val hugged the pillow a bit tighter and made eye contact with Jess - with eyes full of uncertainty and fear.

"Do you want to know why we really came to Erie's End?" Jess asked Val. She nodded quietly, and Jess told her about how things were when they were living with her dad. She was careful not to say where they lived, or what his name was - but she told Val about how he treated them and how her mom found out that he was stealing money from his clients. She even told her about coming home from the movies that night and finding her mom in her room, black and blue from head to toe. She was sitting on the edge of her bed crying. She had jeans on and was holding her t-shirt in her hands. Jess told Val that she didn't think her mom had told her everything, but she knew that her dad was responsible. "Sometimes the worst part of it," she said, "is knowing that he's my blood."

Val was shocked to learn about the reasons for Jess coming to the End. She couldn't believe that after what she'd been through, and having to leave all of her friends without a trace, that she was able to act so happy - and to go on with life. "How do you do it?" she asked her. "How do you still smile, and want to do things, and care about what happens next?"

Jess thought for a minute before she answered. "It's for my mom. I have to be strong for my mom. It amazes me that she endured all of what she did and is still the amazing person she is. She survived my dad - and is still this amazing, strong, funny, caring, smart, encouraging, gift of a woman. I used to believe that couples were supposed to bring out the best in each other - you know, to highlight the good things about each other and make it more possible for those good things to thrive - but what amazes me about my mom, is that her good qualities - they thrive in spite of, and despite my dad. She wants me to have a good life, and with what she's gone through to give me one, I feel like it's my duty to live one." Jess gave Val a warm look of concern. "I hope you don't really want to die," she said.

"No," Val said, "but I do need a way out of my head. I guess I didn't realize how much strength we've all needed over this past year. I think my mom is pretty amazing too." She lay on Jess's bed and admired her hand-painted curtains.

"You are, too," Jess said. "Pretty amazing, I mean - don't sell yourself short. I know someone you can talk to if you need some help sorting the head-mess out. She comes here to help my mom, and I've talked to her a few times too."

"Thanks," Val said. "I've got a doctor's appointment tomorrow; my mom thinks he might refer us for counselling. So hopefully this is the start of my way up from rock bottom."

"Okay, well honestly, let me know if I can do anything - or if you just need to talk, okay?" Jess asked. "Now, should we go see how drunk our mothers are?"

The girls could hear their mothers laughing hysterically, and they wondered if it was due more to the Caesars or the good company. They realized, after returning to the porch, that it was actually a combination of both. Val sat beside her mom on the porch swing and was glad that she came.

∞

There was an unusual feeling in the Cole house. Matthew and Mark were laughing and chanting, "Meg has a boyfriend, Meg has a boyfriend." She was not at all annoyed by the teasing and loved to see her brothers acting like other boys their ages would - boys who didn't have a cloud of grief hanging over their heads. Her dad wasn't wearing sweatpants, he had jeans on, and a button-up shirt. He had shaved and Meg was pretty sure he sprayed some cologne. She was nervous and excited for

Vern's visit and the dinner he was making her family. They hadn't actually had company since her mom passed, and she realized that the dinner tonight was somehow bringing a bit of joyous excitement into the house for everyone.

Mr. Cole looked in the mirror and took a deep breath. When Meg first approached him about Vern making dinner for the family, his internal response was that he would really rather not. He agreed to it, though, because he could see that it meant a lot to Meg. He could see not only that she cared about Vern but how happy she'd been since she starting hanging around with him. He also knew he had to step up as her dad. Vern Kelly was Drunk Doris's son, and it was his job to make sure that she wasn't plunging into a relationship with someone who, if he was anything like his mother, would ruin Meg's life.

The doorbell rang and Meg felt her stomach do a flip.

Mark yelled, "Meg's *boyfriend* is here!" and Meg laughed, knowing full well that Vern heard it. She opened the door, with the rest of her family awkwardly standing a few feet behind her.

She smiled at the sight of Vern holding a covered casserole dish, with a cooler bag strung over his shoulder. He was wearing a t-shirt with the Top Gun logo on it, and a brown plaid sport coat with elbow patches. Meg loved how unique Vern was, and how he just seemed to be able to pull off anything. She also realized that he must have put a lot of thought into that t-shirt. Meg took the casserole dish from Vern and invited him in. He said hello to the family and promptly shook Mr. Cole's hand.

"Nice to see you, sir," he said. "Thank you for having me." He then turned to the boys and said, "You must be Hans and Franz?"

The boys laughed. "No? Then you must be Simon," he said to Matthew, "and you must be Garfunkel," he said to Mark.

Again the boys laughed, and Matthew said, "No, I'm Matt and that's Mark."

Meg looked at her dad and was happy to see that he was smiling; the introductions couldn't have gone better.

"So what's the dinner surprise?" she asked.

"Tonight, my *amici*," Vern said with his best Italian accent, "we will be dining on homemade lasagna and garlic bread, with a Caesar salad on the side - and for dessert, double-chocolate brownies with peanut butter frosting."

The boys smiled at each other and Vern could tell the menu was approved. Meg gave him a surprised look, and he leaned over and whispered, "Dave's mom - don't tell." She giggled. "We need to pre-set the oven," he said. "The lasagna will take about two hours, I was thinking maybe we could play Pictionary in the meantime?"

"Hey, let's use that easel you kids used to paint masterpieces on when you were little," Mr. Cole said, and he and the boys headed for the garage.

∞

When they were out of sight, Meg gave Vern a quick kiss. "Thank you so much for this - they really needed this."

Vern simply smiled. He didn't have the words to explain how good he felt being there. Meg put the lasagna in the oven, and her dad and the boys returned with the easel. Mark was carrying the markers.

"I know," Vern said, "why don't we play boys against girls?" Everyone laughed.

"How about Matt, Vern and me against Meg and Dad?" Mark asked.

"Perfect!" Vern said.

"Before we get started," Mr. Cole said, "can I offer you a beer, Vern?"

Test, it's a test, Vern thought. "No thank you, sir," he said, "I'm not much of a drinker."

Right answer, Mr. Cole thought. "How about a Coke then?" he asked.

"That would be beauty," Vern said. "Okay boys, let's strategize - how are we going to kick their butts? Let's huddle."

The three boys won the game by a long shot. There were high fives flying, and Meg was touched to see her brothers so proud. Mr. Cole had even belly laughed during the game a few times, which radiated to all three of his children. Their house hadn't been filled with so much happiness and laughter and connectedness in a very long time.

As the high fives continued, and Vern taught the boys about *pounding five,* Matthew started to cough. It wasn't long before he was having trouble breathing. Vern didn't know what to do, or if he had caused it.

"It's okay, Matty," Meg said, and put her arm around him.

Vern must have looked concerned, because Mr. Cole put his hand on his shoulder and said, "It's okay, Vern, this happens sometimes - it's the cystic fibrosis, it's nothing you did." He picked Matthew up, and walked out of the room.

Meg followed. "We'll be back in a bit."

"They're just going to calm him down," Mark explained. "They'll probably do some percussion treatments and give him his nebulizer. Percussion treatments are when they try to whack the mucus around and loosen it up, and the nebulizer is his medicine. It might take a while. Oh, and he has a vest - you should ask him to see it, it's kind of cool."

Vern didn't know what to say. He knew that Meg's brother had CF, but he didn't realize what the condition entailed. The mood in the room had changed, and he decided not to let what happened make things awkward. "So this is something that happens a lot?" he asked.

"Yeah," Mark said, "it's an everyday thing." He shrugged his shoulders and gave Vern an awkward smile.

"What do you do when everyone is with Matt?" Vern asked.

"I dunno," he said, "I guess I just wait and try not to feel sad. Sometimes when I'm alone for a long time I think about my mom."

Vern's heart wrenched. "I have an idea," Vern said. "How about whenever it happens and you don't want to be alone, you call me and we can hang?" Mark's face lit up. "I mean, unless that would be too uncool for a smooth eleven-year-old like yourself?" Vern asked.

"No, that would be okay," Mark said, trying to conceal his excitement.

"Okay, so this is what we're going to do," Vern said. "Next time it happens and you don't want to be alone - or just any time you want to hang - you're going to call me, and we have to have a secret code word - and then I'll know it's Vern and Mark time, k?"

Mark nodded. "That's sounds good to me."

"What's our secret code word going to be?"

Mark thought about it for a minute. "Garfunkel," he said.

Vern laughed. "I dig it," he said. "Want to come and help me get the rest of dinner ready?"

They could hear Meg and Mr. Cole giving Matt his treatment, and Matt coughing. Vern did his best to act like it was as normal to him as it was to Mark. "Okay Garfunkel - do you think you could set the table for me?"

Mark agreed and the two of them got to work. Mark set a place setting for everyone. No one had sat in his mom's spot since she died, and he hoped it wouldn't bother anyone. He decided to give the spot to Meg and used the markers from the Pictionary game to write place cards.

"Nice touch," Vern said. Vern worked on mixing the salad and put garlic bread in the oven while the lasagna set. Dave's mom had told him exactly what to do, and he followed her directions to the letter.

"I need the pills for Matt's spot," Mark said.

"Okay," Vern said, catching another glimpse of life's unfairness. "Where do we find those?"

Mark showed him the cupboard that was specifically for Matt's medications. "My mom organized the cupboard," he said. "She put the suppertime ones on the top shelf. The bottles say supper. He needs to have five of them."

Vern grabbed the bottles and handed them to Mark. "You are the best sous-chef around, dude," he told him.

Matt dragged his feet slowly into the kitchen, looking like he hadn't slept in three weeks. "Sorry," he said.

"It's all good, my man," Vern said. "I've got some lasagna with your name on it."

Meg and Mr. Cole came into the kitchen next.

"Vern, I'm impressed, it smells amazing in here," Mr. Cole said. "That game of Pictionary sure did give me an appetite."

Meg smiled at Vern and he smiled back, and he didn't know what he was going to do with himself, or how he was so lucky to be in love with the most amazing human being he'd ever known or could ever have imagined.

∞

Jay and Dave sat on the end of a dock that overlooked the bay. It was one of many public docks that local kids went to if they wanted to fish, but didn't have access to a boat. Jay had travelled around a bit with his parents when he was younger. He'd had the opportunity to see a lot of this country, as well as a few others. To him, there was no place he had seen that was quite as beautiful as Erie's End. The beauty lay in the grand old trees that lined not only the horizon, but the streets and paths and beaches. He also loved that no matter where they were in Erie's End, they were surrounded by water, which stretched as far as the eye could see. If it weren't for the one road that led into and out of Erie's End, it would be an island.

Despite the beautiful scenery, though, and the great company, the fishing that day turned out to be futile.

As they packed up their fishing gear, the boys talked and reminisced about old times. Although Dave was enjoying the conversation for the most part, he was preoccupied with the secret he'd been keeping about his involvement with Val. He wanted to tell Jay what was going on - they were best friends, and he felt like the longer he waited to tell him, the harder it would be.

"Oh man, that was embarrassing," Jay said. "Nothing like puking all over your mom's car after that party. I was an idiot!"

"Nah, I thought it was funny, man; you cleaned it up, and hey, it was a special occasion - no better time!"

"True, I guess," Jay said. "Your mom is the best. I was so thankful that she didn't rat me out." They both laughed, and Dave agreed that his mom was pretty cool.

"Anyways, buddy," Jay said as he got up from the end of the dock, "I should head home. I told my grandma I'd be back early tonight. I haven't really been spending much time with them this summer." He gave Dave a fist bump at the end of the dock and started walking towards his grandparents', while Dave started walking in the opposite direction towards his place.

Dave knew that he had to talk to Jay, that it couldn't wait any longer. He turned around and yelled, "Jay! Wait..."

Jay came walking back. "What is it, man?"

"I need to talk to you about something," Dave said, and Jay could tell that he was uncomfortable.

"You okay, man?" he asked. "Is everything okay?"

"Well, I hope it will be," Dave replied. The two of them walked to the circular garden that framed the start of the path that led through the village. They sat on a granite bench that had been donated by the village funeral home.

"I've been meaning to tell you about this for some time now," Dave started. "Jay…" He took a deep breath and let out a long sigh. "I have feelings for Val, really strong feelings."

Jay didn't say anything, and Dave couldn't tell what he might have been thinking. His expression didn't change.

"I actually have for a really long time, for about as long as we've known her - I often wished I was you when the two of you were going out."

"That's cool, man," Jay said, "we can't help who we have feelings for, but why are you telling me this now?"

"Well, I've been spending some time with Val lately, just the two of us. And well, some stuff has happened between us."

"What kind of stuff are you talking about?" Jay asked. "Like you kissed her?"

"Yeah, I've kissed her," Dave said, "and…"

"And you fooled around with her?"

"Yeah, I fooled around with her," Dave said, and then he took another big, deep breath in preparation for the rest of what he was about to divulge.

"No." Jay shook his head. "You and Val didn't…?"

"I wanted to tell you right after it happened, man, I swear, but Val asked me to keep it between us. She was going through so much, and it kind of just happened, out of nowhere. I really care about her. But, it's also been killing me to have kept it from you. Please tell me you're not mad, bro?"

Jay sat silent for a while. Dave's nerves were eating away at his gut. He felt like he'd betrayed the person who'd been his best friend since kindergarten, and he couldn't tell if that was how Jay felt too.

"Listen, Dave," Jay said. "Val and I broke up, and for a moment, I was devastated. Of course I care about her, and I always will - which is why it's good that she was able to turn to someone who could be there for her when she needed it. The rest is details, and those details are between you and Val. I want you both to be happy. After the breakup, and Jess, I realized that although Val's got this forever spot in my heart - the two of us just don't work. It's cool, man - thank you for telling me - and don't worry, I know Val well enough to know that this conversation stays between us until further notice."

Dave looked at Jay, feeling a bit choked up. "Thanks, dude," he said, "you know I love you, right?"

"I love you too, man," Jay said. "Now things are getting awkward," he joked. "We're good, I'll see you tomorrow." Jay got up and started walking back towards his grandparents' place.

Dave sat on the bench for another couple of minutes and heaved a big sigh of relief. It had gone a lot better than he'd imagined.

As Jay walked, he allowed his real emotions about what Dave had just told him to come to the surface. He didn't know why he felt so hurt. Everything he told Dave was the truth. He was angry, though. He didn't know why, but he was. He was angry at Dave, and he was angry at Val. Then he was confused. Why was he angry at them? He didn't want Val back. He was really happy with Jess. He just walked, confused and hurt, and feeling like he got sucker-punched in the stomach.

CHAPTER 19

I will never understand what just made me speed away in the middle of that wicked storm - I knew deep down that the snow would cover my tracks. I didn't know she was dying. I didn't know the extent of what I had done. My life flashed before my eyes. I knew if I stopped I'd be charged with a DUI, and all I could see in that moment was everything going away - the trust fund, my future -the fucking yacht.

None of that matters now, anyway. The next day, everyone in the End was talking about her death. I learned of the family she left behind, her children and their situation. Whatever future I was trying to save by speeding away, is now and will forever be filled with this unbearable grief - no, guilt - and there's nothing that eases it. I left her there, to die, in a ditch. Those few moments replay over and over in my mind, every single day since it happened. The drinking helped dull it at first, but now - now it just makes the replays even more vivid.

I owe that family everything, anything…and nothing I can ever actually give them. I've been watching them from the shadows, hoping that I'll see them one day and they'll all be okay. Hoping that a day will come when I can't see agony in their fake smiles, or tension in their heavy shoulders, or emptiness behind their eyes. I watch, and hope for that day - and I'm starting to realize that it's a day that may never come.

I am still a coward. I cannot turn myself in. Any decent human being would turn himself in. But I am not decent. I followed him to the garage. I knew that his truck was on the verge of non-repair. What I wanted to do was buy him a new one - to replace it. But there was no way for me to remain anonymous. Instead, I paid cash for the repairs - and left enough for another lifetime's worth of repairs should he need them.

They were so trusting at the garage - I included a typed note with instructions. And that was it. Still, the guilt consumes me. I hoped helping in some way would relieve even just the smallest bit of it - but that thing, that thing inside just keeps eating at me, and I think it could very well kill me.

-A.D.

CHAPTER 20

"Garfunkel," said the shy voice on the other end, followed by a stifled giggle.

"Ten-four little buddy," Vern replied, and he looked at the clock on his side table. "Eight oh-three." He rubbed his eyes. "On my way," he said with a yawn, into the receiver of his see-through phone, a coveted item for teenage girls of the 1990s. Vern threw on the same shorts he wore the day before, and his now-favourite t-shirt, with the Top Gun logo on it. It was his favourite because of the smile he got from Meg every time he wore it. He thought it would probably be a good idea to wash it soon.

He grabbed his backpack and stuffed the bologna sand-wiches he'd made the night before inside. He added a few cans of soda, some cheese strings - and a package of peanut m&m's, which he had learned were one of Mark's favourite snacks.

Since the night of the dinner, the two of them had been spending a lot of time together. Vern's offer that night was sincere, and he didn't mind that Mark called nearly every day and said "Garfunkel" each time Vern picked up the phone. He enjoyed the feeling of being like a big brother; it was something he'd never experienced before. He was usually the one that others felt the need to take care of, so it was different for him to be in the opposite role.

He looked across the trailer from the kitchen to his mom passed out on the floral couch in the wood-paneled living room. "Bye, Doris," he said, knowing that she wouldn't hear him.

At first, he'd found it difficult to spend so much time with Mark and still maintain Mr. Johnson's property. The first Saturday, in fact, the old man noticed that some of the work Vern usually did had been neglected.

"What the hell, kid?" he asked. "I thought I was wrong about you, but I guess your true colours are showing. Maybe you are a slacker after all."

The words stung, because Vern had started to feel proud each week when Mr. Johnson came, and Vern could see that he was impressed with his work. They shared a lot of good talks when he came to check on things every week - they talked over iced tea, until predictably, the old man rudely and abruptly told Vern to "get the hell outta here." Vern decided it was endearing. He also decided that he was glad Mr. Johnson came into his life.

He had explained to Mr. Johnson last Saturday why the work hadn't all been completed. He told him about the night of the dinner and the promise he made to Mark, and how he'd kept it, and intended to keep it as long as Mark needed him to. He could see, as he was explaining to Mr. Johnson, the lines of anger on his crotchety old face begin to soften.

"All right," he said. "That kid needs someone after what happened to his mother - why the hell the universe sent him you, I'll never know," he jabbed, and the two laughed.

Vern poured the iced tea, and promised that the next week Mr. Johnson would see two week's worth of progress.

"Shut up, kid," Mr. Johnson replied. "Don't make promises you can't keep."

Vern smiled and sipped his iced tea. He could see a smile sneaking out the corner of Mr. Johnson's mouth, too.

This day with Mark was going to be devoted to showing him all around the End - like he was one of the guys. Vern had promised him that he would take him around and show him where he and Dave and Jay, and even his sister, hung out sometimes. Meg told Vern a few nights earlier that she was so grateful to him for being there for her brother. She said that she couldn't believe how much he'd come alive since they started spending time together, and that she was so happy to have her brother back.

"How grateful are you?" Vern had asked, and Meg punched him in the arm.

"Grateful, but not *that* grateful," she teased.

Vern hopped up the three concrete steps that led to Meg's front door. He could hear Mr. Cole, and Meg, and Matt, and the cystic fibrosis treatment in progress. Mark was ready and waiting with his backpack on, and he was wearing the flip-up sunglasses that Vern had bought him.

"Stylin', my friend," Vern said, and he flipped up his own shades to match. "Taking Mark to do some manly-man stuff today," Vern yelled out.

"You show him how it's done, Mark," Mr. Cole yelled back, and Mark stood there grinning.

"I'll have him back before dinner," Vern yelled.

"We're having barbequed burgers," Meg shouted back. "You might as well stay when you get back."

"Okay, we're leaving!" Mark shouted. Vern laughed and the two walked out the front door.

∞

"So, my friend," Vern said, "you up for some major walking today?" Mark nodded. "I'm going to show you all the places the guys and I hang out. It's kind of been our thing since we started hanging out. First, I'm going to show you where we usually meet up, at the lookout. Have you ever been to the lookout?"

Mark nodded again. "My parents used to let us run up to the top when we'd go on family picnics," he said.

"Yeah, we love it up there," Vern said. "It's wicked how you can see water from every direction, the bay and the lake. When I was a kid, I used to pretend I was a pirate, and was on the lookout for thieves who would steal my treasure."

Mark laughed. "No way dude!" he said, sounding an awful lot like Vern. "I used to do that too."

They got to the lookout, and climbed the steep stairs, which changed direction halfway to the top. "So, should we look for pirate thieves?" Vern asked.

"Nah," Mark said, "I'm kinda too old for that."

Vern laughed. "Yeah, I guess I am too." He explained to Mark that he and Dave and Jay came here a lot when they had to talk about stuff. "If there's ever anything you need to talk about," he said, "we could come here, too."

Mark smiled. "Sounds good," he said. "Who do you think wrote all this stuff?" There were messages scribbled on the warning signs of the lookout, some with black sharpie, some were beautifully graffitied and some, carved into the wood itself.

"I guess people who had something to say," Vern answered.

Mark took his backpack off and started rummaging through it.

"What are you looking for, Garfunkel?" Vern asked.

"I just want to write something too," Mark said, "since we're here." He pulled his little Swiss Army knife out of his backpack, and held it up to show Vern.

"Whoa!" Vern said. "You're not going to write it with blood, are you?"

Mark laughed. "No," he said, "I want it to last; I'm going to carve it into the wood."

"Okay," Vern said, "but don't bleed. I think your dad might already want to hurt me, because he saw me kiss your sister the other day."

Mark groaned. "Uggh, that's so gross!" he said, laughing at the same time.

Vern opened up his own backpack and started pulling out some snacks. It was hard to believe that he was already hungry and eating their lunch and it wasn't even ten in the morning yet. Mark got to work carving what he had to say into the wood, and Vern understood that this was something he needed to do on his own without answering a lot of questions in the moment. He left him to it while he sat and secretly looked out over the lake for pirate thieves.

"Done," Mark said after carefully etching each letter into the wood.

Vern crawled over the platform to where Mark was sitting. With his finger he traced the letters Mark had carved. "Through and through," he said. Vern remembered Meg telling him about the story her mom used to read, and recognized that it must have been special for Mark too.

Mark was quiet for a minute, and looked out at the horizon. "It's a book my mom used to read us when we were little," he said. "*I Love You Through and Through*. Now that she's gone, I say it to her. You know, when I wish she was here, or when I need to feel like she is, and sometimes I can almost hear her voice saying the words."

Mark shrugged his shoulders, which Vern had come to realize was his way of shaking off his big emotions. Vern felt a bit choked up, but was glad that Mark was talking about his mom. He put his arm around Mark's shoulder, and held it there for a long time. It might have been a little bit awkward except for the fact that it was just what they both needed in that moment.

"Well," he asked, "are you ready to see the next place the guys and I usually end up at?"

Mark put his hand over the words he'd scratched, almost as if his touch was sealing them into the wood. He put his backpack on. "Bring it on."

"Okay, tough guy." Vern smiled while he ruffled Mark's hair. "Let's go."

They walked along the path back into the village. It was probably the most beautiful part of Erie's End, with thick trees lining one side of the path and the water's edge bordering the other.

"You hungry?" Vern asked Mark.

"Starving."

"Shit," Vern said. "I ate both of our lunches up on the lookout."

They both started laughing. "It's okay," Vern said, "I'm going to take you for a Dougie burger."

Mark smiled. "Awesome!" he said. He had never been to a restaurant without his parents.

"We have to stop at my place first, though," Vern said. "I need to grab some cash. You need to know that it won't be pretty, okay?" he asked. "I've never even taken your sister to my place. You know I live in Golden Acres, right?"

Mark nodded. "I think you're the best no matter where you live," he said.

Vern smiled. "And you know Drunk Doris is my mom, right?"

Mark nodded. "That's okay," he said. Vern decided he loved this kid.

Mark stood in the doorway and couldn't help but stare at Doris passed out on the couch. He had never seen an adult, or anyone, in that state before, but especially an adult. It made him feel like he wasn't in a safe place anymore. The world suddenly showed him something he couldn't have imagined, and seeing her like that gave him a sense of apprehension. He was relieved when Vern came out and said he was ready to go. The trailer park was right behind Dougie's Diner, and the two boys were famished.

After lunch they walked around the marina and picked the boats they would want if they were rich. They walked past some of the Slickers' cottages.

Mark said he wanted the orange one with all the big windows, and Vern said that he'd have to move in next door.

"Can you keep a secret, buddy?" Vern asked Mark.

"Of course," Mark said, "I'm great at keeping secrets."

"The only other person who knows about this is your sister. You have to promise not to tell anyone."

Mark said he wouldn't, and Vern took him to Mr. Johnson's place. He showed him the canoe, and he told him about all the work he'd been doing around the place.

"You know, I could use a little help sometimes, if you're interested?" he asked.

Mark felt like he was important to someone - for the first time in a very long time. He smiled, and Vern took that as his "yes."

"One more stop on our tour for today," Vern said as they were leaving Old Man Johnson's place. "What colour do you think I should paint the canoe?"

"Definitely blue," Mark said.

"Definitely, Garfunkel," Vern agreed.

Mark followed close behind Vern as they walked down Mr. Johnson's long driveway. Vern stopped for a second to wait for him to catch up. "Okay, so the last stop of the day is the pier." Vern put his hand on Mark's shoulder. "Sometimes we hang out there, but mostly, this is the place we go when there's serious shit happening. It's the place you go to talk to God, or the Universe, or whoever it is up there. Val broke up with Jay here. It was like she tarnished the sacred place. See, at the end of the pier, if you step down on the right side, you can sit on the concrete and feel like you're just part of it - part of the water, part of the calm, part of the great bigness."

The two got to the pier and Vern asked Mark to read the giant sign that stood a few feet away from the steps leading up to the pier itself.

Mark nodded. *"Harbour Safety Rules:*
1. *No swimming or diving off pier*
2. *No swimming in channel*
3. *Pier out of bounds during inclement weather*
4. *Pier slippery when wet, caution when walking*
5. *Keep off East slope of pier, slippery when wet*
6. *Do not litter or throw garbage in water*
7. *End of pier (lighthouse) strictly out of bounds*
8. *Alcohol prohibited*
9. *Strong current and undertow near pier*
10. *Erie's End Harbour Authority personnel have the right to ask people to leave any Harbour Authority Area."*

"Thanks," Vern said, "I always wondered what that sign said. Do you think it's big enough?"

Mark laughed. The two stepped up onto the concrete pier. Stamped on the concrete were the words *Dangerous Undertow, No Swimming.* "Do you want me to read you that part, too?" Mark asked.

Vern laughed. "It's all good, dude. What it all means at the end of the day, is that we're not going to tell Meg or your dad we came here, right?" Mark smiled and nodded.

The two walked out to the end of the pier. Vern could see that Mark was a bit nervous. The farther out a person was on the pier, the more vulnerable. Vern figured that's why it was such a good place to bare your soul to the universe or God or whoever the hell was up there. The two reached the lighthouse.

"It's strictly out of bounds," Mark said to Vern.

"You're right," Vern said. "Let's do it from right here. The East slope is slippery, and I don't know which way is East."

Mark laughed. "Okay, let's do it from right here."

The two stood on the pier, back-to-back. "I'm telling you, it will feel awesome after." Vern said.

"Okay," Mark said, "Let's do it."

"On three," Vern said. "One, two…a confession you've been holding onto that you need to get out…*threeeeee*…"

Both Vern and Mark yelled their confessions at the same time, at the top of their lungs.

Mark's was "SOMETIMES I HATE THAT MATTHEW'S CYSTIC FIBROSIS RUINS EVERYTHING."

Vern's was "I CHICKENED OUT WITH RILEY POLANSKI IN THE CLOSET."

Mark turned around and looked at Vern with a look that clearly said, *You're kidding?*

"What?" Vern asked. "She was crazy."

The two of them laughed. Vern put his arm around Mark and they started walking back down the pier. "We better get back for dinner - if anyone asks, we didn't have burgers for lunch."

∞

"Can you pass the ketchup please, Mark?" Meg asked. "So, Dad, you have to tell Mark and Vern your good news. They missed it when they were out gallivanting today." Meg smiled at Vern.

"What's the good news, Dad?" Mark asked.

"Well," said Mr. Cole. "It looks like I've got myself a new job." Mark smiled at Meg, and she nodded and smiled back at him. "It's a job here in town, so I won't have to be away for days at a time, like I was with the fishing. I'm going to be helping out at the docks. They need someone to make sure things are running smoothly with all the fishing boats, with people coming in and shipping out. I'm going to be manning the radio too - for maydays and contacting the coast guard for any emergencies that come up. A lot of people at the Harbour Authority know me because of my years as a fisherman, and Joe Mahone called me up and said that they could really use someone like me."

Everyone around the table smiled - it was like the clinking of glasses and saying "cheers" was replaced with smiles exchanged from one person at the table to another. There was a cloud in the Cole house that had been getting smaller and smaller, and on this day, it seemed to have lifted all together.

They all ached for their loss, for the void that remained where she used to be - his wife, their mother. They missed her and felt the distinctive pain of losing her too early, and so unexpectedly. This was the day, however, when they realized that they were going to be okay. Life was going to go on. They were still a family, and they were going to help each other through, and they were going to make it. Mr. Cole laughed - nothing was funny, really, but it felt good to laugh again.

That night, after Vern had left and the boys were in bed, Mr. Cole walked out the front door and sat beside Meg on the front steps. He breathed in the fresh night air. The sound of crickets and toads surrounded them.

"The stars," Meg said, as she leaned into her dad, putting her head on his chest. He held her tight.

"Amazing, aren't they?" he asked.

They both looked up at them for a few minutes, and enjoyed each other's affection. It had taken them a long time to get back to this, and Meg thought this was how it must feel to meet an old friend you haven't seen for years and years - you never want to let them go again.

"Listen, Meggy," her dad said. "I think I'm going to need your help when I go back to work. How do you feel about taking care of Matt and watching out for Mark while I'm working?"

Meg felt so good that her dad trusted her to take care of the boys; it was what she had been wanting since she came back to Erie's End, to know that he thought she could do it. "Of course, Dad," she said.

"It won't be forever," he continued. "Just until I get a couple of paychecks in and then get caught up with all the bills. After that, we can hire help to come in, especially for Matty."

"Whatever I can do to help, Dad," Meg said, "I'm happy to do it."

He squeezed her a bit tighter. The two of them sat on the front step for another hour and just looked up at the stars, and breathed in the air, and thanked the part of the universe that let them be okay on this day. They somehow knew that tomorrow was going to be okay too.

∞

Val rang the Listers' doorbell. She was nervous because she knew that at some point, probably sooner than later, it was going to become obvious to people that she and Dave had started something that was more than friendship. She decided to go over to Dave's to talk to him about it, and to figure out whether they should start telling people that they were together. However, the thought of that made her feel nervous too. Were they together? Was he her boyfriend? What *were* they? She was there to find out, exactly. She also needed to talk to Dave about her doctor's appointment.

It was amazing to her how magnetic he was. He was the one person she wanted to tell everything to; she felt entirely comfortable baring her soul to Dave and knew that nothing she could say to him would drive him away or cause him to judge. He really listened. He knew what to say - and when not to say anything. She hoped that no matter what they were, she would always have Dave to talk to and to trust in. He was the reason she found lust for life again - and she wanted some way, somehow for him to know that.

Dave's mom answered the door. "Hello, Val," she said, "how are you doing, Sweetheart?"

Dave's mom was always so nice to everyone. Val thought she was the kindliest lady she had ever met. "Hi, Mrs. Lister," she said, "I was wondering if Dave is around? He's not expecting me."

"He should be back soon - if you want to stick around," Mrs. Lister said. "He just went out for a run. Come on in, I just finished up some baking. How would you like a cup of tea and some cookies?"

Val smiled. "That sounds amazing."

The two of them sat at the kitchen island. Mrs. Lister put doilies on the plates and then cookies on the doilies - but only after she'd sprinkled them with powdered sugar to make them look even more perfect. Mrs. Lister could have been Martha Stewart herself. Her kitchen was meticulous. Val was amazed by how the blue kitchen utensils were the exact same shade as the blue kitchen towels, and the off-white cabinets were the exact same shade of off-white as the studded leather dining chairs.

"How's your mom holding up?" Mrs. Lister asked. Val knew that the question was inevitable since they had been friends for so long, and she was sure that Mrs. Lister had heard about what happened - but she still didn't know quite how to approach the answer.

"She's a pretty strong person," Val said, "she's taking one day at a time." She smiled politely at Mrs. Lister and took a sip of tea.

"I imagine that we could say the same about you too, Val," Mrs. Lister said. "I mean about being a strong person. This all must be terribly difficult...for you too."

Val could feel her cheeks burning and was sure she was at least a shade of red brighter than she had been the minute before. "Thank you," she said, "I guess I'm taking it one day at a time too; these cookies are so good," she said.

Just then Dave came stumbling into the back door that led into the kitchen. He was sweaty and short of breath, and the smile on his face indicated that he was also pleasantly surprised to see Val.

"I'm so disgusting!" he exclaimed, still catching his breath. "I'm going to have a quick shower."

He gave his Mom a big sweaty hug, and she squirmed and said, "Gross! Hug me after that shower!" Everyone laughed, and Dave winked at Val as he walked by the island.

"Be right back," he said.

"I think he likes you," Mrs. Lister said to Val, and smiled.

Val could again feel her face turn red. "I think I like him too," she said, looking down at the counter, unable to hide her grin. The two of them chuckled.

Hallelujah! Mrs. Lister thought, and couldn't help but admire Val from a new perspective. *My future daughter-in-law,* she thought, and placed her hand on Val's with a warm smile.

Val smiled back and was amazed at how welcome Mrs. Lister could make people feel.

The two made small talk while Dave showered - they talked about the weather, and the beach and how quickly the summer was passing. It was awkward and comfortable at the same time. It occurred to Val that it was nice to sit and chat with a mom who didn't appear to be going through some kind of crisis at the moment.

Dave rushed back into the kitchen, wearing khaki shorts, an unbuttoned button-up shirt, and a Superman towel wrapped around his head - which he must have forgotten about in his mad rush to get back to Val. She and Mrs. Lister both burst out laughing.

"What?" he asked.

His mom pointed to her head. "You have so much hair to keep dry in there," she laughed.

"Oh yeah," he said while removing the towel. "Hi Val," he said, flirtatiously without even realizing it.

"Well, you two have a nice time," Mrs. Lister said as she floated out of the kitchen on her tiptoes. She felt like she knew a secret, and that it was a good one.

Dave leaned on the counter beside Val. "Hi, Beautiful," he said. Val grinned; she loved how cute Dave could be. "What's the occasion?"

"Well," Val said, "I was hoping we could talk about some stuff? Is that okay?"

Dave suddenly felt nervous; he never quite knew where things were headed when Val said she wanted to talk. "You bet," he said. "Mom," he yelled out, "going for a walk - see you later!"

"Okay, have fun, kids!" Mrs. Lister hollered back, with a bit of excitement in her voice that she just couldn't contain.

"Is everything okay?" Dave asked as he put his arm around Val's shoulder.

She wrapped her arm around his waist as they walked.

"I think it will be," Val said.

"What did you want to talk about?" Dave asked.

"A couple of things, but let's go to our spot first?"

Dave smiled; he liked the sound of it when Val called it their spot. The two strolled through the village, until they got to the big oak tree at the outskirts where they had their picnic.

"I didn't bring a blanket," Dave said.

"The grass is good," Val replied. She sat at the base of the tree trunk, criss-crossed her legs, and motioned for Dave to sit beside her. He lay down on the grass and put his arm behind her, resting his head in her lap.

"So, what's up?" he asked.

"First," Val said, "I've been thinking we should probably tell people about us."

Dave had a sense of relief rush through him, as he had been dreading telling Val that he already told Jay. The thought occurred to him that he might not have to confess to her at all now. "I think that's the best idea I've heard in months," Dave smiled up at Val. "What are we going to tell them?"

"Well, that's what I was going to ask you about," she said. "Do we even know what this is? We can't very well tell people what we are, if we don't know ourselves."

"We could tell everyone that you're the love of my life, and I'm your rebound guy," Dave joked.

"Dave! That's not even funny," Val objected. He started laughing.

"I know," he said, "why can't we just tell people that we like each other, a lot, and we're going to see what happens? Some things are better left undefined. It doesn't matter what anyone thinks or knows or thinks they know. At the end of the day, what matters the most is this - us, making us whatever we want us to be."

Val smiled at him. "You're pretty smart for a jock," she said. They both laughed, and Dave pulled Val down to the grass with him and kissed her.

"What was the other thing you wanted to talk to me about?" he asked.

Val began to feel nervous. She knew that she could tell Dave anything, so she just started.

"Well," she said, "I told my mom about how awful I was feeling. She tried not to act like it was a big deal, but she made an appointment for me to go to my doctor. I had to tell him about everything. I told him about walking in on my dad, and then about how I was not myself...and about how I felt like at any moment - if I took just one step in the wrong direction -I'd fall right off the edge of the earth. And I told him about us."

Val paused. She didn't want to hurt Dave's feelings with what she was about to say, but she knew that she wanted everything to be honest and open moving forward, especially with him.

"It's okay," Dave said, sensing her concern.

"I told him that I was having a really hard time, because I know how I feel about you, but in the midst of everything it was like I couldn't feel it. Somehow, everything in me shut off. It was like life was going on around me as it should, but I wasn't there. I could see everything happen, my body was there, but I wasn't feeling any of it. Imagine watching the movie of your life, but not participating in it. It was like it could have been happening to someone else, and I just knew about it...like everything that was happening in my life belonged to someone else."

The two of them sat in silence for a minute, which to Val seemed like eternity. She didn't know if Dave's silence was hurt or if he was processing. He held her hand a little tighter.

"When you say 'everything,'" he asked, "does that mean... *everything?*"

Val nodded and felt a bit of a lump enter her throat. "Yes," she said.

"But you told me it was the most amazing..." Dave started.

"Well first of all," Val chuckled, "do either of us really have a comparison to base *most amazing* on?"

"Good point!" Dave laughed. "But I'm telling you, it was."

"It's like I was playing the part; I was the actress in my own movie," Val continued. "That's what brought on the breakup with Jay, too; I just didn't realize it at the time. Don't get me wrong, I know now that it was the right decision; he and I weren't the perfect match we thought we were - but it's important for me that you know what's been going on, how lost I've been."

Val nervously twirled her hair, and bit her lip before she said, "The doctor told me that I am clinically depressed. At first when he said the words, I was so upset - on top of everything else, my doctor was saying I'm mentally ill. He was saying things to my mom about counsellors and antidepressants. When I got home, I read about depression and as I was reading, I couldn't believe how much of it mirrored my life."

Dave hugged Val. He didn't know what else to do. He wished she wasn't going through any of this. "I wish I could do something, Val," he said, "I wish I could fix this for you."

"That's what I'm trying to tell you, Dave," she said. "Nobody can cure someone else's depression, but it's because of you that I realized I wanted to participate in my life again. It's because of you that I wanted to feel everything again." Her heart was racing; she hadn't been so candid and sincere with anyone, ever. "That first day, when we had our picnic" - she looked at him with tears accumulating in her eyes - "It was the first time, in so long, that I was actually in the moment. It felt so good to be close to you."

"Val," Dave said, "whatever you need, however I can be here for you - you know I'm here. The good thing about jocks is that we have big shoulders," he joked, but he was serious at the same time.

Val laughed. "I don't know where I'd be without you," she said. "I want to live. I want to be present in my life. I want to feel all of it."

"All of it?" Dave asked. "So, does this mean we get a do-over?"

Val laughed and pushed him. "I think that would be *amazing*," she said, "but let's do it right this time - as long as you're okay with being with a crazy person?"

"Val," Dave said, "this does not mean that you're crazy. I'm pretty sure that everyone goes through something like this at some point in their lives. Look at everything that has happened around here lately. Sometimes life spins us in so many directions that we're bound to lose ourselves for a while - maybe that's how we survive it sometimes, and just so you know ... I'm crazy too," Dave said, "crazy about you."

Val smiled, "you're not crazy, Dave," she said, "you're cheesy! ....but cheesy is good, and you're good - so good, and thank you - for you."

The two lay under the oak tree and listened to each other breathe.

∞

Jay was excited for his grandparents to meet Jess, but felt a bit nervous for Jess to meet them. They weren't like traditional granny-and-grandpa grandparents. Perhaps the only thing that was similar about *his* grandparents and the old-fashioned kind was that his grandma was a really good cook. She also liked to go shopping and have her hair and nails done, and she enjoyed a drink or two on sunny afternoons. His grandpa believed that kids should have fun - and even though he believed in respect and responsibility, he thought it was important for kids to not be lectured, and to learn some things from the way of the world and through life experiences.

Jay held the wooden screen door open for Jess and the smell of the lunch his grandma was preparing made both their mouths water.

Jay's grandma had made a salad with veggies from their garden, and grilled cheese sandwiches, and of course, Jay's favourite potato soup. She figured that it would be a test to determine if Jess really was her grandson's soulmate. She'd never met another person who enjoyed her soup as much as Jay did.

"Gram, it smells so good!" Jay said.

She quickly wiped her hands on her apron as she walked towards them. "This is Jess," Jay said.

She put her hands on Jess's shoulders. "Oh, look at you," she said, "you're as cute as a button."

Jess smiled. "It's nice to meet you," she said.

"Frank!" his grandma yelled. "Frank! The kids are here. You have to see how cute Jay's new little girlfriend is." Jess could feel her cheeks turning red. Jay smiled at her. "And look at your dress. I love it. Tell me, where did you get it?"

Jess explained that she had made the dress last year for a project in art class. "Amazing!" Jay's grandma exclaimed. "You know, I'd love to show you an outfit I made, would that be okay?"

Jay was stunned. "Grandma!" he said, knowing exactly the outfit she was referring to.

"Oh, come on now, Jay," she replied. "Maybe Jess and I have something in common. I'd love for her to see what I've done, too."

The two left Jay standing in the kitchen and headed for his grandparents' bedroom. Jess felt a little awkward, but couldn't help but admire how sweet and enthusiastic Jay's grandma was.

Jay's grandma rummaged through her drawers and closet. "Ah, here it is," she said victoriously. She pulled out a matching short suit. The pattern could only be described as 1980s Miami Vice. There were pink ferns and green leaves plastered everywhere, on both the button-up shirt and the elastic-waistband shorts.

"I'm a bit of an artist myself," Jay's grandma explained. She showed Jess the pink flamingos she'd embroidered onto the shorts and the shirt herself, "just to add that little extra oomph." Each flamingo also had a tiny red crystal glued on where its eye should be. Jess politely said how much she loved the outfit, and Jay's grandma smiled with pride.

As the two returned to the kitchen, Jay's grandma said, "I told you she would love it," and in that moment, Jay felt so much love for Jess, knowing full well that she'd handled what could have been an awkward moment with grace and kindness.

Jay's grandpa walked into the kitchen and said, "Smells wonderful, dear," as he kissed his wife on the cheek.

When Jess took her first taste of potato soup, she sincerely told Jay's grandma that it was probably the best thing she had ever tasted in her life.

"This one's a keeper," his grandma said to Jay. "I'm so glad you like it, dear." She smiled at Jay and watched as everyone around the table enjoyed their lunch.

After lunch, Jay asked his grandpa to show Jess his workshop. He led her into the back, where there was a building the size of a garage that was devoted to Frank's tools and projects. Jay knew that Jess would love it. His grandpa loved to make things, and so did Jess. Frank showed her the sculptures he had welded and the woodworking projects he had on the go. He usually worked on many things at once, but right now he was focussing on only one. It was a rolling cabinet for Meg's little brother, Matthew.

"I volunteered at the hospital last year," he explained, and he ran his hand over the smooth surface of the partially finished cabinet. "You know, when you're old and retired like I am, you have to find things to keep yourself necessary," he chuckled. "Matthew had been admitted because of his cystic fibrosis. You know, it boils my blood really, that any kid should have to see the inside of a hospital like poor Matthew has."

He shook his head. "Anyway, while they were there, I would go in to visit Matthew whenever I had a shift - I'd always bring him a little something extra, just to see that smile of his. Mrs. Cole had mentioned that she would love something like the carts they had in the hospital room, for all of Matthew's equipment that they had at home. So, then and there, I decided I was going to make her one. It's taken me almost a year, but it's getting there."

He turned away from Jay and Jess and started organizing his work bench for a moment as a way to hide that he was getting a bit emotional. He didn't mention how heartbroken he was when he heard about Mrs. Cole's accident and how he wished he'd have finished the cart before she died. She always seemed to be doing something to help someone, and he so wanted to do something kind for her. "Well then," he said with forced cheer as he turned around again, "this here is made out of mahogany." He smoothed his hand over the cart's surface again. "And I did my best here to carve the Superman symbol into the front of it. It's on castors so that it can easily be moved throughout the house, and if you look here, these holes in the back are for all the hoses and plugs."

"They are just going to love it," Jess said with enthusiasm. She was in awe of the workshop.

"You know," Frank said, "I keep hearing that you're pretty creative yourself." He put his hand on her shoulder. "Any time you want to come over, I'll show you how to use the tools, and you're welcome to make use of the shop yourself."

"Seriously?" Jess couldn't hide her excitement. "Thank you so much," she said, "that would be incredible!" Her mind started racing with all the possibilities his offer presented. "I'll definitely take you up on that," she said, beaming.

As they walked back through the house towards the front door, Jess thanked both of Jay's grandparents for a lovely afternoon. Jay was pleased to see that they had both fallen for her almost as much as he had. Jess was thinking of all the things she could create in the workshop. She would likely be spending a lot of time with Jay's grandpa in the near future.

The two started walking down the path back towards Jess's place, and as soon as they were out of earshot, Jay couldn't help but tease, "Girl, you should get yourself some flamingo shorts!"

Jess laughed, and said, "Maybe I just will."

∞

It had been a while since Meg and Vern had a chance to spend any time alone together. It seemed like since the night Vern made dinner, Meg's whole family wanted to be around whenever Vern and Meg made plans. If it wasn't the whole family, then it was Mark, who would actually sit between them when they watched movies and tag along on walks. Neither of them minded, but today was going to be just for them.

They had made a lot of progress on the canoe. It amazed Meg, as she walked into Mr. Johnson's boathouse, that the summer was going by so quickly - and that even with everything else that was happening, somehow their secret project was advancing. She looked at the canoe up on the workhorses and realized that it was incredibly significant to her in so many ways. She walked past it slowly on her way to its far end. She smoothed her hand over the now bare cedar. Somehow, the canoe brought her and Vern together - it gave them a shared purpose, and it gave them the opportunity to discover each other.

"Mark said we should paint her blue," Vern said. "I think he's right on the money." He smiled at Meg.

"Definitely," she agreed. "You know we have to name her too, right? All boats have to have a name."

Vern walked over to where Meg was standing and put his arms around her from behind. "What if we name her after you?" he asked. "I think the name *Beautiful* would suit her."

Meg laughed. "It has to be a name that means something to us, but that others won't give a second thought to. My dad said he hates it when people give their boats names that are too simple. He said that a boat's name should have a special meaning - it's like the boat's own personality."

"So, I guess naming it *Boat* would be out of the question then?" Vern asked. Meg laughed.

"This is a hard decision!" she said. "I can't even imagine how parents decide to name their kids."

The two walked over to the sitting area in the corner. Vern turned on the radio and hoped that a Bruno Mars song would come on, knowing that Meg loved his music - but hoping that whatever came on would inspire another make-out session.

Meg leaned into Vern. "I know what you're thinking, but we're not taking any chances today! I can't even imagine what I'd do if Mr. Johnson caught us again."

Vern felt his heart sink a bit, but also laughed at the memory of their first encounter with the old man.

"I've got it!"

"What?" Meg asked.

"Do you know how to make words into Pig Latin?" he asked her.

"Yeah, why?"

"Okay," Vern said, "promise not to laugh. When I first found this boat, I couldn't help but think *hope floats.* That's what we need to name the boat. But clearly, we cannot name my manly boat *Hope Floats.* What would it be in Pig Latin?"

"*Opehay Oatsflay,*" Meg said, "and it's perfect."

The two were about to get ready to put the first coat of blue paint on the canoe, when as Vern's good fortune would have it, "Versace on the Floor" started playing on the radio.

∞

It was dusk and Dave and Val decided they should get back. They were looking forward to time with the group tonight, and each of them had to go home to check in and get changed. They walked hand in hand, no longer afraid that someone might see them. Val thought it was amazing that they could walk in silence and still be totally comfortable with each other.

Dave loved that he and Val had their own spot under the oak tree on the border of town. It was good to have something that was just theirs. A strange feeling came over him as they were walking, though. He loved walking past the *Welcome to Erie's End* sign; it was like stepping over an invisible line that, once crossed, became the entrance to a secret paradise, at least for all who knew Erie's End. But something was different this time. As they approached the sign, Dave noticed that there was a black Mercedes sedan parked beside it. He figured it must have belonged to a Slicker, and couldn't help but admire it. "That's what I'm gonna buy after I sign my first NBA contract," he said.

CHAPTER 21

"Meg - it's me," the cheerful voice said on the other end of the phone.

"What's going on, Val?" Meg asked, pleased to hear the happy tone in Val's voice which seemed to have been all but a memory lately.

"We need to talk, it's important - can you meet us halfway? Jess is with me too."

It was dark, and the boys were in their PJs watching a movie. "I have to stay here," Meg said, "my dad's at work. Can you come over?" Meg wished she could join the girls, but it was almost time for Matt's treatment, and she couldn't leave the boys alone.

"We're on our way," Val said and hung up the phone.

"Okay Matty," Meg called, "let's get your treatment done - you've been coughing like Coughy McCougherson over there."

"Meg!" he objected. "After *Jaws!* It's the part where he's attacking their boat!"

"Come on Matt," Meg said. "You know the rules. We'll pause it - Mark, pause it, would ya?" Meg laughed at the fact that the boys had seen that movie at least three hundred times, and still reacted like it was the first time every time they watched it.

"Was that Vern?" Mark asked. "Is he coming over?"

"No buddy, it was Val - and she and Jess are coming over."

Mark's heart sunk a bit. He didn't know what he was going to do for the next hour while Meg was giving Matt his treatment.

He figured that Vern was probably out with Jay and Dave - and it was kind of embarrassing that he was already in his pyjamas. He decided to go into the kitchen and make microwaved s'mores.

He took the graham crackers, the marshmallows, and the chocolate out of the cupboard. He arranged eight graham crackers on a plate, then placed a piece of chocolate on each one, then a marshmallow, then topped them each with another graham cracker. He had never made s'mores himself before. He put the plate in the microwave, but wasn't sure how long he should cook them for. He figured that since there were eight s'mores, eight minutes would do the trick. He set the timer, and went back in the living room to wait. He picked up the copy of Meg's *Cosmo* that was sitting on the side table, and after ensuring he was alone, turned to the section on page 64 that promised 25 of the Hottest Sex Tips He'd Never Forget.

His eyes widened as he started reading, and he didn't know whether to laugh or be disgusted. Just as he was about to read Hot Sex Tip Number 6, Val and Jess rushed in the door and their chatter and giggles caught him by surprise. Mark threw the magazine back onto the table and grabbed Matt's comic book, then stumbled over to the opposite loveseat, as far away from the *Cosmo* as possible. He could feel the heat in his cheeks, and hoped his red face wouldn't give him away.

"Oh, hey Mark," Val said, "where's your sister? We seriously need to talk to her about something."

"Oh, hey Val," he said. "I didn't even hear you come in." He closed the comic book he was pretending to read. "She's just doing Matt's treatment. Hi, Jess."

"What's that smell?" Val asked

"Uh oh!" Mark groaned. "I was making s'mores - in the microwave."

Val, Jess and Mark ran into the kitchen. Val opened the microwave as a giant blob of marshmallow inched out and slowly bubbled and dripped onto the stove beneath.

"I think I may have cooked them too long," he said.

Val and Jess started laughing. Mark was embarrassed, but kind of glad that it was them and not Vern who witnessed the ordeal.

"I'll clean it up," he said.

"We'll help you out Mark - it might be a big job," Val said. "But I think we should wait till that stuff cools off. Let's just eat the rest of the chocolate first."

Mark smiled.

∞

When Meg and Matt returned to the living room, they found Jess and Mark immersed in a serious game of Battleship. Val was reading the *Cosmo*, and every time Mark looked over at her he blushed. Mark was wearing a sailor's hat and trying to keep a straight face, not to show Jess that he knew he was winning by a long shot.

"You just sunk my battleship!" Jess started laughing. "Did I even hit any of your ships?"

He grinned; little did she know that he just kept moving his ships whenever she called one of his coordinates.

"Okay boys," Meg said. "You two can build a fort in Matt's room and sleep in it tonight." The boys looked at each other with excitement, and they each grabbed couch cushions as they said goodnight and headed out of the living room.

Meg grabbed sodas out of the fridge and plopped on the cushionless couch across from Val. "So, what's going on?"

"Well," Val started, "you know how the guys have their annual camping trip every year? The one where they go out to that island across from the pier?"

"Yeah," Meg said, "aren't they going this weekend? Vern mentioned they were probably going."

"They are," Jess said. "Jay was telling me about it - how they've been doing it since they were twelve."

Val's mouth curled into a scheming smile, "This year," she said, "I think we should crash their party. You know, go out there with them."

"I don't know, Val," Meg said. "That's their thing; would they even want us there?"

"I know for sure Dave would, he's the one who gave me the idea," Val said. "And I'm pretty sure Vern and Jay would both be cool with the two of you going too." She laughed.

"Oh My Gosh," Jess said, "that would be amazing, but I can't see my mom letting me go. She's so strict."

"Just don't tell her the guys are going," Val said. "You could tell her we're having a slumber party."

"I don't know," Jess said. "I mean, I really want to…"

"Let's give our parents some credit," Meg said. "We just have to think of how to ask them - we have to show them that it would be really good for us to go, I mean - they're reasonable, right?"

∞

"It's kind of freaky up here at night," Vern said, staring out into the darkness from the top of the lookout. They'd hung out on the lookout hundreds of times, and Vern loved it during the day when he could look out at the water in every direction and imagine spotting pirate ships, but he always felt a hint of nervousness when they were up there at night, in the pitch dark. He would never fully admit to Jay and Dave how much it freaked him out, because he knew for a fact that they would harass him for his fear of the dark. "I'm jacked for the camping trip this weekend," he said. "It's going to be so sick."

"Sure is," Jay said as he reached into Vern's backpack and grabbed another beer. The one good thing about Vern's mom was that they never had trouble accessing beer, and she never seemed to notice if any was missing.

"I wanted to talk to you guys about the campout, actually," Dave said. "I was thinking it would be sweet if we invited the girls. I was talking to Val about it, and it occurred to me that it would be suh-weet if they could come with us...I mean, tents and girls..." He looked at Jay, suddenly aware that it might be weird for him to be talking about being in a tent with Val.

"I don't know," Jay said, "don't you think it would be weird? I mean, this has always been a *guy* thing."

Dave worried that maybe Jay was saying that because of the whole Val situation, and then wished he'd never suggested it. "Or we could just do the guy thing," he said with fake enthusiasm.

"What?" Vern said. "Weird? No way, it would be fucking awesome! Tents and girls, sign me up!"

"I think it's cool," Jay said, "it's just going against tradition, that's all. I would love to have Jess there, but I can almost guarantee that her mom won't let her go."

Dave felt a sense of relief, and was beginning to think that maybe the Val issue wasn't an issue after all.

CHAPTER 22

"Absolutely not!" Steph said from the armchair she was sitting in on the other side of the living room. "Jessica, there is no way I can let you go camping with your boyfriend. It's one thing when he's here, and I know where you are - but I just cannot allow you to go to that island." She stood up and started walking around the room.

"First of all, you know how difficult it is for me to let you out of my sight for even a moment, but I'm making efforts to do that. I want you to have a normal social life and be a normal teenager - but I just can't imagine the other girls' parents allowing them to go either." She stopped in front of Jess and placed a hand on each of her shoulders, then looked her in the eye. "Secondly -"

Jess looked away from her mom, afraid that she would start crying, and towards the episode of Jeopardy that was playing on the TV.

"Jessica, look at me. That island is a few miles across from the pier - I'm sure it's beautiful, but getting there is dangerous. You would have to take a boat, and I don't trust the water *or* Dave driving you all there in his parents' boat. What if something were to happen? No, absolutely not."

"Mom," Jess pleaded, "please! I'll be sleeping in a tent with the girls, and Dave has years of experience boating. He has his boat license and volunteers with the Coast Guard." She walked over to the TV and turned it off. She sat down in the armchair that her mom had been sitting in, and looked at Steph who was now sitting on the foot stool. "We are all good kids, Mom - this campout is going to be one of those things in life that you remember forever, where you create bonds and memories that stay with you for the rest of your life." She wiped away her tears with her hand. "Remember when you told me about the time you and your girlfriend took her parents' car all the way to New York and then called your parents once you got there?"

Steph felt like a deer caught in the headlights. *Why did I ever tell her about that?* she thought to herself.

"You told me it was one of the best experiences of your life, even though you were grounded for two months when you got back. At least I'm asking you, Mom. This is my life, I want to live it. I respect you, and I love you - but you need to let me start being my own person. These friends I've made here, Mom, they're making this move okay. They're the reason I haven't had the need to contact my friends back home. I'm fine with the fact that we moved here; we had to get away from him - but you have to understand that I left everything else, too - not just him. *My friends.* I left them without even saying goodbye." Jess started crying again, and paused for a moment so that she could finish what she wanted to say without choking on her tears. "So the fact that these people have let me into their circle is more important than you can ever know. I need them, and I want to go with them on this trip. It means everything to me."

Jess looked at her mother with contempt, got up from the chair as her tears started falling harder, and stormed past her to her room, making sure to slam the door behind her as loudly as she could.

Steph sat alone in the living room and could feel a lump rise in her throat. It was the first time she and Jess had really had any kind of argument since leaving Richmond. She never wanted to be responsible for Jess being upset or disappointed, but she knew that at the end of the day it was her responsibility to keep Jess safe. She trusted Jay and she trusted Dave - and knew that he would get them all to the island safely. There was just something in her gut that told her she could not let Jess go. She hugged the throw cushion she was holding a little tighter, and hoped she wasn't just being overprotective.

∞

"I can't go," Val heard Jess say over the phone through her sobs. "My mom won't let me go. She said that she doesn't think it's okay for girls to go camping with boys, and she's worried about Dave taking us all in the boat."

Val felt awful for Jess. She knew how much she wanted to go on the camping trip with everyone. "I haven't asked my mom yet," Val said. "Let me talk to her. If she says I can go, I'll ask her to talk to your mom and explain how innocent it is, and she can reassure your mom."

Jess thanked Val, but told her that she thought it was hopeless.

"I'll give it a shot," Val said, "and I'll call you in a bit." She hung up the phone and headed for the kitchen to talk to her mom. It didn't occur to her until that moment that her mom might actually say no.

∞

"That sounds great, Deb! Oh, it'll be a hoot," Janet laughed, "yes, moral support! I'll call Steph." She placed the phone back on its receiver that sat on the office nook in the kitchen. For a moment, she stared at all the unopened mail on the desk, and realized that she should probably open it at some point. As she turned around, she saw that Val was standing behind her wearing her housecoat and a towel wrapped around her head.

"Just the person I was hoping to speak to," she said. "I just got off the phone with Dave's mom." Janet walked over to the sink and started collecting the dishes from the dish rack and putting them in the cupboards as she spoke to Val.

"Why were you talking to Dave's mom?" Val asked as she opened the fridge door.

"You mean, aside from the fact that we've only been friends since forever?" Janet teased. "She told me that you kids are all planning a camping trip this weekend?"

"Actually, yeah - I wanted to talk to you about that, Mom." Val sat on top of the kitchen table and took a sip of milk from the carton. "Is it okay if I go? It would be Vern, Jay, Dave, Meg and me."

"Val!" Janet scolded, "what has gotten into you? Tables are for glasses, not for asses!"

Val laughed. "Sorry Mom," she said as she hopped off the table.

"And use a glass for God's sake - who are you?" Janet took the carton from Val's hand and put it on the counter. She laughed and hugged Val. "It's nice to see you in a good mood," she said.

Val smiled and pulled a stool out from the island. "Thanks, Mom," she said, "I'm starting to feel better about things. Anyway, about camping, it would be Vern, Jay, Dave, Meg and me. Jess just called and said that her mom won't let her go."

"Well, Val," her mom said, "I do feel a bit hesitant allowing you to go on a co-ed camping trip. What are the sleeping arrangements?"

Val rolled her eyes. "Come on, Mom, it'll be girls in one tent, boys in another, and honestly, what could happen with all of us there - it's not like we're planning a big orgy." She laughed.

"Oh my God, Val," Janet said, "I guess I don't need to have the birds and bees talk with you."

Val smiled. "Sorry, Mom," she said, "I just hate it when parents don't give us any credit." Val looked at her mom, her eyes asking whether she'd be allowed to go.

"My other concern, Val," Janet started, "is that you've been so fragile lately."

"I know, Mom, but honestly," she said, "I told Dave about everything, and I know he'll support me if I'm finding it tough while we're there. I just want to have a good time and enjoy the last bit of summer with my friends."

Janet grabbed Val's hand and held it in hers. "I trust you, Val," she said, "and I am incredibly proud of you - and I want you to enjoy yourself with your friends on this trip. But whatever happens and above all else, use your head - and if you need to come home, come home. Okay?"

Val hugged her. "Thanks, Mom, I got this," she said. "You're the best."

"Did Jess mention why Steph won't let her go?" Janet asked.

"She's just really strict, Mom, she's kind of overprotective. Could you talk to her and tell her what the trip is really about, and see if maybe she's willing to change her mind?"

Janet looked at her daughter and admired her desire to want to help her friend. "Well, Val, it's not really my place to tell another parent how to raise their kids. I'm sure Steph has her reasons, and we have to respect that."

Val was disappointed and hoped that Jess wouldn't be too upset. She thanked her mom and headed up to her room to call Meg and start packing.

When the coast was clear, and Janet could hear the music blaring from Val's room, she picked up the phone and dialled Steph's number. "Oh hi, Steph, it's Janet," she said. "I'm calling about the kids' camping trip this weekend. Has Jess spoken to you about it yet?"

Steph sighed on the other line. "Hi Janet," she said, "yes, actually - I just finished telling her that I don't think it's a good idea. She's so upset with me."

"Oh, okay," Janet said. "Well, I was calling to let you know that the night the kids are camping, Deb and I were planning on a girls' night. You're welcome to join us either way. It'll be a riot, and honestly I think we could all use a fun night."

"So you're letting Val go on the camping trip?" Steph asked.

"You know," Janet said, "at first I wasn't sure about the idea of a co-ed camping trip, but honestly I've known all of these kids their whole lives, and I trust them. They're good kids. I think my hesitation, at least, came from the fact that I had to admit to myself that my little girl is growing up." Janet sat at the office nook and started opening up envelopes while she spoke. "They really don't realize how difficult it is for us when we still see them as the little bundles of joy we brought home." She sorted the mail into piles of bills that had to be paid, junk, and stuff to look at later. "Doesn't it feel like just yesterday we were teaching them how to tie their shoes and spell their names? I have to constantly remind myself," she said, "that I've given Val the foundation to make her own decisions and to now trust her to make good ones - it's harder than it seems sometimes, but I think that's how we're supposed to create confident adults, you know, by allowing them certain freedoms in their youth."

Janet's words hit Steph hard. All she wanted for her daughter was self-confidence and a strong sense of independence. She realized at that moment that by not allowing her to go on this camping trip, she was depriving her of just that. She was allowing her own insecurities to affect her judgement, which is exactly what she had been working hard to avoid.

"What about the island?" she asked Janet. "I mean, I've never been out there myself; and getting there - Jess told me that Dave would be taking them all out on the boat. I'm really worried about their safety."

"Oh," Janet said, "Dave is one of the best boaters I know! He's been raised on a boat. Did you know that he volunteers for the coast guard? You would have nothing to worry about there. And as far as the island goes, it's pretty secluded, but I was speaking to Meg's dad a bit earlier. I called him before I gave Val permission to go on the trip. Meg had asked him, too, if she could go. He really wants her to enjoy her friends this summer, considering everything they've been through - so he said she could go. But he knows Vern is going, and those two are seeing each other, and as much as he wants them to have fun - well, you know…

"So anyway," she continued, "I don't know if you heard, but he's now working for the Harbour Authority, and he told me that he would arrange for HA Officers to check up on the kids throughout the night. I'm much more comfortable sending Val, knowing that we have people checking up on the kids, and they don't have a clue."

Steph smiled on the other end of the phone. "Tell me more about girls' night," she said. "I think I may have just had a change of heart."

CHAPTER 23

"Dad!" Meg said in a panic over the phone. "Dad, you have to come home! Matty was coughing, a lot - he couldn't stop..." - she started to cry - "He was coughing so hard. He turned red. And then, and then, and then blood starting coming out, Dad - when he was coughing, there was blood everywhere." Meg could feel herself shaking. "He's wheezing so hard, I don't know what to do!"

"Meg," her dad said calmly, "I need you to call an ambulance. Matty needs to get to the hospital. I will meet them there - you stay home with Mark and I will call you once I've spoken to the doctor. Try not to worry, sometimes this happens with CF."

Meg hung up the phone and dialled 911. The paramedics arrived in what seemed like an instant. She was still on the line with the operator when they knocked on the door.

"They're here," she said, "thank you for helping us." Meg was trying to keep her tears from falling and her voice from cracking. She didn't want to worry the boys.

She led the paramedics into the living room where Matthew was propped up on the couch cushions, looking exhausted, and sweaty and wheezing so hard that it sounded like he was whistling.

One of the paramedics started examining Matt, and immediately administered oxygen. Mark's eyes widened as the other came in pulling a stretcher. Meg looked at Mark with a reassuring smile, as if to tell him everything would be all right - only, on the inside, she was terrified.

Meg and Mark followed the paramedics out the front door, and watched from the top of their cement stoop as Matt was loaded into the back of the ambulance. The paramedic was about to slam the door when Mark yelled, "Wait!"

He ran into the house, and just as the paramedic finished telling Meg that they really couldn't wait, Mark came running back out with Matt's blanket. It was once blue but time had turned it grey; it was as old as Matt himself. It was tattered and torn, and secure and comforting. Matt didn't drag it around behind him like he used to when he was little, but he'd never gone to the hospital without it.

Mark ran up to the ambulance and handed the flimsy blanket to the paramedic.

"We'll take good care of him," he said as he took the blanket from Mark and handed it to his partner who was sitting beside Matt. Mark looked inside and waved a concerned wave to Matt. A single tear rolled down Matt's cheek and slid behind the oxygen mask.

Mark could tell he was afraid. "Be brave! You got this!" he yelled at Matt. "We'll see you soon."

The ambulance door slammed; the lights and sirens screamed through the quiet neighbourhood. Only when it was quiet and out of sight did Mark turn around and walk back up the steps to where Meg was sitting, wringing her hands. Mark sat beside her, stunned, and worried, and sad. She put her arm around his shoulder, and he rested his head on hers. He quietly began to sob, and the tears Meg had been holding onto now warmed her cheeks as they escaped.

∞

Jess and Jay sat on the porch swing. Jess was trying her best not to let her disappointment ruin their night. She knew that her mom meant well, but couldn't help but feel devastated knowing that everyone else was going.

Steph walked out onto the porch and gave Jess a warm look. Jess smiled at her, knowing that her mom was doing her best.

"Listen Jess," her mom said, "I've been thinking about it, and…" Jess sat forward on the swing, hoping that she knew what her mom was about to say.

"I've decided that you can go on the campout after all."

Jess literally jumped up out of the porch swing. "I can't believe it!"

Jay smiled, and was suddenly even more excited for the campout himself.

Steph sat in the chair across from them. "There are a few conditions, though. First, I need you to both promise me that you will be sleeping in different tents. Second - I want you to leave early, to ensure that there's lots of daylight for you to get there and set up. And third and most importantly - have fun, and make this one of those things." She winked at Jess, who immediately knew what she was referring to.

Jess leaned down and wrapped her arms around her mom. "Thank you so much," she whispered.

Jess turned around and saw Vern running towards them. He had an unusual-for-Vern look of worry on his face.

Jay stood up and yelled down the lane. "Whoa, what's up kid?"

"It's Matt." He barely got the words out through his laboured breathing. "Meg just called me - Matt was taken to the hospital in an ambulance. I'm on my way over to her house. She's there alone with Mark, but really wants to go to the hospital. She hasn't heard from her dad. Mark and I kind of have a thing, so I think he could use some company, and then Meg can go to the hospital."

Jess covered her mouth with her hand. The elation she had just been feeling suddenly turned to fear for poor Matty, and she wondered if Meg was okay.

"Jump in the truck, Vern," Steph said, "I'll drive you over."

∞

"Thank you so much, Jess's Mom," Vern said as he jumped out of the truck in front of Meg's house.

"Keep us posted," she yelled to his back as he was running up the front steps.

Vern burst in the door, and as soon as Meg saw him, the strength she was faking for Mark crumbled and she melted into his arms, sobbing.

"He's going to be okay," Vern assured her. "Jess's mom is out there, she's going to drive you to the hospital. I'll stay here with Mark."

Meg could not speak; she didn't know what to say. She just wanted to know what was happening with Matty. She looked at Vern and her eyes told him everything. He nodded and kissed her on the forehead. She slipped her flip-flops on and headed out the front door with her hand lingering in Vern's before she shut it behind her.

As Vern walked slowly into the living room, he could see Mark on the couch rubbing the tears from his eyes. Mark didn't want him to know he'd been crying. "Hey Garfunkel," he said. "Rough night around here, huh?" Mark nodded.

Vern sat down beside him. "Do you want to talk about it?"

Mark shook his head. Vern nodded to indicate that he respected that. The two sat in silence for a long while, but it didn't feel uncomfortable, just sad.

"I think it's my fault," Mark finally said, and chills ran up Vern's spine. He felt heartbroken that such a sweet kid was carrying so much on his shoulders.

"I promise you," Vern said, "that nothing you did could have caused this." He put his arm around Mark's shoulder. "It is definitely not your fault, Garfunkel."

"But I was trying to make him laugh and he was telling me to stop. He was laughing so much, and then he was coughing and he couldn't stop laughing, and then that's when it happened - when the blood starting coming out everywhere."

Mark pointed to the other couch where Matty had been sitting, and Vern noticed the blood. He was shocked at how much there actually was, and suddenly he felt worried too.

"It's not your fault, buddy," he said, and put his arm around Mark, pulling him close.

"Have you ever seen *The Princess Bride?*" Mark shook his head. "Well, you're in for a treat, my friend," Vern said, and he grabbed the movie from his backpack. He had packed it earlier, before everything happened. He and Meg were planning a movie night after the boys had gone to bed.

Vern put the movie in and came back to the couch and sat beside Mark. "Don't think I'm weird or anything, Garfunkel," he said, "but could you snuggle me?"

Mark cracked a smile and pushed Vern. "You're a dork," he said, but a few minutes into the movie he was leaning on Vern's shoulder, and although both of them were staring at the television, their thoughts were elsewhere.

By the time the end credits were rolling, Mark had fallen asleep on Vern's shoulder. Vern carefully slipped out from behind Mark, rested his head on the pillow he'd been leaning on, and covered him with a blanket. He hadn't heard from Meg and was feeling anxious. He looked over at the spot where Matty had been sitting, and it occurred to him that they might not want to see the blood when they got home. He had no idea what to use to clean it. He thought maybe laundry detergent would work, but didn't want to make it worse.

He picked up the phone and called Mrs. Lister. "Hi, Dave's mom," he said in a sombre tone. "Yeah, I'm still at Meg's - haven't heard anything yet. I was wondering if you know how to get blood out. I was kind of thinking I'd like to clean it up before they get home."

Vern gathered items as per Mrs. Lister's instructions: a bucket of ice water, hydrogen peroxide, salt, dish soap and a scrub brush. He started scrubbing, and it seemed hopeless. He worried that he was making it worse, as the more he scrubbed the more it spread. He remembered that Dave's mom said that would happen, and at that point to add a bit of hydrogen peroxide. He changed the water, and scrubbed and scrubbed and scrubbed, for what seemed like hours.

When he was done and had put everything away, Vern put the blood-stained rags and scrub brush in the garbage, tied the bag up, and quietly opened the front door to take the garbage out. As he shut the door behind him, his phone rang. It was Meg. He warily said, "Hello?" and sat on the steps.

"He's okay," Meg said. Vern let out a sigh of relief, and before he could respond, Meg's tired voice said, "Vern, I love you."

He felt his heart rise in his chest. "I love you too," he whispered, and then heard the dial tone. He put his head in his hands and as his chin trembled, he began to cry.

CHAPTER 24

There were still a few stars barely revealing themselves in the morning dark. The sun would be rising soon, and Meg was relieved that a new day was about to start - a day in which her world would remain, for the time being, unchanged.

As her dad turned into the driveway, he pointed over to the front porch, where Vern was curled up beside the garbage bag on the front steps. She smiled at her dad, and he smiled back and leaned over to kiss her cheek. Mr. Cole motioned with his head for her to get over there, and gave her another smile. He rubbed his eyes, and took a deep breath. It had been a tough night.

Meg quietly walked up the steps and sat beside Vern, who had somehow found a way to make the concrete porch look comfortable. She couldn't help but chuckle at the sight of him. She grabbed his hand and quietly nudged him. "Vern, Vern - do you want to come in the house?"

He raised his head up without opening his eyes. "As you wish," he replied. He sat up and put his arm around Meg's shoulder. "How's Matty?"

Meg smiled. "He's okay," she said. "The doctor said he can probably come home later this afternoon. We're just going to get everything ready for him before we go back to pick him up."

As Mr. Cole approached the steps, he said, "Thanks for staying last night, Vern. You know you could have slept in my bed," he grinned.

Vern stood up and grabbed the garbage bag beside him. "Aw, thanks, Mr. Cole," he said, "but they say hard surfaces are good for the back." He hopped down the steps and over to the garbage bin.

Mark was still sleeping on the couch when they all went inside.

"I'm going to take a shower," Mr. Cole announced.

Meg went over and sat beside Mark on the couch. "Mark," she said while rubbing his hairline, "Mark." He started to stir. Meg held his hand and continued to say his name until he opened his eyes.

He looked at her with downright fear in his eyes. "Matty?" he asked.

Meg smiled. "He's okay, Mark," she said. "He's going to be just fine - he'll be home this afternoon." Mark smiled and gave Meg a hug before rolling over and closing his eyes again.

As Meg got up, she looked over at the spot where Matty's attack happened. She couldn't believe that Vern had cleaned it up; she knew what a big job it must have been, and suddenly the garbage bag made sense. She looked at him with gratitude, and he shrugged his shoulders and winked at her.

"I think I'm going to make you all some pancakes," he said. "You must be starving."

"Actually," Meg said, "I am starving; I bet my dad is too. But you don't mean you're going to make pancakes from scratch? Do you?" she laughed.

Vern laughed. "Good point," he said. "Frozen waffles?"

Meg smiled and said, "You're so good, I'll make breakfast. Why don't you go lie down in my room for half an hour? I can't imagine that you slept too well on the porch."

Vern smiled. "You sure?" he asked. "I can help?"

"It's okay," Meg said. "I want to do this. I'll come get you in a bit."

Vern kissed her forehead, and hugged her tight. He headed straight for her bed and collapsed. The front porch wasn't as comfortable as he'd let on. He wrapped himself in Meg's comforter and breathed in the smell of her.

His eyes were heavy, and he dozed off before his head hit her pillow. He didn't know how long he'd been asleep when the smell of cooking bacon and coffee seemed like it was wafting right under his nose. He looked at his watch, and was amazed that twenty minutes really could make such a difference.

He walked into the kitchen and Meg was at the stove. Mark was in his pyjamas setting the table, and Mr. Cole was sitting at the head of the table with a cup of coffee, fresh clothes on, and his hair still wet from the shower.

"Have a seat," he said to Vern, who obliged.

"So, Matt's going to be okay?" he asked.

"Yes," Mr. Cole replied. "He has a lung infection, which happens from time to time. He's lucky, though - we're lucky - he coughed so hard he burst a blood vessel, and that can be dangerous. But thank God, he's okay."

"You two must be exhausted," Vern said with bacon in his mouth. "When do you go back to the hospital?"

Meg smiled; she loved how Vern was so funny without even realizing it.

"Well," said Mr. Cole, "the doctor administered a strong dose of IV antibiotics last night, and Matt's having a good sleep - but I can bring him home later in the afternoon. I'd like to get back to the hospital soon, though, to be there when he wakes up."

Meg suddenly realized that she was exhausted. "I could use some sleep," she said.

"Garfunkel," Vern said, "what do you say we brush up on our bowling skills after breakfast?"

Mark smiled and turned to his dad, who nodded with approval and gave Vern a look of appreciation.

After breakfast, Meg started clearing the table.

"I can at least do the dishes," Vern said. "Nobody can get food poisoning from me cleaning up." Meg laughed, and he led her to her room and tucked her into bed. "I love you," he whispered, and kissed her for a long time before the sound of dishes clanking reminded him that Meg's dad was just down the hall.

∞

"They're on their way," Meg's voice said on the other end of the phone.

"Okay, we'll see you in ten," Vern said. By this time he and Mark had long finished bowling and were at Dougie's Diner having ice cream. "He's on his way home," Vern told Mark, "let's book it and beat them there. We'll give Matt a royal welcome home."

Mark smiled; he couldn't wait to see his brother and be reassured that everything was going to be okay.

When they arrived, the truck was not yet in the driveway and both Vern and Mark were excited that they'd be there to welcome Matt home. Meg had made a Welcome Home sign and put it on the door. The three of them waited on the front steps for the truck to pull up.

"How are you feeling?" Vern asked Meg. "Did you get some rest?"

"I'm great, thank you for everything. What would I do without you? Honestly, I don't even know how to thank you."

Vern grinned, leaned over and whispered in Meg's ear, "I can think of a way when we're camping this weekend."

Meg laughed and shoved Vern into Mark, who also laughed - not quite knowing what they were talking about. Meg hadn't thought about the camping trip at all since before Matty's attack. She could definitely use a night with her friends, especially now that she knew Matt was okay.

Mark was the first one to see the truck round the corner. "There they are!" he yelled as he stood up on the stoop. Vern and Meg also stood up, and none of them could contain their excitement. They were waving and grinning - and giving Matty the most heartfelt welcome home. The truck pulled into the driveway.

Mark could hardly contain his excitement and jumped from the top step to the bottom. Mr. Cole got out of the truck and walked around to the passenger side where Matty was sitting. He opened the door, and slowly emerged - holding Matty in his arms.

The sight of Matty took all three of the others by surprise. Their grins faded into looks of concern and uncertainty. How could he look so much different today than he did yesterday? He was so frail. His skin was grey, and the bags under his eyes were deep brown. He was still attached to oxygen and a portable IV. Mr. Cole carefully carried him up the steps as Vern opened the front door.

"Hi Matty!" Mark said. "I'm glad you're home."

Matt smiled from behind his oxygen mask and closed his eyes.

"He's a bit tired from the ride," Mr. Cole explained. "He'll be okay; he just needs to rest now. Mark, would you like to watch a movie with Matt?"

Mark nodded. "Hey Matty, have you ever seen *The Princess Bride?*"

Mr. Cole set Matt up on the couch and arranged all of his equipment. Mark put the movie on and sat on the floor beside his brother. He held his hand without saying a word. Matt had his security blanket tucked under his arm, and Mark was happy that he gave it to the paramedic the night before.

Mr. Cole was on the phone calling into work, and Vern could hear him tell them that he was going to take a few days

off, but that he'd be back on Monday. "Thanks for understanding," he said as he hung up the phone.

Meg stood in the hallway between the living room and the
kitchen. She felt lost and unsure. She hadn't expected Matty to
look so frail. She walked into the kitchen where Vern was
sitting at the table and her dad was grabbing sodas out of the
fridge. She sat at the table, and he walked over and handed each
of them a drink.

"Dad," she said, looking not at her dad but at Vern, "I'm
not going to go on the camping trip this weekend. I can't leave
you here alone with Matty like this. You said he's okay, but he
doesn't look okay." She started to cry.

Vern grabbed her hand and gave it a squeeze. He was
feeling concerned about Matty too.

"I want you kids to listen to me," Mr. Cole said. "I am
telling you that Matt is okay. Last night was rough on him, and
it's going to take him a few days to fully recuperate. I promise
you that he will be fine. And I cannot tell you enough, both of
you, how much you've done to help me - I can never thank you
for all that you've both done. This past year has been hell on all
of us. You, Meg, you're the one who pulled me out of a very
dark place. After we lost your mom, I didn't know how life
could go on. I was a shell of a man, and you pulled me out
from the depths." Meg looked up at her dad with tears in the
corners of her eyes.

"You reminded me of all the reasons I have to live, and you
helped me see what I lost sight of. We have to make each day of
this life count. Your mom had a lust for life. All she ever
wanted for us was to live full lives - to get the most out of every
day; to experience fun, and love, and the beautiful details of life
that far too often get missed in the midst of everything else. She
made every day beautiful, no matter what else was going on.
I'm not going back to work until Monday. I will be here with

Matt and Mark every minute. The hospital has arranged for home care over the next few days to check in on Matt.

"Meg," he said, "you only get one chance to be a teenager, and the time passes so quickly. You've already been forced to grow up too soon. You need to do normal teenager stuff. You need to be goofy with your friends, and have fun and gossip and hang out and not worry about your brother, or your dad. You need to spend time with your boyfriend and feel in love. I cannot believe I'm trying to convince you that you have to go camping with your boyfriend; but Vern - you're a good man."

Mr. Cole nodded in Vern's direction, and Vern just wanted to get up from the table and hug him and tell him he was a good man, too, but he decided to stay put and let the moment sink in.

"Meg," her dad said, "you are the most responsible person I have ever known. You need some normalcy in your life; you need to just be a normal teenager, if even just for a weekend. I want you to go on this campout. Please. I promise you that if I need anything, I'll send one of the guys from work out to the island to get you, okay?"

Meg looked at Vern and then at her dad. "You promise you'll send someone, even if it's not a big deal? Even if you're just tired and need a break? Even if for one second either of the boys asks for me?"

Meg's dad smiled at her. "I promise, Meg. But promise me something?" She raised her eyebrow. "Promise me you will go and have fun, and know that I have everything under control."

"Okay," she said, "but I'm not leaving Matty's side until Saturday. And if he's not a bit better by then, I'm not going."

"Fair enough," Mr. Cole said. "Now I'm going to lie down for a bit." He hugged his daughter. "I'm so proud of you," he said.

He walked over to Vern and shook his hand. Leaning in, he whispered, "I'm so proud of you too, son."

Meg and Vern sat in silence at the table with their hands intertwined until they heard Andre the Giant's voice ask, "Anybody want a peanut?" At which point they both cracked smiles.

"I'm going to hang out with the boys for the rest of the day," Meg said to Vern. "You're welcome to stick around."

He smiled at her. "You know what?" he said. "I think I'll let you guys have some time together. I'm going to head over to Old Man Johnson's and get some stuff done, so that it's all taken care of before the campout. I'm glad you're coming," he said. "I wouldn't want to be there without you."

∞

Jay was in his grandpa's garage when he heard his grandma announce that Vern and Dave had arrived.

"Oh, look at you two handsome boys," she said, followed by Vern saying, "You got that right, Jay's grandma."

She laughed and led them into the garage. "Can I get you anything, boys?"

"No thanks, we're okay," Dave answered, "It was nice to see you again."

Jay had just finished packing up the tents. He'd gone over to his parents' house earlier in the morning to get the extra tent for the girls.

"So Jay, you got the tents all packed up?" Vern asked.

"Sure do," Jay said. "How's Matt, and Meg?"

Vern explained what happened and asked the guys to make sure that Meg had a great time at the campout.

"How about you, Dave?" he asked. "Got all the food taken care of?"

Dave laughed. "Yeah, but can I ask why you never bring anything, Vern?"

"C'mon guys," he said, "I'm gracing you with my presence, you should be stoked…and I'll see what Doris has in stock."

"Nice," Jay laughed.

"No...*nice*," Vern over-accentuated, "is what it is."

∞

Meg had just finished updating the girls on Matty's status. "So he seems even more like himself today," she said, "and I feel a lot better about going on the campout knowing that he's improving. I can't even tell you how scary that whole thing was."

Val was lying beside her on Jess's cloud-like duvet. "I'm so glad to hear that he's okay, Meg," she said. "We were all pretty worried. You definitely need this weekend."

Jess emerged from the huge pile of clothes she'd been throwing out of her closet during the course of the conversation. "I'm so glad to hear he's okay too," Jess said. "My mom and I were so worried."

"What do we take on this campout, anyway?" Val asked. All three girls started laughing.

"I am clearly having trouble figuring that out too," Jess said.

"Neither of you have ever been camping?" Meg asked. Both girls shook their heads. "Okay, well," she said, "the less stuff you have to carry the better. Bring comfy stuff - like shorts, sweatpants, t-shirt, sweatshirt - extra socks - and that's it, really. And no, Val," she said, "do not bring makeup camping."

They all laughed. "This is going to be so fun," Jess said, as she dug through the pile and started pulling out her sweats.

CHAPTER 25

I have not yet apologized. I don't know who to give my apology to - not that it would make a difference for any of them - I don't know that it would make it any easier for me to live with myself either. If I had the guts to apologize, I would have the guts to turn myself in. I don't know how these things work - but Mrs. Cole, if you can hear me or see this, please know that I am so sorry for what happened.

You swerved that night. I was tearing straight for you, I didn't even know I had crossed the yellow line, and you swerved, and you saved my life. I know that - you risked...and lost...your life, to save mine. And I am so sorry. I am so sorry for driving drunk that night. I am so sorry for leaving you there. I am so sorry for what your family is going through without you. I am sorry that your kids are growing up without a mother. I keep thinking that you must have been the most wonderful person. Sometimes I wonder if the pain I'm feeling, which I guess is shame and guilt - it is agonizing, and it is unbearable, and sometimes I wonder if this is what it means to be haunted. I hope you are at peace wherever you are. I wish I could do something, anything, to undo what happened. I've been watching your loved ones this summer, and it seems to me like they really depended on you - it seems really like the whole village did. How can I possibly be the asshole who took you from them so senselessly? I'm so, so sorry.

-A.D

CHAPTER 26

It was dark and unfamiliar as Vern and Mr. Johnson sat in silence on his front porch, sipping their iced tea. The only light was the dim glow that cast itself out the front door from the lamp inside the foyer. It was as if the crickets and frogs chirped in time with the flickering of the stars. The breeze was just enough that it made it hard to differentiate between the rustling of the long grass and the waves hitting the beach in the distance.

Mr. Johnson had come into the End that Friday at Vern's request, instead of their regular Saturday. Vern had told him about the camping trip and wondered if they could meet a day early. At the time, Mr. Johnson made a big deal of it and grunted and groaned until he begrudgingly agreed. Without making it known to Vern, however, he chuckled at the fact that it made no difference to him when he came.

The silence was powerful. It wasn't like the times they'd sat together before, not speaking. Vern was shaken but not distraught by what Mr. Johnson had just told him, and the old man's words were still resonating with him. Mr. Johnson's silence was different than his usual calm, too. He wasn't quiet in an attempt to ignore Vern or pretend he wasn't there. He was in a state of reflection, focussed on keeping his heightened emotions in check. He didn't know how this little twerp got to him, but he didn't want to let the kid see him crumble.

From the time they met, Vern had been like an open book with Mr. Johnson. He told him about everything from his childhood to his feelings for Meg, and his struggle to break free from the life and identity he was born into. Mr. Johnson, on the other hand, was locked up like a safe. He did not disclose personal information. Never did he share moments of his life or his experiences or his emotions relating to those things; never until that night.

Their evening had started with the usual tour of the property, and Mr. Johnson, although pleased with Vern's work, pointed out the other tasks he'd like to see completed. As they walked up to the porch for their customary chat, Vern started telling Mr. Johnson about what happened with Matty. The old man could see that Vern was having a difficult time coping with what he'd witnessed, and with understanding the workings and injustices of the world.

"Kid," he said, "you have to know that sometimes this life tries to bury you alive. For some reason it's human nature to expect that the future will bring better, and we forget to appreciate that we're living in the most precious time our lives will know, the present. There comes a point in everyone's life that the world brings you to your knees. The truths that you believed prove to be as far from reality as you could ever have imagined. It happens differently for everyone, and at different times in a person's life.

"Some people, like your Meg, lose a parent and the world is shattered. Sometimes kids get sick, and parents are shattered. Some people fall in love, deep, deep in love with someone who will never love them the same way. Sometimes people die before they even get to live. Some people have unspeakable things done to them by the very ones who are meant to protect them. The beautiful thing about your youth is that in most cases, you get to avoid these realizations and enjoy the dark for a while. You get to live in a world void of the evils and the heartaches, if only for a while - so when you have it, live it."

Vern felt strange, and goose bumps surfaced on his forearms. This was not like any kind of conversation he'd ever had with Mr. Johnson.

"I'm going to tell you something, kid," he said, "because nobody is immune to that day when the world kicks you in the gut, and for a long time I thought it was none of your goddamned business, but I was wrong." The old man appeared to brace himself.

"I was nineteen, not much older than you are now, I suppose. She was the woman of my dreams. I'd never met anyone like her. She was from the city and her father was a bigwig at some corporation. They had just finished building a cottage on the bay, and she was spending her vacation in the End that summer. She was only seventeen, but boy were we in love. She snuck away whenever she could. There was no way her father would allow her to openly date a kid like me. My father was a fisherman, and at that time I was working for the summer at the McNaughtons' farm.

"Ha! You can't even imagine how difficult it is to wash away the smell of pig shit after working in it all day. But you better believe that I cleaned up to my finest every night, just on the off chance that we'd cross paths. Whenever I'd see her, my stomach would feel like there were feathers tickling it from the inside, and my knees would get so weak I could barely stand. She was the love of my life.

"She was all I could ever think about. The night before she was leaving to go back to the city, she was able to sneak out one last time. We walked and walked; we spent almost the whole night talking and laughing and being lost in each other's company. We came to a little clearing just on the outskirts of town, behind the trees that line the beach. We were alone, and in love - and I'll spare you the details, but it was the greatest night of my life.

"Saying goodbye was more difficult than I ever could have imagined. She promised that she'd write, and she did, twice. I received the first letter about two weeks later, but the second didn't come until a week before she would return. There were no letters in between those two, after the first letter - there was nothing, for almost a full year. I wrote to her return address, but until that second letter arrived, my heart was broken.

When I received the second letter, I thought surely it would be a Dear John. All it said was, 'We'll be back on June thirtieth, meet at our spot at midnight.' My days stood still until the day came that I'd get to see her again. On that day, I could not contain my excitement, or tame the damned butterflies.

"I was so anxious to see her and hold her and feel her touch. When I got to the clearing and saw her, I lost my breath. She was resting against a tree, hugging a blanket around her shoulders. All I could do was look at her. She was different, and hesitant. She wasn't speaking, and when our eyes would meet, she would look away so quickly. I asked her what was wrong. She began to cry, and then sob - she was upset to the point that she couldn't speak when she tried. I held her as she trembled. Finally, after a long time, she looked up at me with the most pain I'd ever seen in anyone's eyes in my entire life.

"'I have to tell you something,' she said. 'I'm so sorry. I'm so very sorry.' She paused for what seemed like eternity, and I waited for the same amount of time with bated breath. 'I had a baby,' she said and collapsed again into my arms, 'your baby. A boy.' She could not stop sobbing. I felt the world spinning. I was shocked and elated and confused.

"I asked her where he was, and eventually she was able to explain what happened. When her father found out she was pregnant he was angry and ashamed. In those days, it was shameful to have a baby before marriage. He took her across the country, and didn't let her leave the apartment he rented until the baby was born. He wouldn't allow her to hold him, and he'd arranged for a private adoption immediately after the birth.

"She was devastated, and that night I realized she was suffering incredibly from the pain and the loss. I went to her cottage every day. I demanded to see her - I loved her and I wanted a life with her, and I thought that maybe somehow we could find our son and get him back. They didn't have my permission to put him up for adoption, and maybe there was some chance. Her father threatened to have me arrested, and so I left. But I went back again each day, and demanded to see her, and each time her father threatened to have me arrested. This went on for weeks, until one day she burst past him in the doorway and told her father she loved me.

"He told her that if she went with me, she would not be welcomed home ever again. She said goodbye to him, and hugged her mother. And we walked and we walked, and we mourned the loss of our son, who we tried to find but never could. She became my wife, and many years later we had more children. For so long, we secretly longed for our son.

"After many, many years - and a life that continued to go on without him - the pain lessened. Our children don't know about him. It was a secret that my wife took to her grave, but every so often she would squeeze my hand in a certain way and I would know in that moment that her heart was aching for him. She's been gone twenty years now, my Annie.

"It was about a year after she passed, that I got a knock on my door one summer night. It was strange because people didn't bother with me much. I came to be known as a grump who people would just as well avoid. When I came to the door, a young woman stood there. She was maybe twenty years old. 'Are you Alan Johnson?' she asked. 'What do you want?' I was rough with her. 'Well,' she said, 'I think you might be my grandfather.'

"Her words sent me spinning - it was almost the same feeling I had that night when Annie told me about the baby. I opened the door and sat down on the porch. 'What makes you think I'm your grandfather?' I asked the girl. 'None of my kids have children.' The girl explained to me that her father had been put up for adoption as a baby, and when he passed away she found his journal." The old man put his hand over his mouth for a brief moment. "He had been searching for us, but all he knew was that the names of his natural parents were Alan and Anne.

"I could not believe what I was hearing. I didn't know how she was able to find me, when he couldn't. In a time when you'd think you would feel such happiness and elation, I felt nothing but anger. After all the years we spent searching, and all the mourning, and the nights I heard Annie crying while she thought I was asleep, and the fact that Annie would never know - and he died. I was so angry at that young woman.

"I told her to leave, and to not come back, and to stay the hell away from me. I told her she was wrong and that it couldn't be me. I slammed the door in her face, and that night I sat in my chair and felt the world bring me to my knees.

"I have come to some conclusions in my life, kid," he said, "and they were hard earned. Love means something different for everyone, know what it means for you - and when you have it - when you have love — you do anything to hang on to it. When you have strength, always be willing to share it. And when you need help to make the world make sense, you ask for it. All you have is this moment, right now. You cannot know what is next, or how different your world will be from one day to the next. You will realize that what was important yesterday no longer means a goddamned thing." He looked long and hard into Vern's eyes. "The woman's name, the woman who said she was my granddaughter - her name is Doris."

Mr. Johnson looked away and out into the darkness. "Kid" - his voice cracked as he said it - "go in the house and grab the bottle of Scotch out of the globe in the den. It opens at the top."

Vern did as directed. He stood for a moment in the den, feeling like the wind had been knocked out of him.

"Thanks," the old man said. They both sat in silence. The crickets and the breeze and the foreign emotions gave them each something to focus on. Neither of them knew what to say or do next.

"Now you better get the hell out of here, you've got better places to be."

Vern felt weak in the knees and light-headed, but couldn't stop the impulse to wrap his arm around Mr. Johnson's shoulder and attempt an awkward gesture of affection.

Mr. Johnson quickly placed his hand on Vern's. "Go on, get out of here."

He watched as Vern walked down the path, then poured a small nip of Scotch - and let out a whimper as he cupped his wrinkly hand over his mouth and started to cry.

CHAPTER 27

D eb had just finished packing the cooler with all the food that Dave and his friends would need for their weekend camping trip. She made sure to include some healthy choices like fruit and carrot sticks, but was fairly certain those things would return home in the cooler. She laughed as she reminisced, recalling that her camping trips as a kid were more about marshmallows and hot dogs and junk food, so she made sure there was a hearty supply of those items as well. As the boys entered the kitchen, she was sitting at the island waiting for the batch of homemade cookies to finish in the oven. She had made muffins for them but knew how much they all liked her cookies, so made those too.

"Dave's mom," Vern said as he walked in and nodded in her direction. He was still dazed from the discovery the night before that Old Man Johnson was his great-grandfather. He had managed to compartmentalize it, putting it away for later. Every time he thought about it, the same woozy feeling came over him, and there was too much to feel and too much to process to deal with it before the camping trip. He had decided that he wouldn't talk about it, or think about it, and today would continue as if yesterday hadn't happened yet.

"Oh, Vern." She shook her head. "Dave, I've packed up all the groceries - there are muffins for breakfast, and cookies are baking."

"Thanks, Mom" - Dave put his arms around her and squeezed as hard as he could - "you're the best."

She laughed, trying to escape his grasp. She could hardly believe that he once fit in her arms.

∞

At the marina, the girls were all standing in front of Steph's pickup. As Deb's SUV approached they started waving.

"It's going to be *epic*," Vern said from the back seat with a grin from ear to ear, trying to give the impression that he did not have a care in the world. "Girls and tents."

Dave elbowed him hard in the ribs, and Mrs. Lister started laughing. "Oh, I trust you boys," she said, "and even more than that, I trust those girls. You kids are going to have a great time."

As expected, Steph pulled Dave off to the side and began drilling him about the boat and her precious cargo. Dave respectfully answered all her questions and attempted to calm her nerves by addressing each of her concerns. In the meantime, Jay and Vern started loading the girls' bags onto the boat.

"Val," Vern said, "we're not going to the Ritz. What could you have possibly packed in that suitcase?" He started to laugh. "Well, the good news is, if something happens to the boat, we can empty everything out and paddle home in your suitcase."

Dave handed everyone a life jacket and made sure that they put them on in front of Steph, for a little extra reassurance. She appreciated that he was taking her concerns so seriously. He helped everyone aboard and untied the ropes from their cleat hitches before jumping in himself. He knew that he was probably the only kid his age whose parents allowed him to take their boat, and felt lucky for that. He winked at his mom and took the captain's seat. The weather and the water couldn't have been more perfect.

As the boat picked up speed, Jess could feel the wind in her hair and smiled to herself. Erie's End was the most beautiful place she had ever seen. The fresh smell of the air seemed to magnify on the water.

She looked at Jay, who was across the deck smiling at her. He loved seeing her take it all in with so much pleasure.

Val and Meg were sitting beside each other, laughing about the fact that Val's mom had let it slip about the ladies 'night she was planning.

"I wonder what those crazy kids will get up to tonight," Val joked.

Vern stumbled up the stairs from the galley onto the deck. "All right, all right, all right," he said in a way that made him sound just like Matthew McConaughey. "Who is going to tell these beautiful ladies the first and most-important rule of the annual guys' - and now guys' and girls' - camping trip?"

The guys all looked at each other and grinned, and all together they hollered, "What happens on the island, stays on the island."

They all started laughing, and Vern proudly smiled to himself. "Nice!" he said, before sitting down and putting his arm around Meg's shoulder.

After securely anchoring the boat at the dock on the east side of the island, Dave jumped out and held out his hand to help all the girls step out. Jay and Vern started tossing bags, the cooler and the tents up to Dave.

Vern came out, dragging Val's suitcase. "Seriously, Val? I think if you need anything out of here, you'll have to come onto the boat to get it."

She laughed. "Vern, I need everything in that bag."

It took both Jay and Vern to lift it up to Dave, who thought it was kind of cute that Val came camping a little over-prepared.

Jess was in awe of how beautiful the island really was. She loved the sound the trees made as the breeze danced through them. As the group climbed the narrow trail that led up from the dock and through a forested area, everyone dragged something behind them. They had the tents, luggage, coolers and Val's massive suitcase. They came to a clearing that had obviously been used as a campsite in the past. It was perfect. There was already a fire pit, flat ground for the tents and a little sandy beach just down the slope. As soon as they arrived at the clearing everyone dropped what they had been carrying.

"First things first," Jay said when they had all caught their breath. "Let's set up these tents, so we can have some fun."

After a few minutes, all the parts of the two tents had been laid out in two separate piles. Vern asked the girls if they wanted to take a walk on the beach. "These two," he said, putting one hand on Dave's shoulder and the other on Jay's, "can set this crap up, I trust 'em." He gave them a big Vern grin.

Meg and Val both agreed with Vern and followed him toward the water. Jess went over to Jay. "Sure you don't need any help?"

"Nah, it's fine," he smiled, "you go ahead." Jess winked at him and started away. Just when she was out of his reach, Jay quickly spun around and lunged toward her.

"You okay?" she asked with a laugh.

He didn't answer her. He just pulled her to him, and kissed her with more intensity than either of them were expecting. "Get a room!" they heard Vern yell in the distance, and both smiled while their lips were still touching. Jess gazed up at Jay and smiled; she was flushed.

"Enjoy your walk," he winked at her.

"I can't feel my legs," she whispered as she turned to join the others.

Dave was busy setting up the tents when Jay came back to help out. "Oh, to be Vern - the guy's classic," he said, tossing Jay the sack of pegs.

"Only Vern," Jay said, "only Vern," and they both laughed.

"So, dude," Jay said to Dave, "I know you had no idea what I was going to do when you told me about Val."

"Seriously, bro," Dave said, "you just had this look on your face - I honestly, for the first time ever, had no idea where you stood, I was freaked."

"No, man," Jay said. "It's crazy how things unfold. Who fucking knew? I'm happy for you two, you're cute. It's just crazy how the most unexpected things happen, you know?"

Dave laughed. "Yeah, like Vern and Meg."

They both laughed and felt at peace with where their friendship stood. When the tents were both set up, they each grabbed a beer and admired their work.

∞

Matt's health was improving, and the colour had returned to his face. He was still weak and tired, but more like himself and happy to be home. Under normal circumstances, Mr. Cole would have planned a boys' day out for Mark and Matt, knowing that they were both a bit envious that Meg was going camping. He thought it would be safest, however, for them to stay home and make the most of the day in an environment where Matt could sleep if he was tired, or if he wasn't feeling great they could accommodate him and make him comfortable.

It was a warm, sunny day and the boys were in the living room watching television in their pyjamas. Mr. Cole was still in bed, exhausted; he hadn't been sleeping. He would lay awake at night and listen for each one of Matt's breaths, paying close attention to the rhythm and praying that each time his son inhaled, an exhale would follow. He mustered as much energy as he could and bounced into the living room.

"How would you boys like to have a campout of our own?" he asked with excitement. Matt smiled. "What do you mean?" Mark asked. "I thought we were going to stick around here for Matty's sake? He's still not a hundred per cent, you know." Mark had become quite protective of Matty since the night he was taken in the ambulance.

"Well," Mr. Cole replied, "I was thinking that maybe we could set the old tent up in the back yard, and have our own little campout." The boys' faces both lit up. "Okay," Mr. Cole said, "you two go and get dressed, and I'll go and dig the tent out."

Matt sat in a lawn chair while Mark and their dad set the tent up. It was an older tent, and Mark laughed every time his dad attempted to push a pole through and something didn't match up. The funny part was that each time it happened, their dad would swear, and then correct himself - "I mean, oh shoot," or "fudge!" he would say. "Don't worry, boys, we'll get this figured out."

After about two hours and a lot of swear words, the big orange tent was perfectly positioned in the back yard. There was a welcome mat laid out in front of the zipped-up door, and they even took the time to set up the awning - which was really not necessary but added to the real-camping feel. The boys gathered blankets and sleeping bags while Mr. Cole inflated air mattresses.

Mark packed the cooler with food from the fridge and the cabinets, and collected a few comic books and board games. It was turning out to be the most fun he'd had with his dad and his brother in a really long time. He was happy to see Matt having so much fun too.

When everything was finally in the tent, the three of them took off their shoes and left them on the mat outside the entrance. Mr. Cole helped Matty in and helped him get settled, and Mark followed.

"What should we do first?" their dad asked.

"Let's play Monopoly!" Mark suggested.

"Well then, it's decided," said Mr. Cole. "Mark, why don't you set up the board? Setting up the ol' tent really tuckered me out. Sound good, bud? I'm just going to rest my eyes for a moment."

"No problem Dad!" Mark agreed with an air of purpose.

"I'm going to take a little rest too," Matt said. "So I can kick your butt," he chuckled.

Mark meticulously placed the board on the four milk crates they put in the centre of the tent as a table. He counted out and separated all the money, and ensured that all the properties and houses were in order. He picked out the player pieces - the ship for his dad, the shoe for Matt, and the top hat for himself. He held the thimble in his hand for a long time. It was always his mom's piece.

He announced that the game was ready and looked over to find that his dad's arm was wrapped around Matty, and they had both fallen asleep. Mark chuckled to himself, realizing that the whole setup procedure must have taken a lot out of both of them. Leaving the game set up, he grabbed a comic book and crawled on top of his own air mattress.

He would enjoy the peace and quiet until they were ready to play. He flipped through a few comic books, listening to Matt's quiet wheezing and his dad's not-so-quiet snoring. It seemed like time was standing still. He was getting bored, and it didn't look like either of them would be waking up any time soon.

Mark decided that it wouldn't be a proper campout without s'mores. He knew that his dad would make a fire for them later when it started to get dark, and Mark had realized, when he was packing the cooler, that he used all the marshmallows when he tried to make microwaved s'mores the other day.

While they slept, he decided, he would sneak away and go to the general store to buy more marshmallows. He quietly unzipped the tent, and put his shoes on. He went into the house and grabbed a twenty-dollar bill out of his stash. He put his backpack on and got his bike from the garage. It was a good feeling to be so independent; he felt like he was not such a little kid.

∞

It was the first time Janet had agreed to a social outing since her split with Kent. She was trying hard to be strong for Val. Knowing that Val had her own battles to fight, she didn't want her to see that she was hurting. She had done what she could to make life seem as normal as possible. She wanted Val to feel secure and loved, and she didn't want to let on that the breakup was taking a toll on her emotions. Ladies' night would be a good distraction for her, and it was a great excuse to get out of the house and at least attempt some fun.

She stood and stared at her closet for a long time. She didn't think that anything would be the right thing to wear. She felt tired and frumpy. She wondered, for a moment, if the ladies would notice if she wore her pyjama pants. Janet sat on the corner of her bed, trying to shake the melancholy away. She took a deep breath and remembered the words of the British receptionist she worked with long ago, before she was even married.

She'd been having a terrible day at work that day. She had just graduated from college and was working as a dental hygienist. The dentist she was working for, although an excellent dentist, had terrible people skills. He often insulted the hygienists, was rude to patients, and seemed to enjoy inflicting misery. On this particular day, Dr. Florence was fierce, and his words made her feel like she was two inches tall.

She stepped out to the reception and the look on her face must have given her away. Jennifer, the receptionist, said, "Darling, on days like this, there is only one thing you can do. You put on your red lipstick, you keep your chin up - and you tell whatever is troubling you to bugger off."

Janet laughed at the memory, and at how true the advice turned out to be. She walked over to her closet and picked out her silky red camisole, and a black pencil skirt. She threw on a jean jacket and suddenly felt like she was twenty years old. It was going to be a great night. Just before she opened the front door, she stopped at the mirror in the hallway and applied her red lipstick.

∞

"How do I look?" Deb asked her husband as she spun around in her ladies-night dress. It was a plain green dress that she wore for every occasion. If she needed to dress it up, she put a blazer over it; if she needed to be casual she wore flip-flops with it. It had been to weddings, funerals, graduations, and all of the events that required formal attire. Tonight was its ladies' night debut.

"Looks great as usual," Hank said, looking away from the Saturday paper just long enough to notice and give his wife a wink and a smile. She felt blessed having such a wonderful partner in life. Knowing what Janet was going through, and hearing that Steph had left her husband, caused Deb to be even more grateful than usual for the fact that she and Hank were just as much in love today as they were when they got married, if not more.

She walked over to him, kissed his forehead, and said, "See you later - much later," with a giggle.

"Use your head, young lady," he said, and returned to the sports pages.

∞

Steph stood in front of her full-length mirror and felt a pang in her stomach. It wasn't a pang of nervousness or anxiety. What she was feeling was excitement. She was looking forward to ladies' night and was surprisingly comfortable that Jess was camping with her new group of friends. Things were turning out all right in Erie's End. She thought for a moment about how far she had come.

She was no longer under the control of her maniacal husband. It was amazing, she thought, how her perspective had changed since she left. She felt sad but sympathetic for others who remained trapped in vicious relationships. Nobody really gets it, she thought. It's like the difference between looking at a tornado from inside the eye of the storm and watching the weather report on television.

She was proud of herself, for finding a way out and for learning to cope with the damage that he had done. Erie's End was the place where Steph had been able to find herself again. The self she believed was destroyed, was actually still buried deep inside her, and this place and her counselling, and her ability to think about things from outside the storm, were bringing her back. She was starting to think that maybe her fears were irrational, that maybe she was wrong. She hoped she was. She looked in the mirror at her new black dress and silver flip-flops. She had borrowed some of Jess's homemade silver jewellery. She felt like a million bucks and was ready to celebrate. As she double-checked her ice supply, Steph heard a knock. She smoothed out her dress, took a deep breath, and walked over to open the blue door.

CHAPTER 28

The campout was turning out to be the most fun the six friends had had together all summer. They spent the afternoon swimming, playing Holey Board, laughing and just enjoying each other's company.

"You'll have to thank Doris for this amazing supply of beverages," Jay said to Vern.

Normally, Vern would have laughed, but he couldn't help but think that maybe Doris hadn't always been Drunk Doris. It occurred to him that perhaps that night at Old Man Johnson's was when the world kicked her in the gut, and that maybe she wasn't equipped to know what to do next.

"You bet!" Vern laughed with fake enthusiasm, and tried quickly to put his momentous new knowledge back in its compartment. "Let's all take five with our ladies," Vern said. "I can tell by the look on Meg's face that she wants to make out with me."

Meg smiled at Vern, and he was surprised that she didn't disagree. The two of them walked hand in hand, Meg's head on his shoulder, toward the boat.

"Are you having fun?" he asked her.

"I'm having the time of my life," she said, "but I can't help but wonder how Matty is doing."

"I'm sure he's okay," Vern said. "Mark's been a superstar taking care of him since he got back from the hospital."

Meg laughed. "You're right," she said. "You've really given him a huge confidence boost, you know." She smiled at him.

"Who, moi?" Vern asked, and kissed Meg just because he couldn't stop himself. As he helped her step onto the boat, he started singing "Take My Breath Away," from the *Top Gun* soundtrack.

"It's not going to happen, Vern," she laughed, knowing what he thought that song would ultimately lead to.

"Hey, you guys!" Vern yelled. "If the boat's a-rockin', don't come a-knockin'!"

∞

Dave and Val were about to sneak into the guys' tent. He unzipped the tent and said, "Wait right there, for one second." Dave went in, and Val could see that he was rifling through his backpack. "Okay," he said, as he turned around, stepped outside and simultaneously held the tent's flap open while reaching his hand out to help Val as she made her way inside. He was such a gentleman.

They both lay on top of his sleeping bag. Val put her head on Dave's chest; he grabbed her hand and held it, feeling each one of her tiny fingers between his. "So, how are you doing?" he asked her.

Val looked up at him and smiled. "I'm doing okay. I'm having a great time, but I do have to admit that there were a few times this afternoon that I started to feel anxious out of nowhere, when I should have just been having fun. They pass, though, those drive-you-insane-at-the-moment feelings of panic, if you ride them - they pass. It helps to have distractions."

Dave raised the hand that he was holding and kissed it. "I have something for you," he said. He reached into his pocket, and while keeping whatever it was concealed in his fist, he said, "This is supposed to help get you through those drive-you-insane-at-the-moment moments." He took Val's other hand and placed the object in it.

She looked down and saw that he had given her a smooth round stone. It was dark grey and glassy smooth. In its centre was a hand-painted picture of a cloud. "It's a worry stone," Dave said. "You're supposed to rub it between your fingers if you're having trouble with anything or if you're feeling uneasy."

Val felt warmth rush through her. She was touched by Dave's thoughtfulness. "How do you know just what I need?" she asked him. "Thank you, for this …." she said, as she rubbed the stone between her fingers.

They stared into each other's eyes for a long time. They both felt as though time stood still and they didn't want it to start again. Val couldn't believe how wonderful it felt to get lost in Dave's eyes. She felt at peace.

∞

"Let's get a fire started," Jay said to Jess. "I bet everyone will be ready to eat some spider weenies pretty soon."

Jess laughed. "spider weenies?"

"Oh yeah, City Kid," Jay said. "You must not have any experience with spider weenies. They're a delicacy around here. You take a hot dog; you cut slits in each end and then put it on a stick for roasting. While it's cooking over the fire, the ends curl up and your hot dog ends up looking like a spider."

Jess laughed; she loved how excited Jay got about things like spider weenies.

Jay showed Jess how to build a proper campfire. They gathered kindling from the wooded areas around their campsite. Jay told her that his secret to the perfect fire was all in building perfect teepees out of the wood. It took them no time at all to get the fire crackling. They pulled up three large pieces of driftwood from the beach and set them up around the fire so everyone would have a place to sit.

"Have you seen *Stand by Me?*" he asked her as they sat and enjoyed the fire they built together.

"No," she said, not taking her eyes off the flames.

"Okay, it'll be our next movie night," Jay said. "It has a great campfire scene in it, but I don't want to ruin it for you."

Jess smiled and looked at Jay with adoration, and he leaned in and kissed her.

"Who's ready for dinner?" Vern's voice bellowed from the boat as he made it known that he and Meg were returning to the campsite.

Jay stopped kissing Jess for a second and noticed that she was blushing. He brushed the hair off her forehead. "To be continued," he said, and kissed her quickly before helping her up to her feet.

"The fire is crack-a-lackin' as usual," Vern said, as he and Meg approached.

"Jess, are you hungry?" Meg asked. "I'm starving."

Dave and Val heard the chatter outside the tent and came out to join their friends.

They all made spider weenies. It started to get dark, and nobody knew or cared what time it was.

Jess wished this night would last forever. She scanned everyone's faces and noticed the content on each and every face. Some were laughing, some were staring at the fire, some were talking - but they all looked so happy, and Jess knew that she must have as well.

When the boys started talking about fishing, Val got up. "Do either of you ladies want to join me for some stargazing? I'm in love with the Big Dipper and I've always wondered what it would look like from out here."

Both girls were game. Jess grabbed a big blanket from their tent, and the three of them walked off to find a good spot. They walked farther up the trail they came in on, each holding a flashlight, and each feeling a little nervous about how dark it was.

"Trust me," Meg said, "I remember my dad taking us up here one time to watch a meteor shower, there's another clearing up at the top of the hill - it'll be worth it, I promise."

The girls were all a bit relieved when they arrived at the hilltop. Jess laid the blanket down and they all lay on their backs - amazed by the myriad of stars above them.

∞

"This day went way too fast," Jay said to the guys. "I wish we didn't have to go back tomorrow." Dave nodded in agreement.

Vern said, "Don't worry, my friend," as he put his hand on Jay's shoulder, "the night is young. Let's go and join our ladies."

The guys decided to sneak up on the girls, just to give them a good old-fashioned campout scare. When they heard the girls' voices in the distance, they turned off their flashlights and moved as quietly as they could. When they were only a couple of feet away, they shook tree branches, and stomped loudly on the ground. They knew that what they were doing was working - the girls stopped talking, the panic in their voices revealed that they really were scared. Vern let out a loud growl to mimic a wild animal, and Val screamed. Then the boys all jumped out at once - and could not stop laughing.

Once they were forgiven they joined Meg, Val and Jess on the blanket. They lay and looked at the stars in silence, each appreciating the moment.

Vern was reminded of what Mr. Johnson said about living in the moment, and didn't want to let any more of that conversation creep into his thoughts.

"I love you guys!" he said in his silly Vern way to the group, and started laughing. "Seriously, though," he said, "how did we all get so lucky to have such a great group of friends?"

"Yes," Meg said, "you're the lucky one in this situation, Vern."

Everyone started laughing, and Vern sat up, put his hand over his heart, and gave everyone the saddest puppy-dog face he could muster.

"I'm kidding, obviously, Vernon," Meg said.

"Vernon?" Dave asked and laughed.

"Yeah, his real name isn't actually Vern!" Jay laughed. "Want to know what it says on his birth certificate?"

"Sorry, babe," Vern said as he steamrolled over Jess, who was between him and Jay. "Dude," he pleaded, "please do not -"

"His name is Laverne!" Jay announced, and Vern grabbed him and put him in a headlock.

"You had to do it, you just had to do it," Vern laughed. "Say uncle."

"Yeah, like Laverne and Shirley," Dave said, laughing hysterically.

"Really?" Meg asked with a surprised grin on her face. Everyone was still laughing.

"I hate you guys right now," Vern said, "but I'll still let you be my friends. You take this to the grave. I mean it."

"All right," Jay said. "You can trust us, Laverne."

Everyone lay down again and looked up at the stars. "They are so beautiful," Jess said.

"They're pretty awesome," Jay agreed.

"Not as nice as those clouds though, right Val?" Dave laughed.

"No way," Val said, "although you could never think that the stars look like boobs, so that's a plus." They all laughed.

"Hey," Vern said as he pointed to the sky, "follow my finger. I found a new constellation and it definitely looks like boobs." He moved his finger along the stars as if he were connecting the dots in a colouring book.

Meg pushed his arm down. "You're such a dork," she said and laughed.

"Hey guys," Dave said, "that day when Val noticed the boob clouds -"

"It wasn't me," Val interjected. "You think every cloud looks like boobs."

Dave laughed, and continued. "Anyway, that day when we were walking home, I saw a slick black Mercedes parked at the Erie's End sign. It looks like there might be a new Slicker in town. Have any of you seen it around? As much as the Slickers suck, I would love to ask for a spin in that ride."

Jess quickly turned her gaze from the stars to Dave and sat up suddenly. "Wait, what?" she said in a panic. "Was there anything hanging from the rear-view mirror?"

Dave had thoroughly checked out the car as they walked past it that day, and he remembered thinking how pompous the owner must have been, because hanging from the rear-view mirror was an air freshener that looked like a hundred-dollar bill.

"Yeah," Dave said, "the douchebag hung a C-note from his mirror."

Jess looked at Jay - her eyes widened and filled with tears, and her body felt like it was frozen in place. She started to cry. She was shaking as Jay held her tight in his arms.

"We have to go right now," Jess said to Jay through her tears, "he found us. My mom is not safe; we need to go." She started to cry hard.

"Jess," Dave said, "I'm really sorry, but I can't drive the boat right now, I've been drinking all day."

Jess stood up. She started pacing, and wrapped her arms around herself. She sat down, she stood up. She was terrified, and all of her friends could tell - but they didn't understand.

"What's going on?" Meg asked.

"My dad found us; he probably wants to kill my mom!" Jess yelled. "That's why we're here, that's why we came to Erie's End; that's why we have to leave right now. He found us, and I'm afraid he's going to kill her."

∞

Steph had turned her kitchen counter into a bar fit for ladies night. Janet and Deb had complimented her in the past on her ability to make the best cocktails they'd ever tasted. She did not want to disappoint tonight. She set up a margarita station, set out all the ingredients for Caesars, martinis, cosmos, and was about to get everything ready for Sex on the Beach, when the thought of Jess alone with Jay entered her mind. She laughed to herself.

"They wouldn't," she said, and smiled.

When Deb and Janet arrived, they complimented Steph on how great she looked. They had never seen her done up, and both of them were struck by how beautiful she was.

"You're going to make me blush," she laughed. "And look at you ladies; we're a bunch of hot mamas tonight." The ladies all raised their glasses and toasted to their hotness.

After a couple of hours, a lot of laughs, and margaritas, martinis and cosmos - the ladies decided that they were going to take their party out on the town. Janet had mentioned that it was retro night at the bar, and they decided they wanted to go.

"I can't believe we're doing this," Steph said with a laugh, as they walked down the road towards the bar.

"Look out, bar-goers of Erie's End," Janet squealed as her flip-flops smacked the pavement. "Here we come." She was so glad she decided to put on her red lipstick and join in on ladies 'night. She was having the time of her life.

They ordered a round of Long Island Iced Teas, and just as they'd each finished a sip, "Personal Jesus" by Depeche Mode started playing. Janet grabbed Steph's hand, and motioned for

Deb to follow them onto the dance floor. This was just what they all needed, and it couldn't have been a more successful ladies' night. They stayed on the dance floor for "Love Shack," and then decided it was time to go back to the bar for a refill.

They had managed to get a table, where they sat for their next three drinks. They were laughing and having a great time. Steph sat facing the bartender and couldn't help but notice that he reminded her of Tom Cruise in the movie *Cocktail*. She laughed to herself and thought, boy, I've been spending too much time with Jay. Janet looked behind her to see what it was that Steph was looking at.

Janet turned back to Steph and laughed. "Honey," she said, "he is such a player, trust me - stay away from him."

Deb laughed. "Yeah, he's got a bit of a reputation," she said. "But there *is* a man over there" - Deb pointed behind Steph - "who hasn't taken his eyes off you all night."

Steph turned around; she couldn't see who they were talking about. "Where, which one?"

"The one in the suit," Janet said, "he hasn't taken his eyes off you. He looks very distinguished, the guy with the salt-and-pepper hair? Right, Deb?"

Deb started looking around Steph. "Yeah, that's the one," she said, "but it looks like he's gone."

Steph turned back to face her friends and gave them a shrug. "Oh well," she said, "I'm not really in the market anyway, and besides, this is ladies' night."

∞

Jay held Jess, not knowing what else he could do to comfort her as they all hurried back down the dark path towards their campsite. Dave ran to the tent to grab his cell phone out of his backpack. He turned it on, but couldn't get service. He walked along the shore, holding it up, hoping to get a bar - but nothing. He knew he had to get Jess back to make sure her mom was okay. The others tried as well, walking to different spots, holding their phones in the air, but nobody could get a signal.

It occurred to Dave that he could go to the boat and use the VHF radio. Maybe someone would be listening. He called everyone back to the fire. "Hey guys," he said, "we're not going to get any service out here. I'm going to go back to the boat and send out a mayday."

"Good thinking," Jay said and handed him a flashlight. Dave started walking towards where the boat was docked, while everyone else waited by the fire, unsure of what to do or how they would get back.

As he approached the dock he noticed a boat in the distance, coming toward the island. It was a police boat. Green and red lights lit up the bow, but he knew it was the police from the blue and red lights on top of the bridge. Dave flashed his flashlight toward the boat - three short quick flashes, followed by three long flashes, and another three short. They responded immediately, flashing their lights back. Dave ran back to the group.

"The police patrol boat saw me," he yelled. "Let's go, they'll take us back. We'll come back tomorrow for our stuff. Let's just go."

Jess was relieved and terrified. Jay put the fire out with the buckets of water they collected earlier in the day. The group hurried to the dock, and Dave shone his flashlight again toward the boat.

As the police boat approached, Dave called out, "Over here," and waited for an officer to toss the docking rope. As Dave tied the rope to a cleat hitch, the officer jumped off the boat onto the dock.

"How did you kids know we were coming?" he asked.

Jess looked at Jay with tears of defeat. "We didn't," Jay said. "Why did you come?"

The officer's partner had just joined the group on the dock. "There's an emergency at home," he said. "Meg, your dad asked us to bring you all home. Your parents are waiting at the marina; they'll explain everything when we get back. They're the ones who should tell you what's going on."

As they boarded the boat they all felt a chill, the kind of chill that runs down your spine and forms a rock in the pit of your stomach. Jay held Jess wrapped in a blanket. She was sobbing. He wanted to tell her that everything was going to be all right. He wanted to, but he didn't know if that was true.

Meg sat at the back of the boat, hugging her knees. When Vern approached to sit beside her, she told him she just wanted to be alone for a minute. He kissed her forehead, and respected her request. He knew that when she was upset, she preferred time alone. She needed to process things on her own, and when she needed it she would seek comfort.

She sat and felt sorrow rip through her. She knew what it was like to lose your mother. She knew that if something had happened to Steph, Jess would be left with a gaping wound - a void that could never be filled, and the kind of pain that would take a lifetime to cope with. She knew that Jess would feel guilt for going on the campout and would blame herself for the rest of her life. She hugged her knees as tears streamed from her eyes. She yearned for her mom, and hoped she would be strong enough to help Jess.

As much as she felt pain for whatever might have happened to Steph, Meg also felt guilt for being relieved that this emergency had nothing to do with Matty. If it hadn't been for Dave and Val telling everyone about the Mercedes, she would have inevitably thought the police showed up to tell her something terrible happened to Matty. She wished the thought hadn't entered her mind. She knew that more than anything, Jess would need her friends when they got back.

Meg wiped her tears away and made her way over to where Vern was sitting with Dave and Val. "She's going to need us," she said quietly to the group.

Nobody said anything, but they knew that Meg was right. They would all need each other. As they saw the marina up in the distance, Meg rested her head on Vern's shoulder. He put his arm around her and held her close. Jess felt sick to her stomach. She didn't want the boat to get there, but at the same time it couldn't get there fast enough.

The officers got off the boat first. As Meg, Vern, Dave and Val stood up, they knew that the weakness in their knees had nothing to do with sea legs - but everything to do with the nervousness they all felt. They were afraid to face what was waiting for them. They felt sick with concern about what Jess would suffer when the news of whatever had happened reached her ears.

Jess was having trouble mustering the strength to get up. She was sobbing and Jay was crouching in front of her, giving her the encouragement she needed to face what was coming. He put his arm around her waist and helped her to her feet.

The others waited on the dock until they were all standing together. "Okay, I'm ready," Jess said with tears spilling down her cheeks.

As the kids approached the group of parents who were standing at the end of the dock waiting for them, Jess's worst fears were confirmed. She scanned the faces. She saw Janet, and Mr. Cole, and Deb. She did not see her mom. She felt the blood rush from her head to her feet. She felt heat in her face, and fear like she had never experienced, as she approached Deb and forced the words to come out: "Where is she?" she pleaded. "Where's my mom? He found her! Oh my god, what did he do?" She collapsed into Deb's embrace.

"No, Sweetie," Deb comforted her. "What do you mean? Your mom is at Meg's."

Jess backed up and looked at Deb with confusion. "She's okay?" she asked. "My mom is okay?"

Deb nodded. "She's just fine."

Jess continued to cry. Her fear had shifted to joy and gratitude. Her physical reaction to her emotions was still trying to catch up.

Suddenly Meg had the wrenching realization that if Steph was okay, this emergency had to do with Matty after all. Steph was at home with Mark, and her dad was here on the dock. She grabbed her dad's shoulders. "Matty?" was all she could say.

Her dad did not answer. Meg began to cry. "Dad!" she insisted. "Where's Matty? What's the emergency? Tell me what's going on!"

Mr. Cole looked weary. He put his arm around his daughter. "Meg," he said calmly, "Matty is just fine. He's at home with Steph."

"Then what is going on?" Meg yelled. "Do you know what you've put us through?"

"It's Mark," Mr. Cole said. "We fell asleep this afternoon, and when we woke up he was gone. I figured he went for a bike ride to kill time because his bike was gone from the garage when I checked. But when he didn't come back at dinner time, I started to get worried. Matty and I drove around for hours looking for him. But we haven't been able to find him. I thought maybe he tried to get to the marina before you left and tag along. I told the police that if he wasn't with you, I needed them to take you all home. We need your help to find him. I'm afraid he might have gotten lost in the dark."

Although everyone was worried about Mark, a sense of relief rushed through each of them. They had been spared the devastation they were expecting.

"We'll start walking back toward Meg's house," Jay said as he took Jess by the hand, "we'll see if we can spot Mark along the way."

Jess wanted to help look for Mark, but also really wanted to see her mom for herself, and somehow figure out a way to tell her what Dave and Val said at the campout. Although they were safe tonight, they would have to face the fact that he had found them and really was in Erie's End, and really had left the gift, and really was going to do something terrible.

Val and Dave said that they would take the route towards the village limit, and look along the trails. Janet and Deb offered to walk the main stretch. "Have you checked the cemetery?" Meg asked her dad. "Maybe he went to see Mom?"

Mr. Cole shook his head. "Let's go," he said.

Meg rushed over to Vern who was at the end of the dock. "I'm going with my dad to see if maybe Mark went to the cemetery. I have to do something," she said with urgency and uncertainty. "Call me right away if you find him, okay?"

Vern kissed her forehead and said, "For sure, you call me if you find him first."

∞

Vern sat at the end of the dock. He was worried about Mark being lost and alone in the dark. He pulled his cell phone out of his pocket and turned it on. Everyone agreed that as soon as they found Mark they would send a mass text. He looked at the screen as his phone came back to life and saw that there were three missed calls, and one message. They were all from Mark. He couldn't dial into his voicemail fast enough. He hoped that Mark's message would give some kind of indication about where he was.

"Garfunkel," Mark's voice said, and that was all. Vern hung up the phone.

"Where are you, Mark?" he said quietly to himself. And then it hit him like a ton of bricks. He got up and started running.

Vern was running so hard that his lungs were burning. He couldn't catch his breath but he didn't care. His head was spinning. He felt like his feet were failing him; *faster,* he urged them. *Go. Faster.* He'd never been so afraid in his life. *Not the pier,* he thought, *please not the pier.* He knew what "Garfunkel" meant. It meant that Mark needed to not be alone. It meant that he was reaching out, and it meant that Vern wasn't there today when Mark needed him.

The pitch darkness as Vern approached the pier was intermittently interrupted by the green glow of the lighthouse. Vern tried to call Mark's name. He couldn't catch his breath. "Mark!" It came out as a ghost of a scream. "Mark!"

Vern started to cry. The emotions he'd been compartmentalizing were all coming up at once. He leaned forward with his hands on his knees, trying to catch his breath and reassure himself that Mark wouldn't have come here on his own.

He took a deep breath. "Mark!" he yelled. His voice sounded foreign, but at least it was working.

"Mark!" Vern ran the length of the pier calling Mark's name, his voice now magnified over the water. He hoped if Mark was at the lighthouse that he was safe, and that maybe he just got scared and didn't know how to get back onto the pier.

"Mark! Where are you?" Vern's voice echoed. He carefully stepped down the east side of the pier. It was difficult in the dark to see exactly where the concrete ended and the water began. He walked carefully around to the front of the lighthouse, but Mark was not there. Vern was both relieved and worried at the same time. He thought for sure that this was where Mark would have been.

He stepped back onto the pier. As he walked, his head was throbbing. His chest and his legs were still burning. His face stung. He hadn't even realized he'd been crying. He wiped his face with his sleeve. "Where are you buddy?" he said first to himself and then out loud.

As Vern stepped down from the base of the pier, he noticed the dark shadow of the big warning sign. The one that Vern had

Mark read, the day they did their tour of Erie's End. Something was preventing him from taking his gaze off the sign. As the green light passed over it, Vern felt like he'd been struck by lightning. He ran over to the sign. He hoped his eyes were playing tricks on him. But they were not. Leaning against the back of the sign, and hidden from view from any other vantage point, was Mark's bike.

Vern started screaming Mark's name. *"Maaarrrk!"* He did not think about anything. He felt numb. *"Maaarrrk!"* His feet seemed to move by themselves. Vern turned back and this time slowly walked up the pier toward the lighthouse. *"Maaarrrk!"* His voice was cracking. His throat was burning. Chills ran up his spine; he felt like he was going to be sick. *"Maaarrrk!"*

As Vern approached the halfway point on the pier, the light hit the water on the east side. Just for a second, but just long enough for Vern to see a backpack bobbing in the water. "No!" he screamed. "No! Mark!" He started running. He jumped down onto the ledge on the east side of the pier. He had to get closer. He leaned on the concrete that sloped into the water. He could feel the strength of the current around his ankles.

Vern reached for one of the rusty brackets mounted on the concrete. The backpack was just below him but if he reached for it without hanging on, he'd be swept under. He grabbed the bracket with one hand and reached with the other. As the light passed over again, he could see that the backpack had been hooked onto a broken bracket. He reached, and as his hand made contact with the strap of the backpack, he knew that it was still attached to Mark.

He let out a howl that sounded inhuman, a sound that only those who have experienced the worst kind of pain could ever understand. He unhooked the backpack, and with every ounce of strength he had, he hoisted Mark out of the water and onto the pier. "Mark! No!" He could not breathe. This could not be happening.

He crawled over to Mark and rolled him onto his back. He was sobbing. He knew it was too late. He took his cell phone out of his pocket.

His fingers shook as he dialed 9-1-1. "I found Mark Cole. At the pier. Send an ambulance." His voice was raw.

He put his head on Mark's chest. "I'm so sorry," he sobbed, "I'm so, so sorry," and again that inhuman, uncontrollable shriek of pain escaped Vern's lungs and echoed over the water. Vern picked Mark's lifeless body off the concrete. His wet, heavy, swollen body became more and more difficult to carry with each step.

As Vern got closer to the end of the pier he could hear the sirens and see the lights of the ambulance light up the dark sky. He stood frozen on the pier, not able to take another step. Not able to let go of Mark. Not able to understand. Not able to catch his breath.

Vern did not notice the ambulance pull up. He did not notice the paramedics get out and wheel the stretcher up onto the pier. He did not hear them say, "We'll take him from here." He didn't want to let Mark go.

"We've got this," the paramedic said again to Vern, and pried Mark out of his arms.

As they lay Mark on the stretcher, Vern heard the paramedic say, "It's been hours." He stood, still frozen. He watched the ambulance door slam. He watched the paramedic get into the passenger side. He watched the ambulance turn the corner, and it was in that moment that he collapsed, and in that moment that the world brought Vern Kelly to his knees.

CHAPTER 29

V ern leaned against the shower wall, letting the water rush over him. He didn't know how long he'd been sitting at the pier when Jay and Dave showed up in Deb's SUV. They didn't say anything. Nobody knew what to say. When they got to Dave's, Deb put her arm around Vern's shoulder, and he did not absorb the words that she blubbered through tears. He simply allowed her to guide him up the stairs, with her arm around his shoulder. She started the shower and kissed his forehead, then shut the door as she left the room. He undressed and stepped in, and he just stood and waited for the water to wash it all away. It wasn't until it turned cold and felt sharp against his skin that he turned off the tap.

Deb had left a towel and a change of clothes on the counter for Vern. He went through the motions and got himself dressed. The raw pain occupied every move he made. He needed to see Meg. He knew that she, and Matty and Mr. Cole, must have been shattered. He knew that he needed to see her, and hold her and be there. Deep down he knew that he needed her to hold him just as much.

He rounded the corner into the living room to find Deb, Hank, Jay and Dave all sitting quietly. They all looked anguished in their own ways. Deb's face was red and her eyes were swollen. It was clear that she hadn't been able to stop crying. Dave and Jay looked blankly across the room - probably trying to keep it together, mustering the strength to keep their emotions from spilling out, wanting to be strong for each other.

Hank looked worried; Vern knew he was the kind of dad who would have wanted to provide comfort, but was probably struggling with the fact that in this moment, there was no way to do that. The silence was uncomfortable and sad.

As Vern entered the room, everyone's gaze turned to him. For the first time in his life, he did not want all of the attention on him. He knew that they were all concerned, and he loved them for it, but he couldn't bear to be around them.

"I'm going over to Meg's," he said as his voice cracked. "I need to see her." He put his hands in his pockets and looked at the floor.

"I'll drive you over," Deb offered, and started to get up from the couch.

"It's okay, Deb," Vern said, "I think the walk will do me some good."

Deb couldn't help but start bawling again; it was the first time in his entire life that Vern had called her Deb, and not "Dave's mom." Her heart broke, knowing that he would never be the same Vern, ever again.

As the Listers' door closed behind him, Vern could feel the tears swell up in his eyes. As he walked, he cried and felt a weakness that his body was not accustomed to. His muscles still ached, and his head still pounded. The closer he got to Meg's house, the sicker his stomach felt. From a distance he could see a police cruiser parked out front and Meg's grandparents parked in the driveway. He didn't know what he was about to walk into, but he knew that he just needed to be with Meg.

He rang the doorbell and felt a stab of sorrow rush through him with the realization that Mark would not be running down the hall to get to the door first.

After what seemed like eternity, the door was opened by Meg's grandfather. He stood behind the screen. "Yes," he looked at Vern with a blank stare, "what is it?"

Vern could see past him into the house. Meg and her grandmother were sitting at the kitchen table, her grandmother rubbing Meg's back while Meg nestled her head into her shoulder.

"I was wondering if I could see Meg," Vern asked.

"It's not a good time," her grandfather said, and started to close the inner door.

"Meg!" Vern called, and the door shut.

He sat on the front steps. He did not know what to do. He needed to see Meg. After a few minutes the door opened, and as he heard it creak, he turned around hoping to see Meg. As he looked behind him, however, Mr. Cole stepped outside. He sat down beside Vern and rested his forehead on his folded hands. Vern felt frozen, he did not know what to say. He was still crying silently, and didn't try to stop or hide his emotions.

"She doesn't want to see you, Vern," Mr. Cole said with a tired, weak, raspy voice. Vern didn't say anything but let out an audible sob; he couldn't help himself. "Mark told Matty about the day you took him out to the pier, and tonight when the police asked what he might have been doing out there, Matty told them about it. I don't blame you, son," Mr. Cole said as the sobs he hadn't been able to contain all night long started again. "I don't blame you, but right now Meg does."

∞

Steph and Jess were silent as Steph steered the pickup slowly around the corner. They had stayed at the Cole home until Meg's grandparents arrived. Steph didn't want to leave Mr. Cole alone. She'd never seen a grown man in such a state of devastation. She'd also never known a man who'd experienced so much tragedy and loss.

As they drove, every bump in the road acted as a reminder for their stomachs to be uneasy. They weren't heading back to their happy little cottage with its blue shutters. Although they were exhausted and emotionally drained, they weren't heading back to the cottage; they were heading to the Erie's End police station.

Before anyone knew where Mark was, and while everyone else was still searching, Jess and Jay mustered the courage to tell Steph that Greg was lurking. They'd expected her to have a panic attack, like the ones she'd had in the past. But Jess was surprised by her mom's calmness.

Steph was also a bit surprised, but somehow over the course of her summer in Erie's End, she had amassed enough dignity and fortitude to prepare for the fight of her life. What had once left Steph paralyzed with fright was now the driving force behind her desire to live a life without fear. She didn't know exactly when the switch flipped, but she had realized that Greg only had power over her because she gave it to him - and she was ready to take it back.

"How much more can you handle?" she asked Jess with caution in her voice.

"What do you mean, Mom?" Jess asked, still shaken, and overwhelmed by the fact that things were actually about to get worse.

"I know I told you that your dad hurt me that night. But, I promised myself - I swore that I would never tell you what really happened. Dr. Taylor has been urging me to tell you since the very first time I met her - but I refused. I wanted to protect you. I know that tonight, of all nights, tonight is not the night - but if I'm going to make sure that he never comes near us again, I'll have to tell the police. And if I'm going to tell the police, then I want you to know first. I want you to hear it from me. But Jess, it's big, and you've been through so much. And tonight, of all nights, why does this have to be tonight?"

Steph pulled the pickup over to the side of the road and put it in park. She put her face in her palms and her shoulders began to tremble. Her emotions had caught up with her. She wasn't afraid of Greg. She wasn't going to run from him. She knew she had the nerve to fight him now; but she was afraid of what it could do to Jess. She had been afraid of Dominik too, but finally came to the realization that she had to tell the police. It was the only way to keep her, and Jess, and so many other people safe.

"Mom," Jess said softly as she grabbed one of Steph's hands and held it. "Mom, listen to me. There is never going to be a good time for this, but I am so proud of you for finding the courage to face it." She took off her seatbelt and turned so that her back was against the door of the pickup. She criss-crossed her legs and sat facing her mom. She rested her elbow on the dash and leaned her head into her hand. "What happened to Mark tonight is devastating for all of us. And I am so, so sad and shocked and worried about Meg and her family. But it happened - and the amazing thing about this place, about Erie's End, about these people - is that somehow, they will help each other get through it. One painful day at a time, everyone will figure out how to live again and how to breathe and how to make it not hurt so much. It will happen, and it won't be easy for anyone. I don't know how we're going to move past this night." She put her hand on her heart. "I feel like my chest is on fire, and I've never felt anything like this. But it will happen - everyone will help each other move on; and maybe, just maybe one day we will all laugh again. But the only way any of us are going to get through it is with each other."

Jess was now crying hard too, but her words had to come out; she needed her mom to know that she could handle whatever it was. "It's the same thing with what Dad did to you, Mom. The only way we're going to get through it, is one day at a time - and with each other." She slid across the bench of the truck so that she was as close to her mom as she could get. Steph was still sitting in the driver's seat, staring out the windshield through her tears. Jess reached over and turned off the radio. Steph turned her gaze toward her and Jess could see that she was trembling; her lip was quivering.

"Please Mom," she begged, "you can tell me anything. I need you to know that you have made me a strong person, without even knowing it - you've shown me how to believe in myself and how to cope with the world. Whatever it is, I will be okay. I love you more than anything - and I already know that whatever he did to you is so bad. It has to be bad if you've been so afraid to tell me. I know you - and for it to have demolished you the way it did - I have known there was more to it since your first panic attack." Jess grabbed her mom's hands, and held them, and could feel them still trembling. "So Mom, please understand that you can tell me. I'm prepared for whatever it is to shock me and hurt me. I am ready to face that, to face whatever comes with it - please, Mom. You have to know that as long as we do this together, we can face anything."

Steph put her arms around her daughter and held her for a long time. They both cried, supporting each other and depending on each other at the same time.

Steph pulled away, wiped Jess's tears and took a deep breath. She put her hands on Jess's shoulders, her voice shaking as she spoke. "You know that he thought I told on him for stealing money from clients, and that's why you think he hurt me, right?" Jess nodded. "I didn't tell anybody a thing. I was too afraid of what would happen if I did tell. Dominik found out somehow, about what your dad was doing, probably because he's a smarter man than your father."

Jess pulled away a bit. "Wait, are you talking about Dom Bakowski? The creep who owns the deli on Ancaster?" Steph nodded. "Whoa," Jess whispered, "I have heard a lot of rumours about that guy." She continued to look into her mother's eyes - and tried with everything she had to look unaffected by what she was telling her. "He was a client?"

"Yes," Steph said, "they made a deal," she started to cry again - knowing that this would be the hardest thing she ever said to her daughter, ever. "Your father told him that he could..." Steph paused; she did not want to finish the conversation. She put her face in her hands and her tears turned to sobs.

"Mom," Jess said softly, "it's okay - he told him he could what?

Steph wiped her eyes. "Everyone knew that Dom hung around with strippers. In fact, in addition to the deli, he also owned a strip club. Is that one of the rumours you heard about him?"

Jess nodded. "Yeah," she said, "and I heard that some senior from school went to work for him so that she could save money for college, but he made her do more than just stripper stuff with him and lots of other men."

"Your father was such an idiot for even taking him on as a client, let alone stealing money from him. I am still baffled by how stupid he was to steal not only from his regular clients, but from such a dangerous person. He is a dangerous, dangerous man, Jess. I found out later that it was much worse than I could have imagined. Dominik is actually involved in human trafficking. Have you heard that term before?" she asked. "Human trafficking?"

Jess nodded and felt the knots tighten in her stomach. "Mom," she forced the high-pitched words out, "what did my father tell Dominik he could do?" She put her hand over her mouth.

"Oh Jess," her mom cried. "He told Dominik he could sell me for sex to pay off his debt. I had no absolutely no idea. So, that night - after you left for the movies, your father pulled a gun on me, and tied me to our bed - and he waited outside our room while Dominik and two other men..."

Jess had to get out of the truck. She fumbled with the door handle as her hands shook. Finally, she flung the door open and left it open as she ran to the side of the road. Everything was spinning around her. She thought she could handle it - she thought she would be okay - but she didn't know how to hear what her mom was saying. This kind of stuff didn't happen in real life. She sat down on the dirt and leaned against the front driver's-side tire. Steph carefully got out of the truck and sat down in the dirt beside her. Jess put her head on her mom's shoulder.

"Mom," Jess whispered through her tears.

"That's why we had to leave," Steph said. "That's why I didn't just call the police and have your father arrested. I was afraid of what Dominik would do. With human trafficking, sometimes the traffickers drug their victims to the point that they don't even know they're tied to a bed in a hotel room for a week at a time. Sometimes the girls are so afraid of their traffickers, that they do what they have to do to survive. And customers come and go, over and over again."

Steph could not believe that she was having this conversation with her daughter. Only a few short weeks ago she had worried about giving her coffee because she wasn't old enough yet, and now she was explaining pure evil to her. She felt like she was robbing her of her innocence - she didn't want her daughter to know that the world could be like this.

"I've been so scared, Jess, because human traffickers don't usually target moms in my age group - they usually set their sights on girls your age." Steph whimpered, "Jess, I was so afraid he was going to go after you."

"So," Jess looked up at Steph, "Mom, are you telling me that dad is after us because his debt to Dominik isn't fully paid yet?"

Steph wrapped her arm around Jess's shoulder and pulled her close. "Well, I don't know for sure - but yes, Jess - that's what I've been afraid of."

∞

They walked into the police station just as Officer Parker was walking out. He stopped them.

"What a terrible night - how are you two holding up?" he asked.

Steph recognized that the concerned look on Officer Parker's face was a reaction to the fact that she and Jess were both covered in dirt, had puffy, reddened eyes and looked thoroughly dishevelled.

"It's tragic - what happened to Mark," she said. Her throat was dry and her voice was coarse. "But we're here about my husband."

Officer Parker suddenly looked as if he was on alert. "Why, did something happen?" he asked.

"Well, yes," Steph said, "but I see you're just getting off. We can just go in and talk to someone on duty."

"Absolutely not," Officer Parker said. "I'm all yours." He held the door open for Jess and Steph, and followed them into the station.

∞

After the news of what happened to Mark, Val met her mom outside the Loft Café, which had been closed for hours. They had both been crying, and were shocked - like everyone else. They walked in silence most of the way home. It was strange how quiet everything was. The houses lined the streets like dark shadows. People inside were peacefully asleep, not yet aware that something horribly wrong had happened.

"Mom," Val said, and she stopped walking. She couldn't say anything else. She began to sob and tremble. It was in that moment, in front of the black outlines of the darkened houses - that the reality of what happened hit her. All she could do was cry, and shake, and feel the searing pain of her realization rush through her. She crumpled into her mom's arms, and the two of them sat on the curb and cried.

"It hurts so bad," Val whispered through her sobs after leaning into her mom for a long time.

"Oh honey," Janet said. "I wish I could make it better, kiss it away, but you need to feel this hurt; you need to feel it." Janet was now sobbing too. "But you don't have to feel it alone. And I promise, baby, that one day it won't hurt so bad." Janet rubbed her daughter's back, then picked herself up from the curb and extended her hand down to Val. "Let's go, Sweetie," she said, "we're almost home."

They walked the rest of the way, again in silence. As they approached their own house (it was the only one on the street with the exterior light still on), they both noticed Kent's Jeep Cherokee in the driveway. He spotted them and stood up from where he had been waiting on the front porch.

"What is he doing here?" Val asked her mom, not wanting anything to do with him - especially now.

"I wish I knew, Val," Janet said.

"Kent," Janet said with tired frustration, "it's really not a good time."

"I know, I know," he responded. "Listen - I heard what happened. I wanted to come and see how you two were doing. I know I'm probably the last person either of you want to see right now. I just -" Kent got a little bit choked up, cleared his throat, and then continued, "I just think each day that goes by, is a day that we can't get back. And I'm sorry. And I wanted you both to know that I love you so much. Jan, maybe our marriage wasn't destined to be forever - but I will love you forever, and I'm truly so sorry for hurting you. And if you ever need anything - I hope you can find it within your heart to see me as a friend. I know it might take time. And Val - I wish I could turn back time and stop that day from happening. I will never forgive myself. You mean the entire world to me, and I let you down."

Val started to tremble and sob again. She was so confused. She hated him, but all she wanted to do was crawl into his arms and feel them wrap around her.

"Oh, Kent," Janet said as she sat on the steps of the porch and motioned for him to do the same. "We have such a long road ahead of us. We have so much healing to do - and I don't know if we'll ever be able to call each other friends. But we are parents; we will always be the parents of our two amazing children - and somehow, I think we can manage to do that without hating each other. However things go between you and the kids will be between you and them."

Kent looked over at Val, who was leaning against the railing at the top of the porch stairs, not far from where he and Janet were sitting. "I love you," he said, "and I don't want another day to go by that you don't know how much." He started to cry, and his voice cracked as he said, "You're my little Vallerina."

Val slowly started to walk towards her parents. She sat down beside Kent. She was still crying, but looked up at her dad, and through the tears and the knots in her stomach she said, "I am so mad at you, Dad; you broke my heart. I am so mad at you...and I still love you too."

He pulled her close and she rested her head on his shoulder. Janet reached across his lap and held Val's hand. They all sat in an awkward embrace, and for the first time in a long time, Val felt like she knew where she would find her strength.

∞

Although Vern had always been on his own, he had never felt as lonely as he did after Mr. Cole went back inside the house. He wasn't prepared for the possibility that Meg wouldn't want to see him. He felt like his soul had been ravaged, like everything he loved was suddenly gone. He didn't know what to do or where to go. He didn't want to go home. He felt like he was about to be swallowed up by his agony. He started walking.

As Vern made his way up the path to Mr. Johnson's front door, the stars were fading and the birds had started to chirp. He wished they would shut up. The Wagoneer was still parked out front, and Vern was relieved to see it.

He banged on the door with all the strength he could muster. He called Mr. Johnson's name over and over - and banged until his fist hurt, until finally the door opened.

The old man stood there, and just as he was about to give Vern a piece of his mind - he realized that the boy was in rough shape. "What the hell happened to you, kid?" he asked, and guided Vern inside the house.

It was the first time Vern had to say the words out loud, and he couldn't make them come. He put his head on the old man's shoulder and whimpered. He was exhausted and felt sick, and everything seemed foggy.

"For God's sake, kid, what the hell happened?"

Mr. Johnson had his hand on Vern's shoulder and walked him into the den. Only when he was sitting in the leather armchair was Vern able to mutter the words. "Mark is dead. I found his body at the pier. Meg won't see me." He stared blankly across the room.

"Oh Jesus Christ." Mr. Johnson cupped his mouth with his hand.

He walked over to the globe and opened it up. He took out the bottle of Scotch and a bottle of whiskey.

Vern sat in the chair, and continued to stare across the room. He hardly noticed that the old man had gone into the kitchen. Mr. Johnson came back with a nip of Scotch for himself and handed Vern a glass.

"This is a hot toddy," he said. "It'll help you sleep - right now you just need to sleep."

Vern took the glass and forced himself to take a sip. It was warm, and tasted like cider. It had cinnamon and lemons, and the harsh whiskey was countered by the sweetness of honey. It seemed to warm his insides, and before long, he started to feel a little bit woozy. When his glass was empty, the old man showed Vern up the stairs, and pulled down the covers on the bed in one of the bedrooms that hadn't been used in years.

"Get some sleep, kid. The best thing you can do for yourself right now is to get some sleep."

Vern lay in the bed. He was spinning, but it wasn't because of the hot toddy. He closed his eyes - it was the first time he had in almost two days. All he could see was the flashing green glow of the lighthouse. He curled into a ball. His fatigue finally conquered him and Vern dozed off.

∞

Officer Parker sat in shock after listening to the full account of what had happened to Steph, and the real reason why she and Jess had moved to Erie's End.

"I'm sorry," he said. "All this time, I assumed that what you had been going through was simply a bad breakup. I mean, I knew you might be at risk for a domestic or something, but I had no idea…"

"I know," Steph said, "I was trying so hard to hide it all - you couldn't have known. I didn't want anyone to know." She was too tired to cry.

"God, I hate to admit it, but at some point I thought the protection we were offering you was extreme. I had no idea how serious the risk actually was. Some cop I am - I am so sorry, Steph."

"Please," she said, "you have no idea how much you have done for us."

Officer Parker put a call in to the department in Richmond. "I've just put out an APB," he said, "but I need to speak to a detective right away." He looked at Steph and gave her a reassuring smile as he waited for someone to pick up the phone.

"Yes, it's Officer Parker from Erie's End. Listen, I just put out an all-points bulletin, but I need you to check on something for me right away. I have a woman and child here who are in danger. Can you send a car out to…"

He covered the mouthpiece of the phone and asked Steph for the addresses of both their home and the business. He wrote them down as she said them. "Yeah, I need you to send cars to 103 Werrington Street - that's the house" - he looked at Steph and she nodded yes - "and the other one has to go to the Carmichael Investment Firm on King Street. You'll see the details on the APB, but if Greg Carmichael is at either location, he needs to be taken in immediately. There's also a warrant out for Dominik Bakowski, please keep me posted." He paused, "Okay, you got the APB - yeah - it's un-fucking-imaginable what they did. I'm willing to bet Bakowski…" he reconsidered what he was about to say with Steph in earshot, "you know what man - we'll talk later - but please get those cars out right away… Thanks brother, I appreciate it," he said, and hung up the phone.

Steph felt chills run up her spine. Knowing that now it was out in the open, and that people knew what had happened, both horrified her and gave her an immense sense of relief.

The chief walked in and saw Steph and Jess. Steph could read the look of pity and concern on his face.

"What a night," he said wearily to nobody in particular. "We'll have a cruiser on watch around the clock at your place," he said directly to Steph, "and an officer will remain inside the house at all times."

He moved his gaze away from Steph. "Parker, I just got the call that all is clear at the cottage. Why don't you take these two home? They've had a hell of a night."

As Officer Parker held the door for Steph and she started to walk through, he gently put his hand on her shoulder. "We will find them," he said. "You did the right thing by reporting everything."

Jess could not wait to get home. She wondered how Jay was doing, but realized that she needed some sleep before she could even think about being around anyone. She could not wait to get into her bed and wrap herself up and turn the world off.

As the cruiser pulled up in front of the cottage, Jess felt nauseated - her dad had managed to desecrate their perfect sanctuary. Police officers were standing speaking to each other on the front steps, and there were two more cruisers parked on the street in front. The lights appeared to be on in every room. It looked so out of place compared to all the darkened cottages that surrounded them.

CHAPTER 30

I t was late in the afternoon when Vern opened his eyes and found himself in the floral bedroom where Mr. Johnson had left him. It took him a second to remember how he got there, and why. He felt his breath escape him and his chest become heavy with anguish. He lay there and wished he could turn back time. As much as he wanted to stay still forever, and never face the world again, he knew he had to get out of bed. He knew he had to do something.

He found Mr. Johnson sitting in his chair on the porch. "Thanks," Vern said as he sat in the weathered Muskoka chair, not looking at the old man, but out over the horizon.

"Okay," Mr. Johnson said, without taking his gaze off the horizon either.

"I hated you," Vern said, "after you told me about how you turned my mom away that night. I think I hated you. It occurred to me that she probably only became Drunk Doris after that happened. I had decided that after the campout I was going to come and tell you off. But I was wrong. I don't hate you. It's the opposite, really."

Vern didn't change the direction of his gaze. "They say you're supposed to trust your gut instincts. Well, when you told me, and I realized that you're my great-grandfather - I felt happy, I felt like it was a good thing - and I think I even wanted to hug you." Vern, although still overwhelmed with grief and sadness, smiled to himself knowing how Mr. Johnson would react to a hug. "Last night, I lost two of the most important people in my life." Vern's voice started to crack as the lump in his throat seemed to pulse every time he tried to talk. "And I just want to say -"

"Okay, kid," Mr. Johnson said. "Shut it. It's mutual." The old man looked over at Vern and could see the agony in his face. "Now listen to me. You have not lost anyone. That little boy, although he is not on this earth anymore - he is with you. Think about that." He paused for a moment and sipped his iced tea. "And as for Meg - if you're willing to admit defeat already, then you do not deserve her. I went to Annie's cottage every day when her father wouldn't let me see her. I went every day, on the off chance that I would get a different result from the day before. And every day that I couldn't see her, it hurt like hell. But I kept going - and you know the rest of the story." He turned his gaze from the horizon to look directly at Vern. "Don't you dare give up on her now. It's her prerogative if she doesn't want to see you. Hell, she's probably at home wishing it was you who drowned instead of her brother. But I'll tell you something - if you love someone, if you truly love someone - you don't give up." Mr. Johnson was twisting the wedding ring he still wore on his left ring finger. "You do what you have to do. I'm not saying you force it. I'm saying that this kind of love doesn't come around so often; and if you're feeling it, there's a pretty good goddamned chance that she is too. That poor girl is still coping with the death of her mother. She doesn't know what to do with the loss of her brother. She needs someone to blame. You don't give up on her. You go, every day - and try again. You leave when she says she doesn't want to see you. You respect her. You go back the next day, but don't you dare give up on her now. And when you're hurting like hell, and feel like your life has no purpose - you give it one." The old man could tell that Vern was trying hard not to cry, so he paid no attention when Vern started wiping his eyes with his hands. "You can stay here this week, on the condition that you finish that godforsaken canoe. I know you feel like you're dying on the inside - and kid, I can tell you there's only one way to get past that feeling, and it's to feel the pain, grieve, and live your goddamned life."

"Okay," Vern said as he stood up. He looked Mr. Johnson in the eyes, and the expression on his face revealed an understanding that no words could. "I'll be back."

He made his way down the porch steps toward the boat-house. He stopped outside the door and took a deep breath before he entered. He walked past the canoe, running his hand along its newly smooth surface as he went. He sat on the couches in the corner for a long time while staring into nothing. Then, he forced himself to get up, to lock the door behind him, and to start walking towards Meg's house.

As he approached her house he saw that Meg's grandparents were still there, and realized that they probably would be for quite some time. He rang the doorbell, and was again reminded and saddened that Mark would not be racing to the door to open it. It was Mr. Cole who opened the door. He clearly had not slept, and looked the worst that Vern had ever seen him. Vern realized that it must have taken him so much strength to get dressed at all.

Mr. Cole stepped outside and closed the door behind him. Vern felt his heart sink, knowing this meant that Meg still wouldn't see him.

"Can you just tell her I came by?" he asked.

"I will," Mr. Cole said and sat beside Vern, with his cup of coffee. "My in-laws think I'm going to go bat-shit crazy. They don't think I'm going to be able to take care of Meg and Matty. They want to take them both back with them."

Vern felt sheer panic come over him. He could somehow cope with Meg not wanting to see him; he could get through the days with that bit of hope that maybe, one day, she would. But he could not imagine her leaving Erie's End again.

He couldn't bear the thought of it, and the pain in his reaction made that apparent to Mr. Cole.

"I told them there was no way that was going to happen," he said. "I told them that we just got to a place where we were helping each other muddle through my wife's death and that we needed to be together, now more than ever." Vern's heart rate slowed slightly, and he was relieved. "I'm not sure they're convinced, but I just can't let them go."

"Is there anything I can do?"

Mr. Cole shook his head, and stood up. "I'll let you know about the funeral arrangements," he said. He opened the screen door, and as Vern started slowly down the stairs, Mr. Cole turned around. "Vern, wait - there is something you can do."

"Anything," Vern said.

"Forgive yourself," Mr. Cole said - and went into the house.

Vern stood there and felt himself crumble again. He had been feeling so many emotions, so much pain and sadness, but he didn't realize until that moment that what hurt the most was the guilt. It seemed that with every breath he took, another *if only* entered his mind. *If only I had answered my phone, if only I hadn't been stupid enough to take him out to the pier, if only I'd checked in with him, if only, if only....*

He needed a distraction. He needed something to focus on. He felt like he wouldn't be able to survive this, and he needed something to help him turn down the volume of his thoughts and heartache. He decided to go to Golden Acres. He needed clothes and wanted to see if the special paint he ordered for the canoe had arrived.

Doris was awake when he got there - and dressed. He didn't want to take the time to find out what was going on. He grabbed the box that was addressed to him off the counter. The marine paint had arrived. He went into his room to pack some clothes. As he was loading everything into his backpack, Doris appeared in his doorway.

"Too bad about that kid," she said timidly.

Vern looked at her and nodded. She came and sat beside him on his bed.

"I'm sorry," she said.

Vern lost his composure, put his head in his mother's lap and started sobbing. She rubbed his hair and felt helpless. This was new territory for her, and she didn't know what to do.

Vern stopped at the lookout on his way back to Mr. Johnson's. He climbed up to the top. He sat and looked over the water. He hated that something that looked so beautiful could have the capacity to cause pain and death. He could see the pier in the distance, and it made him angry to realize how unchanged it was. It looked the same as it had the day before - but no-one and nothing else in Erie's End did.

He found Mark's carving on the lookout and traced it with his finger - *through and through.* He held his knees to his chest, and he whispered, "I'm so sorry, Mark - I am so sorry."

Vern wanted nothing more than to go to bed when he arrived back at Mr. Johnson's, but he went to the boathouse instead. He unpacked the box with the paint - and then he sat on the floor for a long time and gazed at the canoe. He decided to take the old man's advice. He had to finish it.

∞

Vern continued to wake up in Mr. Johnson's floral guest room each day. And he continued to force himself to get out of bed and get dressed. He forced himself to sit and eat breakfast with Mr. Johnson - usually in silence, although it was a comfortable and supportive silence. Then, he would force himself, with knots in his stomach and the convoluted fusion of sorrow and hope in his heart, to walk to Meg's.

Each day, she would refuse to see him. Each day he would have a short exchange with Mr. Cole. Each day, he would notice that Mr. Cole looked a little worse than he did the day before. And each day, Vern would come back to the boathouse and work on the canoe.

Mr. Cole told Vern about the funeral arrangements. He said that the funeral would be on Saturday. He said that it would be the second time he'd be saying goodbye to a closed casket. Vern could tell that his pain was intensifying as the days went on.

The day before the funeral arrived, Vern woke up and forced himself to get dressed, to eat breakfast and to walk to Meg's. He expected it when Mr. Cole said that she wouldn't see him. He expected it when he looked worse than he had the day before.

"Can I ask you something?" Vern said after they had been sitting in silence on the concrete steps for some time.

"Shoot," Mr. Cole replied without any tonality in his voice.

"I was hoping it would be all right if I said a few words at Mark's funeral tomorrow."

Mr. Cole, for the first time all week, took his eyes off the cement steps, and looked long and hard at Vern's face. "I think that Mark would be honoured," he said, and looked back down at the cement.

"Meg?" Vern asked.

"She'll be okay," Mr. Cole said, without looking away from the blood-red stone that seemed out of place, embedded in the concrete on the second step.

"Vern," he said. It appeared as though he was in deep thought. His pause seemed unusually long. He took a deep breath. "Meg and Matty are going to live with their grandparents. They're leaving after the burial tomorrow."

"No!" Vern couldn't contain his emotions. He started to cry. "I love her so much - I can't lose her too." He looked at Mr. Cole with desperation in his eyes. He wasn't expecting this.

Silent tears started to stream down Mr. Cole's cheeks. "Turns out I have gone bat-shit crazy," he said, "and I can't take care of my own kids." He stood up and ran his open palms over his face to clear the tears away. "It'll be really nice for you to say a few words tomorrow." He placed his hand on Vern's shoulder, turned around and went back into the house.

∞

Jay lay in bed for a while, re-familiarizing himself with his surroundings. It was the first night he had slept in his room at his parents' house all summer. They had come home early from Guiana when they heard about what happened to Mark. Nothing looked different. The same movie posters hung on the walls, the same drapes hung from the windows. Everything just felt different.

As Jay moved his vintage Spider-Man sheets out of the way and got out of bed, it occurred to him that this feeling was directly related to the fact that today was the day of Mark's funeral. His heart plummeted, and as soon as his feet hit the floor he felt like they were weighing him down, like he could sink right into it, as if it were quicksand. He knew that this day was coming but wasn't prepared for it to be here.

After he ate breakfast and showered, and confirmed plans to walk to the funeral with Jess, he went back into his room and saw the suit his mom had put out for him. His nerves were getting the best of him. He felt uneasy and uncomfortable. He started getting dressed as his mind wandered. He looked in the mirror and realized that he must have grown a bit, as his sleeves and pant legs were a bit short. He hoped that nobody would notice. *What would it matter if anyone did?* He felt a burning in his throat, the precursor to tears.

∞

Val sat on Kevin's bed as he looked in his mirror and attempted to knot his tie for the tenth time.

"Dad used to always do it for me," he said.

Val got up. "Here, let me try." She tried a few times but couldn't make his tie look presentable either.

"Maybe I should ask Mom?" he said.

Val laughed and said, "I know." She untied the tie completely and threw it on Kevin's bed. She fixed his collar. "Perfect."

They both laughed, and it seemed to hit them at the same time that today was not a day for laughing. Val felt a pang of guilt for having done so at all. "Oh God," she said to her brother, "how is this even happening?"

He put his arm around her and pulled her in. "Sorry I haven't been here for you. I know you've had a really tough few months." Val could feel herself getting choked up.

"What could you have done? You're here now," she said, and smiled at him. "It's just crazy how you can go from having it all, to waking up one day and realizing that your life is absolutely not what you thought it was. I don't know what Meg must be going through. Her mom died, and now Mark. She won't talk to anyone. I wish I knew what to do for her. I wish I could make it not hurt for her. She helped me so much when I was going through my darkest - and I don't know what to do to help her now."

"You're doing it," Kevin said. "You're a good friend, Val. People cope with things in different ways. Meg has always been so independent. She needs her space, for now, and you'll be there the instant she's ready. She knows you love her and that she's got your shoulder when she needs it. Things like this make the world seem fucked up. Somehow though, we all have it in us, some kind of mechanism or something that makes us endure and carry on...and survive."

Val was glad her brother had made it home for the funeral. He could be a jerk sometimes, but when it really counted - he seemed to know just what to say. He gave her a soft punch in the arm before she left his room to go and get ready too.

∞

Deb stood in the doorway to Dave's room with curlers in her hair, wearing her slip. She had bought a new dress to wear to the funeral. She couldn't bring herself to wear her green dress. Although it was her go-to dress for all occasions, it was the dress she was wearing the night it happened.

"Thanks, Mom." He took the freshly pressed suit from her and hugged her, wishing he could comfort her. She had been crying all week. He loved that his mom was such a caring person - during good times it was the reason she made everyone feel so welcomed and loved; but at times like this her big heart caused her a lot of worry and agony.

Dave got dressed. He knew it wouldn't be an easy day for anyone. He thought it would be good for all of his friends to be together after the funeral, to be there for each other. He started by calling Jay and suggesting a Dougie Burger in Mark's honour after the service. Jay agreed, and suggested it to Jess, and Jess called Val. None of them had been able to get in touch with either Vern or Meg all week, but they knew they would see them at the service.

∞

Jess couldn't get used to the fact that there was always a police officer around. All she wanted to do when she opened her eyes was get out of her own bed and crawl into her mom's. Instead, she decided to get dressed before leaving her room. She put on her black dress. It seemed wrong - to be wearing a black dress on a sunny summer morning. She decided on no makeup, knowing that she wouldn't be able to contain her tears. They'd been sneaking out all week, no matter how she tried to control them. She could be brushing her teeth, or putting on socks - her tears just kept coming. She couldn't wrap her mind around what happened to her mom. She couldn't understand how, if her mom's suspicions were correct, her own father would be willing to trade her life to save his own. And she couldn't turn off the aching sensation in her heart, for what happened to Mark. None of it seemed real.

Steph was already dressed too when Jess went into the kitchen. She had just finished serving the officer coffee, and asked Jess if she wanted one. They all sat at the kitchen table, quietly sipping their coffee, feeling a strange sense of discord between the sunshine outside and the darkness they felt within. The officer was the first to break the silence.

"Officer Parker called earlier and said that he would take the two of you to the service today."

Steph smiled and said, "That's great, thank you. I really hope they find them soon - I hate to be such a nuisance to you guys."

The officer's expression didn't change, but he said, "It's no trouble at all ma'am, that's what we're here for."

Jess looked at her mom, and was nervous to ask, but said, "Mom, I was hoping I could walk over with Jay. He was going to come and pick me up."

Steph looked at the officer for approval.

"I think that would be all right," he said. "We'll be close behind."

Jess was relieved, as she hadn't really spent much time with Jay over the past few days and was certain that just seeing him would somehow ease the turmoil she'd been feeling.

It wasn't long before Officer Parker showed up at the door. He wasn't in uniform but dressed in a full suit. He was attending the funeral too, as he knew the Cole family well and wanted to pay his respects. Steph was relieved and felt a sense of comfort - she hoped that he would sit with her during the service. She felt comfortable and safe with him.

Jay was next to knock on the blue door. As Jess opened it, she couldn't control her tears. What they were about to face suddenly became more palpable, and she didn't know how she would hold it together. Jay couldn't stand to see her so upset, and the lump in his throat emerged again. He wanted to be strong and supportive, and he forced his own uneasiness away and put his arms around Jess. She cried into his shoulder and he held her tight. When she pulled away, she said, "Okay, let's do this." She squeezed his hand and they started walking.

Steph and Officer Parker followed. "Can you please make sure all the deadbolts are locked after we leave?" Steph asked the officer who was staying behind in the cottage. She looked at the blue door as she walked out and hoped that the deadbolts would be enough to keep them safe.

The officer did as directed and watched as the black sedan pulled away. He had been uncomfortably waiting for everyone to leave so that he could use the washroom without feeling awkward. He took the newspaper from the kitchen table, and with a sense of relief locked the bathroom door behind him.

The happy-looking cottage had felt foreboding all morning. Steph and Jess had both attributed it to the fact that it was the day of the funeral and they were now sharing their home with police officers around the clock.

Greg waited across the street, where he'd been watching the cottage all week. He was quite pleased with himself and his ability to hide in plain sight. He'd rented the cabin from the old couple who owned it. They had it advertised on an Airbnb site. They were travelling across the country to see their grandchildren and would be away for the entire summer. He had been watching. He knew the shift changes. He knew the officers. He knew which ones took their posts seriously, and which ones considered this assignment an easy way to get paid for some R and R. He also knew that Jess had a habit of leaving her bedroom window open.

When he first found out where they were, he planned on simply coming to get them and bringing them home. Nobody could leave him the way she did, and he would make sure that she never left again. He promised Dominik that his wife would make him enough money to pay back everything he'd embezzled and more. But after that night, Dominik told him that Steph was too old, she wasn't marketable. That the only way it would work was if his daughter came to work for him. Dominik wanted Jess.

Greg wouldn't let that happen - he wouldn't give his daughter to him. But he wouldn't let Steph get away with ruining his life either. He had to go into hiding, or Dom would kill him.

All he could think about was making Steph pay. Then he would disappear. How dare she? She ruined his life. She told Dominik about the embezzlement. She did this to herself, and then dared to leave him without a solution. All he could think of was wanting her to die and wanting to watch her suffer. After all that he had done for her, he couldn't believe she would put him in such a situation.

He quietly lifted himself into Jess's room. He closed and locked the window behind him. He knew there was an officer in the house but wasn't worried. His only objective was to find and get to Steph's room unseen. It took him no time, as the washroom door was closed, which left only one other option. He quietly opened the shuttered closet door and stepped inside. He closed the door behind him and felt a sense of conquest with the realization that he would be able to see Steph through the slats in the door when she returned home.

He sat on the closet floor. The confined space made him even more agitated. He was sweating. His eyes were bulging. He could hear his heartbeat as though his heart was actually in his ears. He started whispering to himself. "That fucking bitch is going to beg me to kill her." His plan made perfect sense to him - anyone else would see that he had gone perfectly mad.

He grabbed some of Steph's clothing that was in a pile beside him on the floor. He held it up to his nose and inhaled her scent for a long time. He started laughing as he put the clothes back down. He pulled the rope he bought from the Erie Mart out of his shirt and laid it on the closet floor.

He wanted her to suffer. She ruined him. She had to suffer. He wanted to hear her say she was sorry. She disrespected him...*nobody disrespected him.* His adrenaline surged as he reached for his Glock in its holster. It gave him a sense of power - she was so wrong to think she could take him down. After releasing his grip on the gun's handle, he reached to the other side of his belt and felt for his knife. He hadn't decided whether to shoot her or use the knife to slit her throat. He whistled quietly, waiting for her to get home.

CHAPTER 31

Vern took a deep breath as he approached the church. He saw groups of people congregating outside. He looked up at the steeple. His chest ached. He had made it through the days that led up to this one. But he didn't know how he would make it through this. He gulped and felt his stomach sink.

Dave and Jay saw him approaching and came to greet him. They knew that he was not in a good place. Each of them put a hand on his shoulders. Without saying anything to each other, they all walked into the church.

The sight of the casket with Mark's picture on top was enough to conjure tears in most of the guests. Vern felt his own wanting to escape, but used all the strength he had to prevent them from gushing out. He had to make it through this first. He had to say the words that he needed to say. He sat in the pew and struggled to keep it together. He listened as the minister delivered what most would say was a beautiful service. Vern concentrated on blocking out the sounds of people weeping. He could hear Meg's audible sobs, and his heart broke as he longed to hold and comfort her.

It was when the minister said, "...and now, if there is anyone from the congregation who would like to say a few words..." that Vern's heart started to race and the tears he'd been holding back felt like they were going to come. He took another deep breath. He told himself to keep it together. He mustered the strength, and he stood up.

As he slowly walked up the aisle, he felt his stomach churning. He could hear people whispering, but didn't know if what they were saying was about him being Drunk Doris's son from Golden Acres - or if they blamed him for Mark's death. He stopped and bowed his head in front of Mark's casket, and willed his tears not to come. He adjusted his bowtie, and made his way to the podium.

He looked over to where Meg was sitting. He didn't want to upset her by speaking if she didn't want him to, and gave her a pleading look that she recognized as a request for her blessing. Although tearful, she looked up at him and gave him a single nod. He cleared his throat.

"I only really knew Mark for a summer. He quickly became like a brother to me." Vern's voice cracked and was weak. He paused for a minute and locked eyes with Matty. "Just like you did too, Matty," he said, and took another deep breath. He was hurting, but had to continue.

He gathered his nerve, and his voice became stronger and more confident. "Sometimes in this life, I think we're meant to find certain people. The universe was smiling on me when it somehow led me to the Cole family. Each person in this family, in some way, taught me about love - like I had never known. I spent a lot of time with Mark this summer. He was the kind of kid who sat back and took everything in - and doing that, made him wise beyond his years. He just got it, you know? During all of the time that we spent together, I thought I was teaching him, and taking him under my wing. But as it turns out - he was the one who taught me."

Vern paused again, fighting back tears. "One day, Mark and I sat on top of the lookout and we searched the lake for Pirate Thieves. Luckily, there were none." Vern smiled to himself at the memory. "But while we were up there, Mark carved three words into the wood where people who visit the lookout leave their legacy. He carved the words *through and*

265

through with his Swiss army knife. At the time I thought it was a sweet reference to a children's book that his mom used to read to all of the Cole kids."

Vern looked over at Meg, who was sobbing into her handkerchief. His heart broke for her, and when she looked up at him, he gave her a look that expressed so much care and loving concern.

"I realize now, however, that it was so much more than that. It was the way that Mark lived his life. It was how much he cared about people. It was how much he wanted everyone else to be happy. It was how he wanted people, and friends, and most importantly, his family - to be together - to be with each other. It was how he loved. And it was how he changed my life...through and through.

"I haven't been able to prepare myself for this day. I can't bring myself to say goodbye to him. In my darkest hour, after we lost Mark, someone who I look up to told me that even though he is not on this earth anymore - Mark is still with me. Those words have given me the strength to get through this week, and the strength to say goodbye. Those words have given me the choice to live the rest of my life as a better person because I had the privilege of learning how to live my life through and through - because of Mark - and I will carry him with me every single day."

Vern looked over at the casket, and the picture of Mark. He spoke to it directly. "Mark - your time on this earth was too short. You taught me that what is most important in this life is the people you share it with. You taught me to love with all your heart - and when you love, to love through and through. I want to thank you for so many things. You're my hero, my friend, my brother and my teacher. So, Garfunkel, as we all say goodbye to you on this day - know that the world has lost a light, but those of us who knew you - will carry yours with us forever."

Vern could no longer hold back his tears. "I love you through and through…yesterday - today - and tomorrow too."

He stepped down from the podium, and as his tears burned his cheeks, he walked down the aisle, past the congregation, and out the door. He sat on the steps of the church and leaned against the cold brick wall as the sobs he'd been hanging onto escaped at once. He felt like his heart was catching on fire. He wished he could rip it out of his chest.

The wooden door of the church opened. The service had ended. Most people began to gather in the church hall to eat egg salad sandwiches and drink coffee and discuss what a beautiful service it was.

Vern didn't look to see who was coming out of the church until Meg's feet stopped beside him. He looked up at her as he wiped his tears away with the sleeve of his suit. She sat down beside him and leaned into him. He put his arm around her, and the two sat and cried, and felt comfort in each other for the first time since Mark died.

"I'm so sorry," Vern said after a long time.

Meg squeezed his hand. "Me too," she said, "this was not your fault. He loved you so much." Vern held her close.

"We're going to bury him now," she said, "just Dad, Matty and my grandparents. That's how Dad wanted it. I don't think he wants everyone to see him fall apart."

Vern looked at Meg. "Do you want me to be there?"

She looked down at her feet. "Yes," she said, "but it's better if you don't come. My grandparents are taking me and Matty back with them. We're leaving right from the cemetery, and I can't say goodbye to you right after I bury my brother." She started to sob again. "Check on my dad, ok?"

The church door opened again, and Meg's grandfather said, "Meg, it's time to go, the limo is waiting."

Meg stood up, and Vern stood with her. He did not know what to say. He was devastated.

He hugged her tight and through tears he whispered, "I love you."

She started to walk towards her grandfather, and Vern tried with all of his might to hang onto her hand to keep her from going. But he knew that she had to. As he felt her hand slip away, he let out a whimper. He watched the big wooden door close behind her, and he sobbed "No," out loud, but to himself. He started to run - he knew what he had to do, and his legs wouldn't move fast enough.

∞

Jess found her mom sitting with Deb and Janet in the church hall.

"How are you doing, sweetie?" Steph asked.

Jess just shrugged her shoulders. Her puffy eyes and red cheeks gave her away. "Mom," she said, "everyone is thinking of going to Dougie's to have a burger and just be together. Is it okay if I go?"

Steph looked over at Officer Parker, who was sitting at the table with them. "I'll send a cruiser over to sit across the street from Dougie's," he said.

"Okay," Steph said, "but don't be too long, okay?" Jess nodded and gave her mom a long hug.

Dave and Val, and Jess and Jay gathered together outside the church. "I hope Vern is okay," Val said to the group.

"That speech was hardcore," Dave said with weakness in his voice.

"I think we should give him a little bit of time, but then we have to go and find him," Jay said. "He shouldn't be alone today."

As they started towards Dougie's, they were all quiet. Dave and Val walked hand in hand, and so did Jess and Jay.

"Did you guys see the guy who stayed behind in the last pew?" Jay asked the group. "I've never seen him before, but he was crying like crazy."

"Are you talking about the guy who was holding the leather journal in his hands?" Val asked. "I noticed him too, but I have no idea who he is. The initials on his journal were A.D. Is he an Ender or a Slicker?"

After a few minutes of silence passed, Val said, "I can't believe Meg is leaving again." No one else said anything; no one knew what to say.

∞

Vern ran up the steps and into Mr. Johnson's house. "Hey!" he yelled abruptly. Mr. Johnson was startled awake from the nap he was taking in the leather chair in the den. "I need to stop them!"

"What are you talking about, kid?"

"Meg and Matty are leaving - they're going to live with their grandparents. I have to try to stop them," he said. "Can I take the Wagoneer? Please."

"Do you even have a driver's licence, kid?" the old man asked.

"Well, no," Vern said, "but please - there's no other way - there's no time."

"Sorry kid," Mr. Johnson said. "There's no way I'm going to let you take my car. You don't have a driver's licence and I can't in good conscience let you drive in the emotional state you're in. Absolutely not."

Vern's heart sank. If this couldn't happen - there was no way to stop her from leaving.

"And don't you dare even consider taking the keys off the kitchen counter," Mr. Johnson continued with a wink. "Don't you even think about it."

Vern ran into the kitchen and grabbed the keys. He burst past Mr. Johnson, who was now standing by the front door.

The old man watched as the Wagoneer jerked out of the long driveway. "Go get her, kid," he said to himself as he smiled and hoped that Vern would figure out how to actually drive the damn thing.

The whitewall tires squealed as Vern lurched the Wagoneer to a stop in front of Meg's house. He didn't see her grandparents' car, and hoped he wasn't too late. He saw Mr. Cole's truck in the driveway and hoped it was just because they'd been chauffeured to the cemetery in the limo. He knocked on the door, but there was no answer. He was frantic. He tried the knob - and it was open.

"Hello?" he called, as he entered the house. There was no answer.

"Anybody home?" he called as he anxiously searched the house. Nobody appeared to be there. He stopped suddenly, outside the half-closed door to Mark's bedroom. Mr. Cole was sitting on Mark's bed. He was sobbing into Mark's pillow - falling apart. Vern opened the door, and slowly walked over and sat beside him on the bed. He couldn't believe how unreasonable it was, and how cold, and how callous - that Meg's grandparents would leave Mr. Cole alone and devastated immediately after burying his son.

"They're gone," Mr. Cole wept, "all of them - they're all gone."

"When did they leave?" Vern asked.

"You missed them by ten minutes."

"Listen," Vern said with urgency. "I know you feel like you can't do this - like you won't get through this. I know that it takes every ounce of strength to take a breath sometimes, because it hurts so much. But the only way you, and Meg and Matty are going to get through this is together. You need each other. You can't let them go."

"I know," Mr. Cole said, "I know - but it's too late, and I don't know if I can be strong enough for them." He held Mark's pillow a little tighter.

Vern put his hand on Mr. Cole's shoulder. "Listen to me," he said. "You are one of the strongest people I know. You can do this. You are strong enough for them, and when you aren't - let them be strong for you. They need you. I need you. We need to do this together. Mark would want the three of you to be together."

Mr. Cole looked up at Vern, his eyes widened as it hit him - he knew that Vern was right.

"Let's go," Vern said, "I'm driving." They rushed out of the house and Vern pointed to the Wagoneer. Mr. Cole looked at him with a puzzled expression. "I'll explain later," he said, "hop in."

Vern sped through the village and past the *Welcome to Erie's End* sign. He'd never thought about how crazy it was that there was only one road in and out of the village. It was as if they lived in their own secluded world. Once he hit the highway, he pushed on the gas pedal with as much force as he could.

"Vern," Mr. Cole said nervously, "my in-laws drive ten below the speed limit - let's take it off warp speed."

Vern eased his foot off the gas pedal, but made sure he was going at least twenty over the speed limit. He had to catch up to them.

After what seemed like an eternity of Vern's crazy driving, they could see the sedan driving slowly ahead. "There they are, up there, that's them," Mr. Cole said.

Vern started honking the horn frantically and sped up again. He continued to honk. He saw the brake lights come on, and Meg's grandfather put his hand out the window and waved for Vern to pass.

"He's probably calling you a goddamned asshole right now," Mr. Cole said.

Vern pulled to the left and steadied the Wagoneer in parallel with the sedan.

Mr. Cole unrolled his window, and saw the shock on his father-in-law's face. "Pull over!" he yelled out the window. "Pull over!"

The sedan pulled onto the shoulder, and Vern made his way to the shoulder a bit farther ahead. His abrupt stop caused them to jerk forward. He shifted into park and clumsily started pressing the release button in the centre of the old metal seatbelt buckle. "C'mon, c'mon," he said out loud as he saw Meg in the rear-view mirror. He got out of the Wagoneer and started running back towards the sedan, towards Meg. Mr. Cole was close behind.

Meg had gotten out of the car, and when she saw Vern running - she began to cry all over again. She started to run towards him, running and crying, and just wanting to get to him. They finally met each other between the two vehicles on the shoulder of the highway. They wrapped their arms around each other.

"I can't lose you too," Vern said.

Meg leaned into him. "What's happening?"

"I talked to your dad," Vern said. "He knows that you all need to be together, that going with your grandparents isn't the answer and isn't going to make it any easier. We came to stop you."

Vern and Meg looked back at the sedan and could see Meg's grandfather and Mr. Cole having a heated discussion. They saw Meg's grandmother get out of the car and put her hand on her husband's arm. She said something to him. He looked at her and she nodded. Then Meg's grandfather shook Mr. Cole's hand, and gave him a hug. They walked to the back of the car, and after Meg's grandfather opened the trunk, they started unpacking luggage and Matty's equipment.

"Get the car a little closer," Mr. Cole yelled over to Vern. "We're going to transfer everything and go home."

Vern looked at Meg with relief, and then with panic. "I've never had to go backwards," he said.

Somehow, he managed to back the Wagoneer up the shoulder so that it was close enough for them to transfer the luggage and the equipment.

Meg hugged her grandma and grandpa and opened the door to the back seat. "We're going home," she said to Matty. He smiled, and it seemed like it was the first time anybody had seen a smile all week.

∞

As Vern pulled into the driveway, Mr. Cole said, "Thank you, Vern - thank you for making me see..."

Vern gave him a look that showed his own gratitude. He didn't have the words, but he was so grateful that Mr. Cole took him seriously. He helped unload, and when Matty went into the house, he asked Mr. Cole if it would be okay if he took Meg back with him to return the Wagoneer. He promised that he'd walk her back right away.

Mr. Cole looked at Meg, who nodded that she wanted to go. He shook Vern's hand. "Thank you again," he said. "I think Matty and I could use a little quality time. You know, we've got to start somewhere."

∞

"It was really a nice service," Officer Parker said as he and Steph drove back to the cottage. "That Vern Kelly surprised me, who knew he was such a sentimental kid?"

Steph smiled. "They're all a pretty great group of kids, aren't they?" She was trying to act light-hearted for Officer Parker's sake, but couldn't shake the melancholy she was feeling. She wondered how Mr. Cole was coping with things, and if it would be appropriate for her to recommend Dr. Taylor to him.

As they approached the cottage, Steph wished that Jess was with her. She knew that it was important for her to be with her friends right now, but she just didn't want to be alone.

"Would you like to come in for a bite?" she asked Officer Parker as she reached over to undo her seatbelt.

"I'd love to," he said, "but I took time off to attend the service, and now I have to report for duty." He could sense Steph's disappointment. "I'll tell you what," he said, "I'll meet you back here and relieve the officer who's stationed inside, what do you say?"

Steph smiled and felt relieved. "Sounds great," she said. "That'll give me just enough time to get changed and get dinner going."

She inserted her key to unlock the first deadbolt, and heard the others being turned from the other side of the door. She figured that the officer had been watching as she came up the steps.

"Well hello there!" he greeted her cheerfully as he opened the door. Steph supposed that she couldn't expect everyone to feel as glum as she did. It was so strange to be welcomed into her own home by a stranger, but at the same time she was grateful for how seriously the Erie's End Police Department was taking her case.

"Any signs of him?" she asked.

"Nada," the officer replied. "It's been a very quiet afternoon around here."

"In that case," she said, "Officer Parker will be back soon to take over, so I don't mind if you want to take off a bit early." Steph was so tense, she just wanted to take off her dress and sit down and close her eyes, and be alone. She knew nothing would happen with a cruiser still parked right outside.

It had been a long, boring day for the officer and he was thankful for the chance to leave early. He quickly walked through the house and poked his head in each room as he did. "Well, all is clear," he said to Steph. "Davis is still in the cruiser outside - if you really are sure, maybe I'll head out?"

Relieved, Steph said, "Yes, that's fine. Thank you for your help."

As he walked by the cruiser parked outside, the officer said, "I'm leaving, but Parker's on his way - I've been having issues with my stomach all day."

The other officer laughed. "Maybe you oughta lay off the coffee."

Steph walked into her bedroom and sat at the end of her bed. She had no idea that Greg was watching from behind the slatted closet doors, waiting to make his move. He was just waiting for Steph to turn her back.

Steph took off her heels and felt the sweet instant relief that comes when feet are set free. She got up to put on her flip-flops, and as she started to walk towards the head of her bed, she heard her closet door open. For a split second she froze. She knew it was Greg. She knew this was it. The rest went in slow motion.

She screamed for help as loud as she could, hoping that the officer who was still outside would be able to hear her. He didn't.

Greg grabbed her by the back of her hair and pulled hard. "You stupid bitch," he said as she let out a wail, "did you honestly think I wouldn't find you?"

He pushed her down onto the bed with so much force that she bounced when she landed. He raised his hand above his head to gain the momentum it would take to hit her hard. She took the opportunity to kick him as hard as she could. She didn't know where her foot made contact, but she heard him groan and ran for her bedroom door.

She grabbed her cell phone out of the pocket in her dress. She autodialed Jess's number. Just as it started to ring, she felt Greg's sudden, sturdy grasp on her ankle. She fell forward and her face slammed into the corner of her dresser. She felt waves of pain burning and bursting through her whole body. She pleaded with him as he pulled her by the ankles. She had dropped her phone but could hear the distant sound of Jess saying hello.

"Jessica!" she screamed. "Don't come home! He's here! Don't come home!"

"Mom - no!" She heard the terror in her daughter's voice on the other end.

Greg sat on top of Steph, preventing her from moving at all. He hit her in the face over and over. Each time his fist made contact, it felt like a burning-hot wrecking ball that was smashing into her, trying to break her. The taste of copper filled her mouth and she thought she might choke on the blood. Her vision became blurry, each time she blinked - it seemed like all she could see was Greg's knuckles like a hammer, plummeting toward her - but she kept fighting back. She dug her nails into his flesh and scratched him and tried with all she had to reach for his neck or his eyes. He was so much stronger, she couldn't reach any part of him, but she could not succumb to him. She heard Jess screaming from the cell phone that was still across the room.

She mustered the strength to push him off her, and as he lost his balance, she started again for the door.

∞

Jess answered her phone at Dougie's and screamed, "Mom - no!"

Jay jumped to his feet. "Is it him?"

Jess nodded and covered her mouth as tears of panic rushed down her cheeks.

"Hey!" Jay yelled to the officer who was parked across the street. He started waving his arms. He could hear Steph screaming from Jess's cell phone. "Hey!"

The officer turned his head toward him. "What's going on?" he yelled back.

"Her mom is being attacked! She's being attacked at the cottage."

The officer immediately flicked on his sirens and sped off toward the cottage.

"Oh my God!" Jess screamed. "Mom!" She could hear her mom whimpering and saying over and over again, "Jess, don't come home," as she cried. She could hear him threatening to kill her, and she could hear every contact his fist made with some part of her mother's body.

"Come on!" Dave said as he jumped over the patio railing. "Let's go."

∞

Steph picked the phone up off the floor. "I love you so much, Jess," she slurred into the receiver, and she pressed the *End Call* button, not wanting Jess to hear what might happen next.

Greg had grabbed the rope from the closet floor, and before Steph made it to the bedroom door his hand had a firm grip around her arm. He pulled her across the room; he pushed her down to the floor. He stood with one foot on her back, as if to claim victory and he started loosening the rope. As she tried to make her sight come into focus, with her head pressed to the carpet, she could see pools of blood throughout the room. She felt the wet warmth and knew that another one was spreading beneath her.

He bent down and pulled her hard by the hair, causing her to rise to her knees. He picked her up by the collar of her dress and slammed her down onto the antique chair in the corner of the room. She kicked at him and struggled as much as she could, but he had a tight hold on both her wrists. He wrapped the rope around her wrists, then fed it behind her through the slats in the chair and tied it around her ankles. She couldn't move. She tried screaming again, hoping that the officer outside would hear.

"Shut up!" he yelled at her.

Steph cried as he sat on the edge of her bed and started to whistle. She knew she should be afraid, but she was numb - although not numb enough to give up. It was the same tune as before…it made her sick to her stomach. He had literally gone insane, and she was about to die, but she wouldn't let him get to Jess, she couldn't.

"Please don't do this," she pleaded. "I know you're here for Jess. I know you're going to give her to Dominik." Her words sounded strange and garbled as they left her swollen lips. "Greg, she's your daughter, your blood. She's your child - nothing is worth what he will do to her, what will happen to her if you give her to him." She cringed and writhed and burned all over - the pain she felt throughout her bloodied body was nothing compared to the agony that cursed through her at the thought of what could happen to Jess.

"She will live, she'll be fine," Greg said. "I'm on the run from Dominik now - because of you. He will kill me if I don't pay him back what I took over the years, and I can't - this is happening because of you. The only one who won't live through this is you - and that's because you couldn't keep your big mouth shut." Greg got up from the bed and slowly walked over to where Steph was tied up in the chair. He stood in front of her, looking down with lunacy in his eyes, and placed his hand on the knife in its holster.

"I didn't tell him," Steph cried, knowing he wouldn't believe her, "I never told a soul."

"You did this to yourself," he said and started to whistle. Steph closed her eyes for a moment, she willed herself to be strong. When she opened them again - all she could see was the blurry outline of Greg's hand gripping the base of his gun. As her sight sharpened - it occurred to Steph that the last thing she would ever see was the barrel of a gun.

Jess couldn't catch her breath. She was so afraid it would be too late when they got there. She was so afraid of what they would find. As they approached the cottage she saw the cruisers outside with their lights flashing. She hoped they made it to her on time. She hoped that her mother was still alive. She heard the ambulance in the distance and started running faster toward the house.

Just as she neared the walkway up to the blue door, she heard what sounded like a crack of thunder. It took her only a second to realize that it was a gunshot. "No!" she screamed and ran toward the door.

Officer Parker had just arrived. He ran up and intercepted Jess. He held her back. "It's not safe for you to go in there," he said.

"My mom!" she screamed. "He just killed my mom!"

The ambulance pulled up, and the paramedics quickly entered the cottage accompanied by more officers. Time stood still while Jess and her friends waited for some news, for someone to come back out.

Jess sat on the curb holding her knees to her chest. Officer Parker was still beside her, with his hand on her back trying to keep it together himself. Jay stood beside them, watching the house, feeling as though everything around them was happening in a movie - that this was not real.

After an eternity passed, the blue door opened. Jess heard the creak of the door, she jumped up and turned around to face the cottage; her knees felt weak and her heart stood still. She took a deep breath and raised her gaze toward the front porch.

Steph stood there, bloodied and beaten. She looked around for Jess, and when she saw her, started to whimper. "Jess!" she cried out with all the strength she had left. "Jess."

Jess ran up the stairs and they both fell to their knees. They melted into each other and neither of them ever wanted to let go. Jess looked into the doorway, and saw the paramedics put a zipped-up body bag on the stretcher.

"Is that him?" she asked her mom nervously.

Steph looked over her shoulder and nodded.

"That's him," she said.

The officer that had rushed away from Dougie's slowly emerged from the cottage and stepped onto the porch. He was dazed and was holding his cap against his chest. Officer Parker hurried up the stairs. He put his hand on the constable's shoulder, "Well done Jones," he commended. Jones slowly shifted his gaze to Officer Parker, and with a delayed uncertain smile he said, "it was my first..." his voice trailed off and Parker could tell that the magnitude of what had just happened was still sinking in.

He knelt on one knee next to Jess and Steph. "I'm so sorry I wasn't here," he said, "I'm so sorry you were alone. They got Bakowski," he said, "that's what kept me at the station. I got a call that they took down his entire trafficking operation in Richmond - they got him. He was into some filthy shit"

Unaware that she was too weak to stand, Steph tried to get up, but felt her legs give out, causing her to sink back to where she was. "Thank God," she cried, "thank God."

"Mom." Jess knelt down beside her. "We're going to be all right." The second ambulance arrived and the paramedics started up the stairs with a stretcher for Steph. "I'm coming with you mom," Jess said.

"Okay," Steph mumbled, "but leave the door unlocked." She attempted a smile with her swollen face - and Jess squeezed her hand.

∞

Vern pulled up to Mr. Johnson's house. The old man was sitting on the front porch, sipping on iced tea. He stood up when he saw the Wagoneer approaching. He waited anxiously, hoping that things had gone Vern's way. He saw Vern get out of the driver's side, and celebrated quietly to himself when he saw him walk to the passenger side to open the door for Meg.

"Way to go, kid," he said quietly. "Way to go."

Vern walked with Meg up the front steps. "You remember Meg," he said.

"Nice to see you, young lady," Mr. Johnson said. "I'm very sorry to hear about your brother."

"Thank you," Meg said, knowing that she would have to get used to hearing those words.

"And you, you little thief," he said to Vern, "where the hell are my car keys?"

Vern handed them over, and Mr. Johnson gave him a wink that went unnoticed by Meg. "Do you mind if I take Meg to the boathouse?" Vern asked. "I want to show her -"

"As long as I don't find you two the way I did the last time, I don't care what the hell you do," he said, and went in the house.

Meg looked at Vern, and for the first time all week, she half-smiled.

Vern felt butterflies as he put the key in the boathouse door. The day had already been filled with so many emotions that he didn't know if it was the right time. He couldn't stand waiting any longer, though. Every day when he worked on the canoe, he'd wished that she was with him - and now that she was, he had to show her. He opened the door and she stepped inside.

She expected to find the canoe in the same state as the last time she was there, upside-down on the workhorses and waiting to be finished. What she saw took her breath away. It looked like a brand new canoe. The blue paint was the perfect hue. It was so smooth, and its shine reflected the light from the boathouse windows.

The wood trim had been re-stained and looked rich and healthy. She walked over to it, and looked at Vern with admiration. She ran her hand along its surface, admiring the quality of Vern's workmanship. Her hand stopped when it came to the metallic gold letters that had been carefully placed underneath the wooden trim at the stern. She traced each one with her finger: G - A - R - F - U - N - K - E - L.

"Oh Vern," she said, "it's perfect." He put his arms around her and they leaned into each other's lips. As they kissed, they both cried - silent tears. Whatever came next might not be easy, but they would face it together.

ACKNOWLEDGEMENTS

The thing about aspiring to be a writer is that it's a lot like being an aspiring rock star. You write because you love to write - but in most cases, you still need a day job. It's thanks to our day jobs that we had the opportunity to chance upon each other. We met at the Goodwill Career Centre while we were both working as Employment Consultants. We were cubicle neighbours and we quickly learned about each other's interests - favourite movies, excellent taste in music, heightened affection for anything 80s, local lunch spots—and before long we also recognized each other's creativity.

Over the course of our cubicle banter - Wade disclosed that he had written a screenplay called *Summer Girls*, which was also made into a web series. We discussed a goal that we both shared of one day writing a novel - and so began our journey - Wade's screenplay would become the foundation for *Escape to Erie's End*. This collaboration has been a gift, and it reinforces the adage that sometimes people come into our lives for a reason. It is so important to us to acknowledge and thank the **Goodwill Career Centre** for being the place where we took our very first steps in this journey.

• • •

They say that there is truth in fiction. *Escape to Erie's End* is a fictional story laced with many of our own truths. There are nods to our friends and families throughout the novel, to where we live, and to bits and pieces of our personal histories.

We would like to acknowledge **Bernadette Rossetti-Shustak** for creating her wonderful children's book, *I Love You Through and Through*. This book is dear to the characters in *Escape to Erie's End*, and helped us round out one of our favourite storylines. It is also the book that Pam has read to her son, Scott, every single night since he was born.

We learned a lot about the writing process throughout the course of this project. Some nights, we would sit in front of our computers and the writing would flow - other nights, we required a bit of added inspiration. We would like to acknowledge **Emm Gryner** for creating such incredible music; her albums were our soundtrack as we wrote, and her song *Summerlong* is mentioned on the novel's first page.

• • •

We want to thank our **Editor, Matthew Godden, from Thames Valley Wordworks** for his attention to detail and for the guidance and expertise he provided throughout the editing process.

The book would be incomplete without the cover, created by **Nathan Yoder** who was able to capture so many elements of the story in his artwork.

• • •

Finally, we would like to acknowledge and thank each other for being dedicated to this novel, for picking it up again when it seemed impossible, for understanding when writing had to be put on hold because of life's trials and tribulations, for motivating each other, for brilliant ideas and plot twists (and the late-night phone calls to discuss them), for arguing about storylines and characters, and names and eye colours - for the long hours, and for the friendship that brought *Escape to Erie's End* from start to finish.

- Wade & Pam

10068464R00160

Made in the USA
Lexington, KY
23 September 2018